Rebellion's Message

MICHAEL JECKS

BLACKTHORN

First published in Great Britain, the USA and Canada in 2019
by Black Thorn, an imprint of Canongate Books Ltd,
14 High Street, Edinburgh EH1 1TE

Distributed in the USA by Publishers Group West and in Canada by
Publishers Group Canada

First published in 2016 by Severn House Publishers Ltd,
Eardley House, 4 Uxbridge Street, London W8 7SY

blackthornbooks.com

1

British Library Cataloguing-in-Publication Data
*A catalogue record for this book is available on request from the British
Library*

ISBN 978 1 78689 497 7

Typeset by Palimpsest Book Production Ltd, Falkirk,
Stirlingshire, Scotland

Printed and bound in Great Britain by Clays Ltd, Elcograf S.p.A.

This book is dedicated to the memory of Beryl Joan Jecks
22nd March 1929 – 4th October 2015
Miss you, Mum.

ONE

There was a man lying on the ground in front of me when I came to. He was dressed in travelling clothes, and I stared with a grimace at the stained and torn cloak, the sun-bleached hat and worn boots. His face, I thought, looked familiar, but for the life of me, at that moment, I couldn't work out why. Mind you, I had a serious lump, at least the size of a duck's egg, on the back of my skull, and there was a series of important questions troubling me just then, not least of which were: Why had someone clobbered me over the pate with what must have been a maul or hammer? Why was I sitting on the ground? Exactly where was I? And why was my knife in my hand?

And what was smeared over the blade? That should have been uppermost in my mind, to be honest, but just then the other questions seemed more urgent.

My companion, on the other hand, had no questions or concerns of any sort. Not any more. He was past caring, since someone – possibly me – had caused him to add his blood to the piss and mud of the ground out there. Yes, I was outdoors, in a small yard, and the noise that now came to me reminded me that I had been in a tavern. From the smell, this was the yard that was the unofficial privy out at the back.

I climbed to my feet, the world spinning lazily. It felt as though a giant had bound me to an enormous bobbin and was twirling it enthusiastically. I don't know whether you have experience of such events, but, to me, waking beside a dead body with my knife besmeared with blood was not looking like a good turn-up for the books. Especially when I heard a door crash wide, steps and a sudden grunt of surprise.

There are many men who are experienced with dead bodies. Some are used to finding them; others are used to finding those responsible for them. Me, I'm more used to avoiding them.

I ran.

Earlier that day

Later, when I had time to think back, life had been so delightfully unremarkable only an hour or so before. It was just an ordinary, everyday Sunday morning.

We had all been sent out at daybreak by Bill, determined to catch the early attendees at church so that we could enjoy a good meal that evening. Yes, it was shameful behaviour to rob the religious on the Sabbath, especially in a church, but we had to live, and pickings had been poor the past week.

Bill? He's our company's fencing cully. There were six of us: Bill, Wat, Gil, Ham, me and Moll – Bill's wench. A man on his own in London nowadays, in the year of Our Lord fifteen hundred and fifty-three – or, if you prefer the new method by which some capricious fools are setting New Year in the week after Christmas, fifty-four – is in danger all the time. There are too many men with knives, clubs, guns and swords, and a fellow on his own is likely to be beaten over the pate and arrested before he's nipped his first bung, but with a man like Bill in charge of the company – a fellow who could fence the goods we found, who could source food and drink, beds and protection – life is a lot safer. I'd been with him for months now. When we stole something, he would find a buyer; when I cut a purse loose, he would take the money and make sure that it was held safe for the good of all of us, with the pelf being split equally. Bill ensured we all got a fair share and none of us would go hungry.

But enough of Bill.

That morning I'd decided to go to the cathedral. I reached the street near St Paul's, down close to Ludgate and the Fleet river, and there I pulled my woollen cap down over my eyes and studied myself as best I could in the limited reflection from a window-pane. Not tall, but not short, mousy hair a little ragged where Piers last cut it because he was drunk. Piers is a pimp and hairdresser working in a brothel, mainly because he lost his wife and house to the ale, but he could still handle a pair of scissors quite well – and better while sober. I suppose, as an apple-squire, he had to know how to keep the doxies looking as well as they could. The wenches there were installed to cater for a better class of client. They never would let me inside, not without seeing the colour of my money first. Actually, if they saw the inside of my purse, they wouldn't let me in anyway.

I suppose it is as well to explain a little about myself. A fellow setting out on a narrative of this kind should naturally inform his readers as much about himself as possible. In that case, since by reading this, my dear friends, you are joining me on the journey of my adventures, I will explain.

First, I go by a number of names. Foremost is Jack Blackjack, since that is the name my father gave me; then there's Jack of Whitstable and Jack Faithful by those who know me well. But I have been known to use other names as I see fit. Peter the Passer, John of Smithfield, Hugh Somerville – all have been used or misused by me. As to the rest of me, I suppose I am well formed, if slender, with a face that inspires trust – which is lucky. It is my face that has earned me my keep these last two or three years: square, with a kind of rugged integrity in my brown eyes and straight nose. True, there is a scar on my left cheek, but that gives me an air of devil-may-care insouciance. I like to tell women how I won it defending the virginity and honour of a maiden – although, in truth, I won it tripping while running from an enraged miller who found me in his daughter's bed. It would have been fine, but when he glared at me and said, 'Who is *he*?' his daughter turned her limpid blue eyes to me and gave a squeal. 'I don't know! I've never seen him before!' Names hadn't mattered the night before, mind, but I suppose she saw no need to overuse the truth. In any case, when telling a tale like that of my scar, it's best to tell most of the truth – just not quite all. I want to entice a gull to listen to me while I snip the strings of his purse.

So, as I said, I studied myself, checked my appearance and walked into the Black Boar tavern, just another slightly scruffy fellow who had entered for a sup of ale, and hardly anyone cast me a glance. Why should they? They didn't know that within the hour I'd be a wanted man, a notorious murderer.

It was dark inside the tavern when I entered, and I almost brained myself on the low ceiling. Smoke curled from the fires, thick fumes choking at the throat and creating a warm fug. It was hard to see from one side of the room to the other.

Men were seated at settles and benches, and I glanced about me as I entered, hoping for a suitable victim. The barman saw me. He was big and red-faced, and had the cheerful look of a man who knew exactly where the club under his bar sat waiting. He raised a leather tankard in a dumb show of offering, but I shook my head briefly. I was there for a different occupation. Besides, I had no money. I pushed past drinkers and a threepenny upright who was haggling with a man who couldn't take his eyes from her chemise top, to where two men were playing dice on a rough tabletop in a window. One was a great bear of a man, with a beard that was as black as a sinner's soul. The other was fair-haired and had a bright smile and youthful grin. Pushing past me, a fellow with a broad-brimmed hat went to the table and sat, his face hidden, and seemed to stare at the murky glass of the window.

There was no point hanging about hopefully. A quick inspection of all the fellows inside told me that there were no pickings in there, not that I'd be keen to try it. I like the Boar and wouldn't want to be forced to seek a new watering hole because desperation had forced me to steal from a customer in there. I wanted to watch the street, but the men near the window showed less inclination to move than dogs at a three-day corpse. The Bear glowered at me while he continued his game, and I leaned against a wall and peered through the window at the yard outside while they exercised their eyes in my direction. I eyed the game briefly, to see whether they were playing with fullams or some other form of loaded dice, but I am not experienced enough to tell. Dice are a mug's game. The sharpers know how to trap a coney and empty his purse in minutes. The three played on, the hatted man seemingly joining in without speaking.

It was hard to see through the window at first, but I knew

that place, and in my mind's eye I could fit the people to the scene, even with the filthy and smeared glass.

The great looming bulk of the cathedral was just down from here. I could make out the steeple against the sky, the roofs of the canons' houses, and even the school for poor boys. And all about them were the people of the city, wandering and bellowing.

There were days when this city drove me to distraction. I come from Whitstable, and the ribald cries of the hucksters and whores demanding attention, the shrieks of the little brats begging for food or coin so they could go and buy drink for idle parents, or to take themselves to oblivion, made me feel sick. The idea of providing a service for money was sneered at, when the lazy brats could win a rich man's coins, but I did not begrudge them that, although I did dislike their habit of picking on a fellow like me. These dregs of society were all too keen on deriding a fellow's dress or sneering at him when he gave them nothing. Still, the wenches selling their pies and apples had busy lives of grim effort, just as I did. They toiled hard, as hard as any scavenger cleaning the streets of refuse. And they were just as necessary, but also dangerous, to a man like me, if they took it into their heads to denounce a fellow trying to nip a bung.

The point was, many new people came every day, expecting to find streets paved with slabs of gold. They arrived from towns and villages all over the kingdom, walking with the drovers bringing their animals to Smithfield, riding on mules, or joining one of the teams of packhorses that made their way from as far away as Exeter or even Durham, attracted by the frenetic lure of sex and money, just like ravens to a corpse.

Inevitably, the newcomers would end up here, in St Paul's on Ludgate Hill. And this is where I'd meet them.

It's where I met him. I really wish I hadn't.

TWO

I was a professional already, and I could spot them a mile off.

Wide-eyed, confused, they'd wander the streets staring upwards with their daft mouths agape at the magnificent tall buildings, rich stonework and expensive carvings. Most of them had never seen a house with more decoration than an annual covering of limewash; here in the city, often a man set store more by how ostentatious the outside of his house was, rather than have any comfort inside, and these places showed it.

Never pick the older ones. That was my first, my hard and fast rule. Older folks would have more experience, and may be on the lookout for a cutpurse. No, I'd always head towards the youngsters, the lads too overwhelmed and befuddled to chew the straw in their mouths. You could promise them much and make a small fortune from their foolishness before they'd realized they'd been gulled.

But there was a problem with this rule: if you always went for the youngsters, you invariably ended up with purses that were almost weightless. They had so little left after a journey here. All their money was spent on the roads heading to London, and robbing them was as pointless as stealing the flame from a candle. It would not benefit me. And I was hungry.

So today I was waiting to find a new target, one who could help me to find a good meat pie and a quart of beer. I had already failed to steal one purse, taken another that contained only a few bone counters that would be suited to a game of merrills or backgammon, and one clipped coin. Not enough for more than a cup of beer.

'You standing there hoping to play?'

This from the bearded man. He glared at me like a miller seeing a rat in his sack.

'Nay, I am waiting for a friend.'

'You keep looking at us as though you're watching our play.'

'I will turn my back.'

'You'll feel my boot in your arse if you don't piss off!'

The fair man was already laughing uproariously, while the man with the hat remained at the table, but any relief I felt at their lack of attention was quickly dispelled as the big man climbed to his feet, fists ready clenched. I strolled away, but as I heard him approach, I hurried.

I swear I could feel his boot at my buttocks as I hurtled through the door and almost into the fellow who was soon to become the fellow I most feared in the whole world.

I'd seen him walking about the street that morning while I was watching for a target. He was loitering like a man of leisure.

Broad-shouldered, he had a thin beard and sallow complexion. His eyes were a little yellowish, like a man who'd spent too many hours out of the sun, and at first glance I would have marked him as a man who had the pox or malaria. It was a false first impression, though. On a second look, he didn't seem unwell. A good thing, too, for else the dainty wench at his side would have dropped him in an instant. She was dressed in sober but fashionable style, with a most lecherous twinkle in her eye when she looked at her man, but when she glanced in my direction, that twinkle died like a snuffed candle.

He was clearly wealthy. There was no chance that this woman would have been with him for long if his purse was empty, for I knew her. She was Ann Derby, one of the brightest, sweetest, shrewdest little tarts who ever lifted skirts for a coin.

I fixed my best and brightest apologetic smile to my face and bowed and apologized most prettily, if I say so myself, and eventually the fellow grunted that he was unharmed, and took his hand from his sword's hilt. However, he was no easy hob ready for a fleecing. I could see that from the way that he set a hand on his purse as soon as look at me. This was not a newly arrived innocent ready to be saved from excessive spending by my swift fingers, and Ann took his arm to walk between him and me, too obviously keen on the idea of liberating his purse herself. She didn't want to share it with me. I was left muttering a curse under my breath.

Turning and looking about me, I saw another face I recognized. On a low staircase that gave up to a shop front, I saw my comrade Bill. It was rare to see him out like this. The fencing cove was happier to keep to his bench where others would bring their winnings to him, but there he was. Good old Bill. If it weren't for him, I would have nowhere to trade my prizes, nowhere to rest my head. He was peering in my direction, but I don't think he saw me. He was searching for someone else. Fleetingly, I wondered who.

However, I had no time to ponder about him overlong. As Ann and her man passed on, I saw another fellow who was clearly perfect, only a short distance away.

He was a younger man with much more money than sense, and the gaudy, fashionable clothes to prove it. Slashed sleeves and more buttons than could easily be fitted to their holes in an entire morning, he was rolling in a manner guaranteed to attract the attention of any number of fly nips or foists. More, those clothes were worn and stained. He was a recent visitor, or I was a Fleming. With his clothing and his general air of dissolute living, I felt sure I had a target worthy of at least one or two meals. His purse looked overfull, which is always a good sign in my eyes.

I carefully took the battered coin from my purse and allowed it to fall, stepping on it in an instant. A man cannot leave a penny lying in the street for two breaths without some thieving urchin snatching it up. As the gull stumbled past, I raised it with a frown. 'Master? I believe you dropped this,' I said. 'Does your purse have a hole?'

The poor, befuddled fellow turned his blank gaze to me, and I held it aloft. Well, who would deny ownership? His stare moved from me to the coin, to the purse at his belt, and he rattled the purse. It chinked delightfully, indicating to anyone who could be interested that here was a most friendly purse, feeling a little overfull and eager to share a pleasant evening in the company of a fellow with a liking for a life of comfort. I knew that purse and I would get along well.

But before I could open my mouth, a flaxen-haired harpy, with the sharp, furious face of an alewife who finds her customer has been drinking all night and now cannot pay the reckoning, stopped before us and screeched at him.

'So there you are! Two weeks, almost, and you've deigned to return?'

'Mistress, you must not . . .'

'Must not, mustn't I? What mustn't I, eh? When my husband goes dipping his wick in another woman's . . .'

'Agnes, in the name of God, go home! You are making an unnecessary scene. Trust me!'

'What? Trust you?' she spat. 'Do you think me a fool? Do you think I'm blind?'

'Don't make a scene!' he pleaded, his eyes darting hither and thither as though expecting a captain and his soldiers to appear at any moment.

'I *hate* you!'

With that, she burst into tears and ran off down the road towards the cathedral.

There are never good moments to intervene between a husband and wife, but this seemed like a heaven-sent opportunity for me. The man might not have been a newcomer as I had first thought, but he was clearly in need of companionship.

'Master, you should have a leather worker look at your purse,' I said. 'There are so many men about here who would steal the teeth from your jaw; if one were to see your money falling so easily, they would cut the strings in a trice and be off to the stews to spend it.'

'But there is no hole,' the man said. His tone was that of a boy told that his favourite toy had been eaten by the dog, fretful and sullen now his woman had gone.

'Mayhap the coin was ejected by the others for being less than sociable,' I smiled, desperately trying to avoid gazing longingly at the purse. 'Are you new to the city?'

'No! I live here.'

'Really?' I had guessed that, of course. Why else would his woman have been here, too? Still, his accent was so slow and dull, it was as bovine as the cattle I guessed he tended. I thought he sounded as though he came from Suffolk. Only later did I learn he came from the other direction, from far-off Devon. But he was speaking the truth: he had been living in London long enough. He had been going to say something else: where he was to, or where he was from, I guessed. It mattered little to me. 'If you don't recall this penny, why do we not go in and have a pot or two of ale as good companions should? Someone else lost it and we can make good use of it.'

'No, I have an urgent duty. I must go and fulfil my task.'

'Perhaps you should visit the cathedral? St Paul's is only just here, my friend. Come, you are cold, and it is warmer inside. Besides, it is always a sound scheme to offer thanks to Him for safe delivery after a long journey.'

'No. I must complete my mission before I rest. I have a message. A most important message,' he said.

'For whom?'

But that was as much as he was prepared to divulge. I smiled and teased and cajoled, but I wasn't truly interested in some message. All I wanted was the opportunity to take hold of that purse. I needed something that day. So far, all I had was a set of bone counters.

I'd even given him my last blasted penny.

THREE

B one counters? Yes. And one clipped penny.

I was not having a good day. Earlier, I had seen a fellow who looked ideal. He was a youth of some eighteen or nineteen years, clad in a jacket that had plainly been made for him two summers earlier, a cloak that had seen the underside of more than one hedge, and the gaping, mazed stare of the newly arrived. However, for all that he was young and new to the city, he had a purse that looked most interestingly full, and I was determined to become better acquainted with it.

It would be tedious to explain my approach to him – the slow, blinking confusion on his ale-bloated features, the slight stumble that allowed me to trip him over my leg, the swift nip of his laces with my concealed knife, and then the profuse apologies and quick assistance to help him to his feet, dusting him with one hand while the other slipped his pleasantly weighty purse under my shirt. I left him to go on his way with a cheery wave and smile, and walked increasingly swiftly in the opposite direction.

There are some gulls who are a problem, and who require hard effort just to be able to speak a few words to them. Others are so suspicious that even a man as apparently honest as me cannot approach within a few feet. This fellow was as easy as a child. Most men who carry large purses can be relied upon to be cautious. They don't get to acquire large purses by giving away all their wealth like this lummox.

I soon discovered why. His purse was full, but not in a way that would enrich me. Inside there was one clipped penny and many bone counters, the sort that a gambling club might use. They were useless to me, and I almost cast the purse, bone coins and all, into the gutter. But then I thought the better of it. Someone might value those counters. I shoved it back into my shirt and continued on my way.

*   *   *

So, now I had this new gull.

I could see only one way to get near to him, and that involved investing more than my solitary penny. I persuaded the fellow, at length, to join me in a sup or two, and he finally agreed, walking with me back into the tavern from which I had been ejected so recently. I pushed my way inside with the youth trailing behind me. Willing or no, he had little choice: I had the hem of his cloak in my hand.

Inside, I caught the eye of the barman and soon had a jug of ale and two cups. Pushing my guest towards a bench and table in a corner, I began to think that the day was going to go well. I was looking forward to a drink, but I was looking forward with still more enthusiasm to the first opportunity of looking into that purse.

'You again!'

It was the man into whom I had almost run earlier. He and Ann Derby were there, staring at me disapprovingly. As my companion and I stood at the bench, his woman rested her buttocks on the smooth wood with barely a hint of reluctance. It was only natural. The boards were as filthy as the rest of the tavern. I bowed and looked about me for an alternative rest for my weary legs, but only succeeded in catching the eye of the dice-player with the hat. He appeared to be studying me with some interest, and I quickly looked away again. There was something about his gaze that was deeply unsettling.

Since the woman and her gallant had taken our bench, all I could do was stand nearby with my gull. I was happy to be barged into and pushed ever nearer the fellow, and at last I was close enough to filch his finances, but even as I moved my hand, the man on the bench asked my companion to sit beside him. I was to be cheated again! And then I saw that the youth's purse was gone. Fleetingly, with the eyes of a professional, I saw his purse move swiftly in the hands of the man on the bench. He had not only stolen my blasted bench, but he'd taken my bird's money, too. That was pushing arrogance to the limits! But what should I do?

There was only one thing I could do. I sat quickly, forcing the man and woman apart. The alternative would have been for me to take residence on the woman's lap, and Ann clearly had no desire for my closer proximity. Instead, she gave me a fierce glare and reluctantly shuffled along slightly. The man, of course, had no desire to cause a fuss while he had my man's purse in his hand. He gave me a sour gaze, which I returned with a wide smile. And then, as I was considering how to acquire what he had taken, I felt a tug on my cloak, and a moment later something was thrust into my hand.

You must understand that we three were sitting so tightly packed that it was an easy mistake to make. He had thought to pass the purse to his accomplice, you see, and had no idea that my hand was resting there.

I saw all this in a flash and acted accordingly. I grasped the purse of bone counters I had taken that morning, and tugged the lady's skirt. A hand came forward, I thrust the purse into it, took up my gull's purse, concealing it beneath my cloak, and then stood and made my way to the door.

As I did so, the men playing dice looked up. The fellow in the hat stepped forward, blocking my path, and I was struck with a sudden conviction that he knew more about me than I would like. So, with an airy nonchalance, I tacked and went to the back of the tavern. A door there, I knew, gave out into the alley behind, where men made use of the walls for their privy. Once there, I searched quickly for an escape, but there was nothing to be found. I was trapped! In the absence of another idea, I hurried to conceal myself behind a stack of long planks of wood that were set like a pavilion against the wall, with a pile of trash to one side waiting to be taken to the midden. There was little enough space to hide there, but when I reached it, I discovered that, set into the wall behind the planks, there was a doorway. I hoped that it might be persuaded to open. I tried the latch cautiously.

I was not a moment too soon. Almost immediately, I heard the tavern's door shoved wide, and, peering between two long planks, I saw my young victim. He stood with an expression of baffled consternation as he stared about him, and I hastily drew my eye back in case I might be seen. My hand on the latch felt it rise. I pulled open the door, glancing back towards my gull. As I did so, there was a slamming thud on the back of my head, and I knew no more.

And that is that.

As I said, I came to and saw the body. When I was knocked out, I had fallen forward from my concealment, and the man's body lay near me, dead. I heard the door opening and shutting, the loud footsteps, but I had paid them little heed because I was suddenly recalling everything. I had been struck down, and I had a quick panic that I could have been robbed! Patting my shirt, I soon reassured myself that the purse was still there, and I was congratulating myself when I heard the door, the steps and now a gasp.

Perhaps you will have already spotted my mistake. I had paid no heed to the man who had left the tavern, but now I was suddenly wide awake, so it seemed, although with a thundering head. I reviewed the scene that must have met the man's eyes: a fellow dead on the ground; second fellow beside him, gripping a bloody dagger. No, this wouldn't look good.

When I glanced up, wincing, I saw that Ann Derby's friend was standing in the doorway. He was looking at me with a cold face, as though I was a murderer or something. Well, perhaps he wasn't to be blamed for that, but there was no need, in my opinion, for his sudden pulling of the door wide and his bellow inside calling for the constable. And then I saw him draw a short riding sword.

You will have seen fights; so have I. I've seen men fight with sticks, with daggers, with swords, and, if I am honest, I am more than capable of defending myself. I am young, and those who have tried to injure me have tended to be older, slower and, more to the point, generally unaware that I was going to attack them. Invariably, I've noticed, folks can get hurt when their opponent is prepared. I try to avoid giving away any important clues that could allow my enemy to ready himself. More, I have also noticed that when a man with a short knife is attacked by a man with a sword – any sword – the result for the fellow with the knife can be unpleasant.

I didn't intend to find out how unpleasant, which is why I took to my heels. The door that had been behind me was ajar. At the other side, there was an alley full of noisome fumes that proved men didn't always bother to seek a privy, and I was along it faster than a flea finding a new host.

I made it back to our room, a clear half mile away.

I have run from many things in my life. As a boy I learned quickly that it's better to get away than to hang around and receive punishment. I am experienced, but that mad pelting along alleys and up small streets was terrifying. All the way, I fancied I could hear boots in close pursuit, but when I run, I run to win: never look back – that just slows you. One thing you learn early on in a career as a thief is to focus on where you're going. Whence you came matters very little, and those following can take care of themselves.

I ran along to St Paul's, out towards Ludgate, then up an alley beside St Martin's until I was close to Newgate, where I turned right. I had hoped to find – and was glad to see – that the Shambles was packed with people stocking up on meats. Carcasses and barrows of joints were being carried here and there, because the rumours of Wyatt's rebel army approaching London meant many families were keen to feed well in case there would be a siege. I darted in among the people, ran into the yard of St Martin's Le Grand, then took a left and bolted down a lane to St Nicholas's, before nipping down to Paternoster Street. From there it was easy enough to take a circuitous route homewards to the great river.

There are many hovels in the city. For me, the best place always was down near the river. There you get the fresh smells of the water, rather than the foul reek of sewage in the roads. Our place was along Trig Lane, an ancient building that had been used for constructing boats, allegedly, but more recently, from the smell, had been used to fill barrels full of herrings. I shared the large room in the roof with my friends. It was where our company's leader, Bill, conducted his business, and where we all slept.

'What's the matter with you? You look like you're in a dead sweat,' Moll called from her bed. She was lying in a deliciously amorous pose with Bill, as usual.

In the circumstances, I thought hers an unfortunate phrase. 'Nothing,' I said.

'That's the first "Nothing" I've seen that's made you so pale and anxious,' Bill commented. He peered at me as he rose from the bed. 'What's happened?' he said, almost aggressively, as though suspecting that I had led the tipstaff to our home. Apart from being jealous of his bedding Moll, I also disliked his suspicion whenever I came back from an escapade.

'Aye, well,' I said grumpily.

Moll rose languidly, and I stared at her like a lecher twice my age. She came towards me and I could smell the after-effects of lovemaking. She bent past me to reach for a jug and drank from it. 'There's nothing like sex after a good morning, is there?' she said.

'You've had a good one?' I asked.

'Moll's only just back. She took a good purse,' Bill called. He climbed from his bed and pulled a shirt over his head. 'She always brings in more than the rest of you put together.'

'Where was that, Moll?'

'In the cathedral. He kept staring at me,' she said, putting a hand under each breast and raising them with a saucy grin. She could have tempted the Angel Gabriel, that woman.

'What about you, Bill?' I said. 'I saw you up at—'

He cut me off sharply. 'What have you brought?'

I set my jaw. He could be like that sometimes. I tried to be friendly, but all too often he would treat me like a wayward younger brother, one who had little brain. Well, I was not so dim.

'He's not well,' Ham said. 'Look at him.'

'He looks pale,' Moll said. She reached up and wiped the hair from my brow, peering with concern. 'You have mud on your face, Jack. Has someone been flinging shit at you?'

'I fell,' I said.

Bill gave a dry laugh. 'So you came back with nothing? What, you tripped on a loose cobble, did you? We need money to eat, Jack. You can't live here at our expense all the time. I don't want others to run risks just because you're not capable.'

'I can do my job,' I said grumpily.

'Where did you fall, then?' Bill asked.

Moll shook her head. 'It doesn't matter, as long as Jack's all right.'

'Ach, he's not used to such news,' Wat said. 'That's why he's pale. What of it, eh? None of us are.'

'What news?' I demanded.

FOUR

You see, I was so confused and worried after waking next to that body that the main news of the day had passed me by. Apparently, the rebels in Kent were making great advances. They were marching on Maidstone, or *from* Maidstone, or something, and the city itself was fascinated by the predicament. Queen Mary was only recently on the throne, and she had no intention of giving it up, from all I had heard. Yes, this was important news. I was young enough never to have seen a civil conflict, and the idea of an army marching on London would usually have had me shivering in terror.

But today? No! Today I was more concerned by the fact that a man had raised the hue and cry after me because he discovered me beside a dead man, my knife in my hand.

And who was it, I wondered, who had knocked me down? Whoever did that, surely, was the murderer.

I felt sick, and it wasn't only the knock on the head that caused it. I was more alarmed by the idea that someone had tried to kill me, too, and then killed my gull. Mind you, it had also occurred to me that whoever had done that had presumably been the man who drew my knife and put it into my hand.

He had deliberately tried to set me up!

None of the others noticed my concern just now, though. It was probably a good thing.

Ham shook his head grimly. 'Folk are worried all over the city.'

Bill pulled a face. 'News? What news is there? Royalty and all the grand folk arguing among themselves. They live in their palaces, eating the best food off silver plates, drinking the best wine out of golden goblets, and never spare a thought for the likes of us, unless we're caught and held in their courts, and then they order us hanged without a second thought.'

Wat chuckled. 'You think so? What about the rioters?'

'Rioters, my arse! Soon as the queen sends her men, they'll be put to flight.'

Wat had nothing to say to that. Indeed, there was little enough to be said. Bill was right.

Bill Tanner was older than the rest of us, at nearly forty years. He was of middling height, broad at the shoulder, square-faced, brown-haired, and with a scar at the edge of his mouth that made his lips curl upward as though always sneering at the world. His grey eyes held a world-weary cynicism, but since he had been born in the turbulent years of good King Henry VIII's reign, of immortal fame, and had lived through the troubles of King Edward VI's, he reckoned he had earned the right to his cynicism. Most of us couldn't remember the shock and fear when Henry ordered the destruction of the monasteries, nor the discontent when the Nun of Kent was executed for denouncing the king for something or other, nor the fears of invasion – which still prevailed. Bill had. He had survived more dangers and disasters than all of us, his confederates, put together. And he had gathered us together and bound us to each other.

His was a simple creed: we were all one family. And, like any family, there was one father who ruled the rest. Bill was our leader, our father and our guide. What he didn't know about the City of London wasn't worth knowing. He had a finger in every pie, and he could trade anything we brought to him. I don't know what we'd have done without him.

The youngest of us, Wat, was a shorter fellow, with straw-coloured hair and a narrow face. He had suffered badly from scurvy last winter, and his voice had a lisp because he had lost so many teeth, no matter how much meat he ate. When Bill found him, Wat was a child, foraging among the trash on the street, searching for anything to eat. He had been orphaned for years already, and it was a miracle that he had survived as long as he had, living with the rats and cockroaches wherever he could find shelter. More recently, he had become a most accomplished thief and pocket-taker.

Ham was a little older, a large, heavy lad with a face that had been beaten once too often for any of his looks to have survived. His ears were large, bloated things that looked as if they had been added as an afterthought, his nose was twisted and notched like an ancient sword-blade, and his brows were thick from fights. For all his size, though, he was kind and mild with all of us. It was only when he saw one of us in danger that he began to grow angry.

There is another member of our little company, but he wasn't there just yet. Gil – at thirty or more, the second oldest among us – was a proficient thief who could put the fear of the devil into any poor victim on the streets. He certainly did with me.

Since Bill was already up, Moll rose as well. She settled her skirts without false modesty, covering those wonderful long legs, and patted her hair back into shape as she cast a look over at me. It was enough to make a shiver rise all up my spine. She could do that with a look, could Moll. I didn't fool myself; she was unlikely to throw over Bill for a daft country boy like me. Bill was protection and security, and that counted for her. She had fled her home when she was young. Once, she told me that her mother had remarried after her father's death, and her stepfather tried to climb into her bed and 'get to know her better' when her mother was away. She ran from home with the sound of his roars ringing in her ears, she said. I told her then that if he should ever find her again, Bill would kill him, and that seemed to give her comfort. She smiled gratefully. Me? No, I didn't stand a chance, I reckoned, but that didn't stop me looking, and every so often there was a gleam in her eyes that spoke silent promises of what she could do to me if we were ever alone together. I know: I can dream as well as the next man!

She was slim as a willow, was Moll, with hair that glistened in the light as though she had auburn diamonds sparkling in it. Her face was pleasing to the eyes, too, with high cheek bones and slightly slanted eyes, and she had a way of holding her head low and peering up at a man from those big greenish eyes of hers that gave the appearance of a wanton challenging a fellow. I had adored her when I first met her, and since then my infatuation had increased to the degree that it was painful to watch her in Bill's arms. Not as painful as his amusement at my predicament, though.

'What, you want a handful of her, Jack?' he said now. He had a twisted grin. 'She's ripe enough.'

Moll squeaked as he put a mitt on her breast and squeezed. She caught him a slap on the cheek. 'You wait till later, Bill Tanner! And stop embarrassing the poor lad. He don't deserve it.'

'He don't care,' Bill said, his other arm about her waist. 'Come on, give me a . . .'

My blushes, for my imagination was running riot at the thought of grappling with her delectable globes, were saved by the door flying wide. For a brief moment, my arrest and the end of my life on the scaffold flew before my eyes: I heard the judge pronounce my fate for the hideous murder of a man living in the city, I felt the shackles on my wrists and ankles, I felt the scorn of the crowds as they witnessed me pissing myself, the heat of my shame as I failed to make even a momentary speech in my own defence before the noose was set about my throat . . .

And then I realized that the man at the door was no beadle. It was Gil.

'The army! The Whitecoats are marching!'

Yes, the Whitecoats. That was the big news of the day: that the rebels had approached close enough to justify sending a force against them. The City of London's yeomen had been gathered together and were marching against the traitors who dared to challenge the new queen's right to do as she wished. That was fine by me because, as the rest of the company eagerly grouped around Gil and belaboured him with questions until he covered his ears, I was left alone. Only Moll stood near me, eyeing the rest of them with weary and pitying amusement, like an elder sister eyeing her wayward brothers.

Since I had caught my purse, I had not had time to look inside it. Now I took it up and opened the laces. It was a goodly size, with a delightful heft to it. Whoever had made this had expended quite a sum on it. The soft leather had hung from a thicker piece of leather that had been carefully cut through at the base, where it had been secured with a thong. A piece of the thong remained, and I could see the perfect, shining edge where the knife had sliced. It had been enormously sharp, then. For the rest, the purse was secured with a lace that had golden thread in it. Even here it gleamed in the light. I opened it and smiled to see the treasure inside. I had no idea how much money there was, but the sight of that many silver coins brought a smile to my face and a glow to my heart. I soon forgot all about the man slain in the alleyway. It was nothing to do with me, after all.

'What's that you've got?' Bill said.

I had been standing there gloating too long. I would have shoved it behind my back, but there was no point. My guilty face would give me away. 'I won this today,' I said, holding it out.

We had a moderately strict policy of share and share alike in our group. I couldn't keep it back, whether I wished to or not. Not now he'd caught me out, anyway. He was a clever bastard at that sort of thing. Bill could sense when someone was holding back on him.

'Let me see it,' Bill said and took the purse. His fingers shook as he took it, the avaricious old stoat. Bill took all our money and looked after it. That was the price we must pay for our safety here in the house. There was greed in his eyes, and then, I thought, something else, too: anger or hatred, directed at me. At first I thought it was just the way I had held out on him about the purse, but then I saw his eyes slide towards Moll, and that made me wonder. I've always liked Moll, as I said. Perhaps I'd been eyeing her too much. He didn't like to think that anyone could challenge his position as her man, and I didn't like to think that he could take it into his head to remove me as a potential challenger.

I wasn't going to worry about it now. My concerns were more to do with that dead body behind the tavern.

Besides, I would do nothing to risk my place here. It wasn't much, no, but in this season, at the end of January, it was cold and wet outside. In here, at least a man could find a patch that wasn't sodden on which to sleep. A place where a man could lie in the dry, without fearing that rain and snow would hasten his end, was always appealing. Bill had found this place. Yes, it had leaks in the roof, and the stench from the river was foul in summer, but it was mostly dry, and we all felt safe, which is more than most people could say in London.

He took my purse and pulled at the laces. Soon he had a handful of coins and began counting them.

'What kind of a nobleman was he?'

'He was no nobleman! I think he was more a bumpkin. Not a man of note,' I said.

Bill chuckled. 'You think so? Then he had gulled a rich man or robbed him! Look at all this cash! It's enough to keep us in beer and meat for a month!'

FIVE

His words were enough to make me frown. The fellow had not looked inordinately rich. He was dressed more as a servant than a man of property. It was peculiar that he should have so much money, so perhaps Bill was right and he was another thief like me – except a man used to robbing others would have been much more suspicious of a helpful man like me.

Bill carried the coins into a shaft of light, throwing the purse aside. I picked it up, thinking it might be useful to me, and found that there was an odd thickness to the base. I felt the leather and discovered that there were two layers. Without thinking, I pulled the purse inside out and saw that someone had added a second patch inside, as though to mend a hole. But there was no hole. As I manipulated it, I could feel something inside that crinkled.

'What's that?' Bill said. 'Did I miss one?'

'No, I was just looking at it. I thought it would make a good purse for me.'

'You think so?' He looked at me with a sour grin. 'It's a bit good for the likes of you. Mind you aren't seen with it. Anyway, you'll need a new lace.'

'Yes,' I agreed. I knew where there was a spare thong in my bag and went to fetch it. While I knelt, I pulled at the inner patch of leather, and some of the threads broke. Soon the patch was free, and I could see a piece of parchment inside. I took that out and opened it, but there was nothing of any interest, only a series of strange figures. I can read my letters, after a fashion, but this was not any English I had learned.

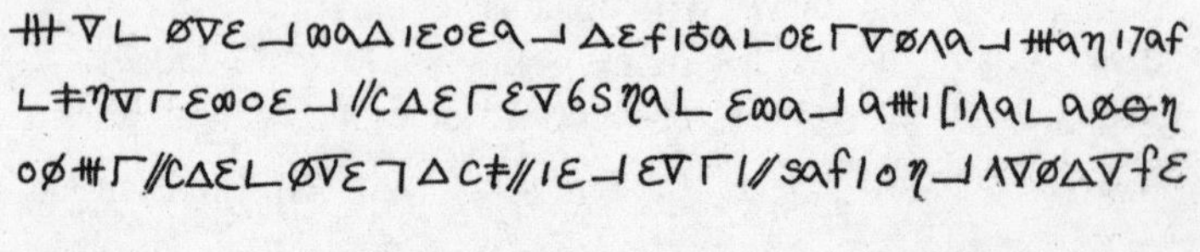

'You can't take that purse,' Gil said. He was bigger than me. Not in height, and definitely not in intellect, but, equally certainly, his breadth was double that of my slender shoulders. He walked to me and snatched the purse from my hands. He smirked at me as he did so. Gil and I had never been friendly, but I didn't want to dispute with him. He was welcome to the purse. It was easier that than me winning a broken nose or worse in a fight with him.

'You take it,' I said. 'It's tatty enough to suit your clothing.'

Which wasn't true, but it made me feel a little better for saying it.

We all went out when the noise of cheering and clapping came to us. The yeomen were marching from the city, and we walked up the road to where the London folk were gathered.

No, we didn't go from any daft sense of pride in the military, but because where the army marched, a man might attempt a little business. A crowd was heaven-sent for us, scoundrels as we were. It meant incautious women and cheerily drunk men. It meant rich purse pickings.

I went along behind the others. Gil was bent, threading my thong through the holes in my purse as he went, occasionally casting a sneer in my direction as if determined to enjoy my discomfiture as much as possible. I never liked Gil. He wasn't a pleasant soul. We hurried along Candlewright Street and caught up with the soldiers as they approached the bridge.

They marched well, all in good order as soldiers should, their weapons slung over their shoulders, their white coats and emblazoned crowns and royal insignia gleaming in the sunlight. Fortunate for them that the weather was holding, I thought. Us, too. The crowds would have been thinner if it were piddling down.

'What will happen?' Moll said.

'The rebels will march here, meet the soldiers and surrender – or get a thrashing they'll never forget,' Bill said dismissively. 'If they're lucky, some will be allowed home. The rest . . . Tower Hill has space for many gallows, and the heads on the Bridge Gate are rotting. They could do with some new ones on their spikes.'

The soldiers were marching like stern retribution, but then, as we craned our necks to see more clearly, one of the men suddenly dropped his arquebus and ran to a woman. He grabbed her and bent her backwards, kissing her, and although his companions continued marching, they raised a roar of approval for his actions. There were cheers from the crowds, too, where men and women cheered and applauded, but the men were needed in Kent, and they dared not delay even a moment. It fell to an officer on horseback shouting at him to get him to rejoin his companions. He went, a shortish, dark-haired figure, running to take up his gun again, and then racing on to catch up with his comrades, while the crowd clapped and hooted. He looked in my direction for a moment, and I saw a young man with the face of an innocent. It was like staring at a child about to go away on an adventure – or a prank. As he and the other men continued on their way, I was left thinking that this poor fool could well be strolling out to his death.

There were not only the Whitecoats. The news of rebellion and the fear of civil war had brought out all the city's martial spirit. There is nothing that the City of London detests more than a war nearby – it plays merry hell with the merchants' incomes – so behind the Whitecoats came another five hundred or more, these a contingent of volunteers from the city, all waving their hats merrily as though leaving to go hunting at Greenwich or beyond, and the women cheered them. There is little that stirs the breast of a woman so vigorously as the sight of men marching off to fight and kill other men, I've noticed.

It's not for me.

Why not?

When I was a young lad growing up in Whitstable, my father had early on tried to interest me in his business, making leather jacks and buckets. It's a good trade, after all. Wherever the Navy has a dock, wherever there is a tavern, there is a need for blackjacks, and few men can have such a guaranteed business. My problem was, the thought of spending all day with my hands in water preparing leather, or tugging the linen thread tight in the stitches until my hand was a mass of cuts, did not appeal to me. My indifference enraged him at first, then infuriated him. I'd never have an income, he swore. He wasn't the most affectionate of men, and the idea that I might have my own ideas about a career didn't occur to him. In any case, if I was to have a trade of any sort, it would be with him, rather than another man gaining an apprentice as cheap labour. It was one more thing that we would never see eye to eye on. So, at his wit's end, he tried to shove me towards the military. He wanted to see if I had the necessary strength and determination, I suppose, but I would have nothing to do with the notion. It's one thing to fight and injure or kill a man; but there's always the other aspect of life in the military: the risk that an enemy would fight back and maybe kill *me*. I never saw the attraction of that. So, naturally, he declared me a coward as well as a rascal. Well, I don't deny it: he was right. He declared me a rascal so often that perhaps the idea took hold and bore fruit. After all, I was now the living embodiment of his fears.

But I would prefer to be a disreputable person of no name, hanging about London and cheering the poor women mourning their soldier-boys, than to be a soldier lying with my belly slashed open on a field of blood and gore. That was never likely to be my choice.

'Any gulls here?' Moll asked, peering about her at the crowds.

Her words brought me back to my senses. With all the excitement, I think we had all forgotten our purpose. While viewing the marching ranks was satisfying, it was not as satisfying as a full belly and a pot of ale in the fist. There were plenty of men and women down in the street with full purses, and if we could liberate one or two, we would have made a good profit on the day.

Without a word said, Bill, Wat and the rest of us dispersed in among the throng.

There were so many there, it was a cutpurse's delight. Men and women were jostling and shoving. A matron gave a squawk and glared at the men near her, but that was not a theft, except of her pride. She had no husband with her, only a manservant who held a club but had no space in which to wield it. I was tempted. While she was glaring at the nearer men, one of whom had no doubt pinched her backside or mauled her bubbies, I could easily sidle past her and filch her purse, I thought, but then I saw her servant watching me closely, and I moved on. There was so much potential here in the crowd that only a fool would concentrate on one who was already prepared to defend herself to the exclusion of all other opportunities. I turned and glanced back a little later, and I was disconcerted to see the man still staring after me. I jerked my shoulders to resettle my jack more warmly about my shoulders and continued on my way, resisting the temptation to look back once more.

I moved along the street and stood at the corner. My costrel had a little ale left in it, and I pulled the plug and sipped. The pitch had flavoured the ale as usual, and it tasted sharper, but that was all to the good. I felt the cool liquid drop down my gullet, and as I pushed the bung back in and tapped it lightly with the heel of my hand, I saw her again: Ann Derby.

She was a glorious woman. Tall, but not slim or boyish in outline. No, Ann was utterly feminine, with curves like a ship of the line, with bosoms between which a man could suffocate, and hips that were built for grappling. Ah, but she was a lovely wench!

Sadly, her demeanour showed that she had considerably less regard for me than I for her. Earlier, when she caught sight of me, the twinkle had died. Now, as she noticed me again, her eyes narrowed. She turned abruptly and moved along the street like a galleon under full sail. I tried to catch up with her, but she turned into an alley, and when I darted into it after her, she grabbed my jack and yanked me in, almost pulling me from my feet.

I squeaked. 'Hold! Wait, what are you doing?'

'I ought to gut you here, you miserable prick!' she hissed.

SIX

Her face was only inches from mine, and I could smell her breath. She had been chewing cinnamon or cloves and her breath was the sweeter for it. I couldn't help but think how plump and soft her lips looked.

Her next words dispelled any further amorous reflections.

'Why did you kill him?'

'What?' If I squeaked before, this time I squealed like a stuck pig. 'Me?'

'Don't deny it! You think I'm a fool? Everyone saw you go out, and moments later he was dead. The gull had realized his purse was gone, and went out after you to raise the hue and cry. You slew him as soon as he accused you, didn't you?'

'You'd blame *me* for robbing him?' I said, and I meant it to sting.

She had the decency to look embarrassed. 'Yes, well, you know how these things are.'

'I saw your confederate take the purse, and he was foolish enough to pass it to me.'

'And you gave me a bag with bone counters.'

'I didn't think your man would know there was anything missing.'

'At least he didn't kill anyone for it.'

I glared at her. 'What happened to the counters?'

She glared back at me. 'I don't know and I don't care!'

I tried to be conciliatory. 'Look, your man robbed the gull. You can't get angry with me when *he* made the mistake of passing the stolen purse to me, can you!'

'Can't I? I was to have a share of the money.'

'That's hardly my fault!' Something struck me. 'Was that it? You were going to share the money?'

'Yes. We were to share it: one third to me, two to him.'

'I see.'

'I held it for a moment and gave it back to him when I

could. I should have guessed. It wasn't heavy enough. I had seen how heavy it was when it dangled from the gull's belt, but when you passed it to me, it was much lighter. And we saw it was different when we looked at it outside. And when he opened it.'

'After I'd left the room?'

'Of course! You think we'd open it while you and the gull were there? After you walked out, we left the gull sitting on the bench and went to the street. We'd begun to stroll towards the cathedral when I gave him the purse, and – and he went mad! I never saw a man become so full of choler so swiftly! I thought he might die of rage – and then he ran back inside to chase after you. I didn't know what had got into him. Not at the time.'

'You hadn't seen I had taken the purse from your man, then?' I said, feeling smug that the switch had been so successful.

'He told me later, after he found you with blood on your hands, standing over the poor fellow.'

'I wasn't standing!' I protested, but she just tipped her head as though I was plainly lying. It was hurtful. 'Your man called the constable, did he?'

'It's usual when a man's found in the act of murder.'

'He waited there? I hope you ran off before the law arrived.'

'No, I stayed. I didn't think anyone would accuse me of anything. I was in the tavern all the while when you killed the poor fool. He seemed to know the constables when they arrived. Anyway, so what? What do his actions have to do with you?'

I didn't like the sound of that. I know some constables myself, but they were the sort of men who had limited senses of humour, and I wouldn't wait for them to appear at a crime. It was odd that a proficient purse-snatcher should be on terms with them. What sort of man knew the officers but could prise a purse? Someone with more money than me to spend on bribes. I reasoned, 'I think he must have killed the gull and knocked me down. He came in from the gate to the alley behind the tavern, broke my head and then killed the gull. Who was he? Where does he live?'

'Do I look the sort of woman who would wait on a man like him?'

'That depends on how much he was paying you,' I said.

She looked at me with withering contempt. 'More than you could afford,' she said pointedly.

I ignored that.

'In any case,' she said, 'when the shouting and bellowing all started and the hue and cry was raised, I made myself scarce. I didn't want to wait any longer than I had to. You were lucky to escape. You should have seen all the men there haring off to catch you. I wandered away before anyone could accost me.'

'Yes, well, the door to the alley was open, so I took it.'

'And you ran. Why you took so long, I don't understand. You had the body there. You were found red-handed, weren't you? Why didn't you flee as soon as you had killed him?'

'I *didn't* kill him! Why should I?'

'Then who did!' she snapped.

That was the nub of my problem, I realized. If no one had seen anyone, other than me, leaving the room, it would make establishing my innocence a great deal more difficult.

'I told you. Your companion came at me through the alley and . . .'

'He didn't. I saw him. He went back inside the tavern. It must have been you.'

A thought struck me. 'The man with the wide-brimmed hat! It must have been him! He did it!'

'What man with—'

'Someone was there,' I said. I recalled the door in the wall, trying the latch, the way it gave way, then the pain of the blow on my pate. 'There were three men in the tavern. One had a hat with a broad brim, but he left the place just as I was rising. I thought he was going to attack me before I could get to the front door, but what if he went out, then came at me along the alley? *Someone* came in from outside. I was knocked down, and I didn't come to – not until your fellow came after me. Whoever it was who came through the gate must have hit me on the head and then killed the gull. That other fellow murdered him, and would have killed me, too, but for the speed of your man coming out, I suppose. I'll bet it was the man with the hat. Your fellow surprised him, I think, and he fled. Leaving me lying injured and unconscious to take the blame.'

I thought I struck the right tone there. Not arrogant, but with just a hint of professional appreciation, as though I was experienced in such crimes. After all, I was the only man who could describe the scene.

'Where?' she said.

'Where what?'

'Show me where you were hit.'

I bent my head and indicated the lump. She felt it without sympathy, with a grudging respect and a fair amount of ungentle roughness.

'*Ow*!'

'Very well. I can see you have been knocked down.'

'So you believe me?'

'Let's say I'm less inclined to disbelieve you,' she said.

'But I didn't do anything!'

'So *you* say,' she said with scorn. 'If someone else was there, no one else saw him. Everyone in the tavern did see you go out there, and the other fellow following immediately after you; when you disappeared, he was dead. It's no surprise everyone thinks it must be you.'

'You could have told them I wouldn't kill a man!'

'And how would I know that?' she spat. I could feel the spittle hit my face, and I closed my eyes and lifted a hand to wipe it away, but as I did so, she thrust me from her and I tripped over a piece or two of trash and fell heavily on my rump. She turned to leave me, wiping her hand on her skirts as though to clean them of my filth.

'Who is he, anyway?' I said.

'Who?'

'Your companion. The man who was with you in the tavern? The man who came out and found me?'

'He called himself Henry, but I don't know more than that.'

'Where did you meet him?'

'He found me on the street. Where else? But I can tell you this: I saw him once at a house in Paternoster Row, near St Michael-le-Querne. I think he lived there.'

'Could you show me?'

'Why? What does it matter?'

'He might know something. He was trying to rob the fellow. Perhaps there was more than money involved.'

'Look! You killed that poor gull, and that is all that weighs in the balance.' She began to walk away. 'You are dangerous. I don't trust you, and nor does anyone else. You're marked as a murderer.'

'Ann!' I called, and she paused.

'What now?'

'You have to believe me! I didn't do anything!'

She curled her lip, but this time more in amusement than contempt. It was oddly irritating to be looked down upon by her. I felt like an urchin viewed by a knight's lady. 'Looking at you now, I hardly think you have it in you to stuff a man full of steel,' she said, 'but there was no one else there that I saw!' and she was gone.

SEVEN

For a long time I remained there deep in thought.

Her words had shocked me. It never would have occurred to me that anyone could think me guilty of committing a murder, and yet Ann thought exactly that, if her face and actions were anything to go by. If *she* believed me capable of killing a man, who would believe me? Especially since I had bolted as soon as the first man appeared. Not that it was my fault: whoever it was who had knocked me down was surely the guilty man. And yet that man had come in from outside the tavern. No one would have seen him arrive.

Panic set in. What was I, other than a rascal who had run to London at the first opportunity, leaving his home and father alone, to try to make his own way in the world by living on his wits? I was quick with my hands, and competent enough at word-play when it was necessary, but I was not capable of killing in cold blood. How could anyone think I would plunge a dagger into a man's belly?

The answer to that was *easily*. This was London. The city was full of men who would draw a knife or sword at the slightest provocation. If a man felt insulted, if a man felt his honour was impugned, if a man felt he was being made to look a fool, let alone if he thought he was robbed, he would be more than capable of killing another. In God's name, I'd seen it often enough.

I had to get back to the house and speak to Bill. He would know what to do.

Yes. Back to see Bill. That was the main thing. I clambered to my feet and set off back the way I'd come. I peeped out into the roadway and sauntered out among the passers-by, making my way back towards the river, treading carefully amid the horse, dog, cattle and donkey dung that liberally covered the whole of the way. It was a way to distract myself – not that it worked. I was deep in thought as I went. The young gull was dead, I was blamed, and I had no idea who was responsible. I didn't know who the fellow was, nor why I had been knocked unconscious before he had been killed.

The only thing that made sense was that someone struck me down to rob me and . . . and robbed him, too. The man with the broad-brimmed hat.

I stopped.

No one would have come through that gate knowing that I was there. Someone appearing behind me would not have known I was there before they opened the gate. Whoever it was didn't want me dead. They were looking for better prey. And the lad had a well-filled purse. Surely it was a man who saw him in the tavern, guessed he would be in need of a piss after a while, and decided to lie in wait. For him and his money.

Except . . . I took out the parchment I'd found in the bottom of the stolen purse. It made no sense to me. Just a jumble of letters and occasional strange symbols, and I peered at it with confusion. No one could make sense of a thing like that, surely. Which was the point, of course. A man who had need of such a code had something to conceal.

And the rebels were approaching London just at the time that this fellow appeared and died.

Somehow this reflection was not reassuring.

When I reached Trig Lane, I climbed the rickety steps to the loft and was surprised to see Bill already there. He was over at the paillasse where Ham and I slept, and he sprang up with a face that turned a deep red as I entered.

'What are you doing back here so soon?' he growled. 'If you're thinking you can have an early night because of one purse, you can think again!'

His aggressive manner drove all thoughts about why he was at Ham's and my bedrolls. I hastened to explain my predicament.

'I can't stay in the streets. I have to talk, Bill. I need help.'

He was mollified by that. He looked at me askance and persuaded me to sit on a stool while he fetched us both wine from a leather flagon. 'Well?' he said when we were both seated.

'Today a man was killed behind the tavern near Ludgate, and people are saying it was me killed him!'

'Why would they do that?'

'I was there. That purse I took?' I explained all about Ann and her companion, then about bolting to the yard and what happened. Bill listened with a frown on his face. I ended, 'I don't know what to do!'

'It was Ann's friend found this man?'

'Yes.'

'And you're absolutely certain that you didn't see whoever it was knocked you down? You don't know him?' he demanded.

'Why are you so suspicious? I don't have eyes in the back of my head!'

'Ann's friend found you, you say?'

'Yes. He left her outside the tavern when he came back in, according to her.'

'Does she know who he was?'

'Who cares? He came through the tavern. He couldn't have flown from the tavern, out to the alley, then back in to knock me down and kill the other fellow,' I said sharply.

'Watch your temper, boy,' he said.

I swallowed my justifiable irritation. 'I just spoke to her and she had no idea what the name of the man was, other than that he was called Henry.'

'Henry? Are you sure?'

'I think so,' I said. I was a little perturbed to see how Bill leaned away, staring at me.

He took a long pull at his wine, wiping his mouth with the back of his hand. I thought his expression was too much like that which he wore when the carts rolled by with men being carried to the gallows: 'There, but for the grace of God,' he seemed to be thinking. Now he wore that same expression as he looked at me.

'You'll have to keep your head low, then. Perhaps you ought to go back to Kent and hide out there.'

'But I can't!' That was unthinkable. 'I can't run away from the city! My father wouldn't have me back now, and I don't know anyone else.'

Bill nodded and shrugged. 'Well, you are going to be hunted

now, and since you're responsible for stealing a rich purse, they'll look all the harder. You'd best stay here, hidden.'

'I didn't even steal it from him. I took it from Ann and her friend.'

'I don't think that will help save you from the rope.'

EIGHT

Bill's view was straightforward enough. Unhelpful to me, but straightforward. He thought that I would be in great danger if I left Trig Lane, and that if I were to be caught, I'd be killed.

'It's either run far away, back home to Whitstable, or at least stay here and keep your head down,' he said. 'Do you still have that purse?'

'No. Gil took it.'

'The shit. Typical of him,' Bill said. He eyed me a while in silence, before nodding to himself. 'Right. First thing is, we ought to find out what's being said on the street. You wait here. Understand me? You hang about here. I'll go and see what I can learn.'

I nodded, feeling only relief to think that he was on my side, glad to know that he would look after me. It was only after he'd gone that I realized I hadn't told him about the strange code in the bottom of the purse. He knew about the money well enough, but the message was hidden. I pulled it out again and stared at it. Someone must be able to understand it, I thought. But I had no idea who. There were magicians and others who had skills in the strange art of deciphering such messages, but they were not the sort of fellows who would frequent the haunts where I was known.

Alone, I was bad company for myself. It was impossible to settle. I meandered about the room, but no matter what I did or how I tried to drive it away, I couldn't get rid of the memory of that man's face, drained of blood, eyes wide, and the sight of all that blood everywhere. Whoever had tried to set me up as the murderer of the fellow had done an excellent job – that much was clear. I sank into a gloomy reflection, convinced that I was doomed now. I would be caught and hanged for a murder that was nothing to do with me.

* * *

I was startled when the door opened and Bill came in again.

'Well, we know a little more now,' he said.

'Are they still hunting me?'

'In the city, yes. But no one seems to have known who you were, so you're safe enough for now, I think.' He eyed me bleakly. 'But it is not good news for you. The fellow who died was called David of Exeter, apparently. He was servant to some family from the West Country: the Carews or somesuch.'

'I've never heard of them.'

He shrugged. 'A thief will not often know the name of his victim, will he? But the rebellion in Kent – that is not the only one, is it? There're many others elsewhere, if the stories are true.'

'But the Kentish rebellion is the only one remaining. The others have all been crushed, haven't they?'

They had. The fighting in the rest of the country was snuffed out before it could take hold. Spies had discovered the conspiracy, it was said. The government was so efficient that the rebels had been defeated almost before they could gather, to the benefit of all. A country ignited by the flames of rebellion was not a safe country for anyone.

He looked at me. 'Yes. But the man who started the rebellion in Devon was a man called Carew.'

'Really?'

'Yes, *really*, and if that is so, what was his servant doing here, do you think?'

'Perhaps he was coming to . . . I don't know!'

'It's likely he was bringing a message to someone, isn't it? Perhaps he had a message – something to tell his co-conspirators, something to do with the rebellion?'

The import of his words struck me. That strange piece of parchment must contain a coded message. I had no idea to whom it was addressed, of course, but if there was a rebellion, and men thought I had hurt one of their messengers, the rebels would want revenge. Not that it was likely. 'There's only one rebellion continuing, isn't there? That'll soon be crushed. We saw the army march.'

'Yes. You are probably enormously lucky,' Bill said.

Yes, I thought. The army would crush the rebellion, and soon the whole matter would be forgotten. There was nothing for me to worry about.

It was already growing dark when the others began to return. Gil was drunk, as usual, and demanded beer as soon as he arrived. He grabbed my costrel and shook it, throwing it at my head when he realized it was empty. I had to catch it quickly before it could hit the floor. So often the leather on a cheap costrel has been cooked too long and will shatter if dropped. Moll and Wat turned up a little after him, and Gil tried to make Wat give him some drink, but Moll got in his way and he backed down with bad grace, shoving me from his path as he went to lie down. He wouldn't want to stir Moll. If she were to go and complain to Bill, he would suffer, and he knew that.

Bill was there as the first men of the watch made themselves heard.

It was strange that throughout the day the only noise in the area was the shouting of men, the rumble of barrels, the steady wash of the waves on the wharves, the snuffling of a few pigs, the squawking of chickens and the constant creaking of timbers and hempen cordage as ships and barges passed by. At night, all those sounds gradually dissipated and were replaced by occasional barking dogs, men singing, shouts and, every now and then, a baby bawling its head off from the place over the lane where a maidservant had been comforting her master too well and too vigorously.

After some food, I sat on the floor and covered my face, wondering what would become of me. Moll saw my despondence and tried to get me to talk.

'You'll be all right,' she said. She walked over and sat beside me. 'The watch will look around for a while, but they'll soon lose interest. How many bodies are found every week, and the murderer never found?'

I knew she was right. 'But I want to find the man who did that. He tried to see me killed.'

'I doubt that. You were knocked down, but he didn't kill you, this murderer,' she said earnestly.

'Stabbing the man with my dagger and putting it into my hand – that wasn't supposed to see me hanged in his place?'

'Perhaps it was just a panicked act? He probably didn't think anyone would consider you a likely murderer.'

I was irritated by that. It sounded as though she thought I was so feeble-looking that no one would think me capable. Then she smiled sympathetically and glanced across at Bill. I thought then she was trying to lift my mood and was worried that he could read too much into our quiet chat. No matter! I was in no mood to listen. She was a woman and couldn't understand this sort of violence. She had no idea how it felt to have been placed in such a position, and in a while she grew exasperated with my grumpiness and rejoined the others about our little fire.

'The Duke of Norfolk was leading the Whitecoats,' Wat said.

Bill snorted. 'Him? He must be eighty if he's a day.'

'He's the queen's most trusted commander,' Wat said.

Gil chuckled roughly. '*Most* trusted? The *only* one she'd trust, more like.'

'If she thinks he will be vigorous enough to stop a man like Wyatt at the head of five thousand men,' Bill said, 'she's going to get a nasty surprise, I reckon.'

'The rebels will fail against real soldiers,' Wat said confidently.

'You think so? Everywhere they go, they win more friends and allies,' Gil said with a sneer in his voice. 'The Whitecoats are marching on Rochester, but when they get there, they'll be cold, tired and inclined not to fight the people, you can be sure of it.'

'You seem to know a lot about these people,' Bill said.

'I had a talk with three men in a tavern, and they knew a lot about it.'

'Who?' Bill said.

'I don't know. They were just men in a tavern. You know how it is.'

'Yes. I do. To go and drink in a tavern, you need money. But I haven't given you any,' Bill said.

'I have money of my own sometimes,' Gil said. There was

an edge to his voice that I heard clearly as a threat. I looked up to watch.

'We all share and share alike,' Bill said, which wasn't strictly true. We shared, and he took the lion's portion. But he was our banker, and we all knew it was to our benefit.

'Yes, and I keep some by,' Gil said.

It was so fast that I almost leaped from my skin and rapped my skull on the ceiling. Bill sprang up, leaped over the fire and caught Gill a blow across the face that sent him sprawling. In his half-drunk state, he could not defend himself as Bill kicked him four times swiftly in the belly, before lifting him and holding a fist to his face. 'You want some more? If you want to stay here with us, you'll have to learn a little more respect!'

'All right,' Gil said, his eyes averted.

'Where's the rest of it?'

'I don't have any.'

'Give me your purse.'

Gil reluctantly removed it from his belt and Bill took it, weighing it in his hand. Then he looked down. 'This isn't yours,' he said. 'It's the one Jack stole.'

'I liked it,' Gil said.

'Make sure you aren't seen with it. You spent all your money?'

'I hardly had to. The men all bought me wine. They had been gambling in the cockpits – cleaned out the house, they said. They were all three buying drinks for me and others. I stayed with them while they were throwing their coins around. Who wouldn't?'

'Three of them?' I asked.

'What of it?' Gil snapped.

'Did one of them wear a wide-brimmed hat that concealed his face?' I asked, struck by a horrible suspicion. You don't survive as a felon for long without learning to doubt the nature of coincidence. Those who lose the critical facility to wonder about men who suddenly appear and buy drinks for strangers often find that their life can become foreshortened.

'What of it?'

I sat up and stared at Bill. 'It's the man from the tavern.'

'Did you tell them where we live?' Bill demanded.

Gil shook his head. 'You think I'm soft in the head like Jack? I wouldn't tell anyone where we live.'

But later, when I glanced at him, I saw his eyes slide away from me. There was something in them. Naked greed, I thought. If someone were to offer him money to hear of my whereabouts, I didn't doubt that for a single silver penny he'd sell me and his own mother as a job lot.

NINE

Monday 29th January

The next day, Monday, the others rose as usual with the dawn. Or near to it. Bill and Moll were awake, but clearly had no intention of getting out from beneath their blankets for quite a while, such was the giggling and wriggling that was going on. I averted my eyes, trying to dispose of the jealousy that threatened to engulf me. Wat was already awake and chewing at a piece of dried bread, blowing unenthusiastically at the coals in an attempt to light the fire, but his tinder was too thin and the cinders wouldn't catch the flame. In the end, I pushed him aside and broke some small twigs to lay it afresh. Before long, I had some charcloth smouldering and a small flame was soon igniting some shavings. Gil, meanwhile, rose like a bear with a sore head, and hawked and spat, narrowly missing me.

I wouldn't react to his ill humour. It was pointless. If he wanted to beat me to a pulp, there was little I'd be able to do to defend myself. Bill could launch himself at the idle git, but if I tried a similar thing, I'd end up sprawling and then be beaten still more furiously. No, I would do better to ignore him.

He had the purse I had pinched, I noticed. It looked entirely out of place on his belt. It was too bright and richly decorated for a man with such faded britches and worn jack. Not that it was my concern. I rather hoped he would be seen. Perhaps someone who knew the dead man, and who would think Gil must have been the killer. That would let me off the hook. Until he pointed the finger at me. Knowing my luck, everyone would assume he was telling the truth, and either hang me or hang us both as irrelevant nuisances.

Bill was eventually finished, and while Moll lay back

contentedly, he rose and dressed himself, hunkering down beside me. He put his arm over my shoulders, which came as a surprise, and spoke almost kindly.

'Jack, you're a good lad. You understand you have to stay here hidden, right? Don't go into the street while the folks are looking for you. If you do, you'll be an easy target. Keep to the house and you'll be safe.'

'Yes.'

'I'll see what I can learn about this man who was so friendly with Ann.'

'What of the other three? The man with the wide-brimmed hat and his friends?'

'They showed bleeding poor taste, wasting their money filling Gil with beer and wine, but apart from that I don't see that they come into this. They just happened to be in the tavern.'

'In two taverns. It's strange that the same men should appear in both taverns.'

'*If* they were the same three men,' Bill pointed out. 'Don't go thinking that every fellow with a wide-brimmed hat must be the same man. There are enough men who wear hats like that in London.'

'I suppose so.'

'You stay here, keep away from beadles and constables, and it'll soon blow over, I expect.'

Bill patted my back, and then called to Wat and Gil. 'Come on, lads. Time to get to work.'

I watched them enviously as they trooped from the door. They would be going to church later. Bill liked to visit St Paul's, while Gil and Wat had a liking for St Mary Magdalene's and St Augustine's. All tended to have full congregations during Mass, and the opportunities for filching a purse were excellent. I just wished I could go with them.

Moll stretched like a cat as the three shuffled their way to the door. Bill peered out, and then they were gone.

'Well?' Moll said.

'Eh?' I shot her a look, and I must have reddened like a fresh beetroot from the thoughts that flashed through my head.

'Are you going to do as he said?' she asked, and then caught sight of my expression, I suppose, because she lifted the blanket up over her breast and gave me a disapproving look.

'I . . . er . . . yes, I suppose so,' I said. But at that moment the only thing I was certain of was that I had to get out before my attraction to her became any more obvious. 'Um,' I said. 'I'll be back later.'

'Why are you going? And *where*?'

At that moment I wasn't sure I could respond without embarrassment. I stood at the doorway and stared out. From here, the hill rose before me: Ludgate. It was a rising mass of shingled roofs, and in the early morning sun the smoke rose from a thousand hearths, mingling with the steam as the sun warmed the hoar frost.

I couldn't stay there alone with Moll. She was a temptation too far. I would inevitably have to say something that would make life impossible for both of us. No, I would have to go and cool down somewhere. It was impossible to go into the city after Bill's warning, so I chose the other path and wandered down to the river. I sat, dangling my legs over the wharf, chilling my buttocks on the freezing boards, watching the ships passing by. Every now and again a wherry would float past, and a stream of rich curses would be hurled in my direction; one bit his thumb at me; other sailors on their ships would wave or make obscene gestures, depending on their mood. The attitude of sailors to landsmen never ceased to amaze me. They all seemed to think that the fact of their living or working on water gave them some kind of advantage over ordinary men, that they could take the piss on a whim.

It left me feeling distinctly bitter. The whole world seemed to be taking the piss out of me, as far as I was concerned. I just hoped that the news of the murder would soon die down, so that I could go about my business same as usual. After all, it was all so unreasonable! No one who knew me would think I would risk the rope. Not for a purse.

Who was the dead man? He was just a scruffy-looking fellow, when all was said and done. He was a pain, too – that was sure. I wished I'd never caught sight of him. I wanted only to get back to my work. I'd need new clothes first, though. Looking down at my comfortable jack and britches, it was clear that, while I continued to wear them, any description passed around by Ann's 'Henry' would be bound to come back to me. London was a vast city, but not so vast that a man like me would go unnoticed around Ludgate. I was plainly not a rich man, and my height and appearance would be broadcast by now. What was I to do?

By the time I returned to the house, it was gone noon, and Moll had left. I sullenly stared inside, feeling very hard done by. It seemed that even she had deserted me. I was all alone in the world. Perhaps they were all gone, never to return. That would be typical.

Hearing steps, I turned to see Gil swaggering down the lane. Behind him, I saw three men. One wore a broad-brimmed hat.

TEN

In the time it took me to recognize the man from the tavern, I realized that Gil had betrayed me. Quick as a kingfisher, I sprang down the stairs before either man could see me, and was out on the wharf, hiding behind a stack of barrels, hoping to attract the attention of a wherryman so I could cross the river, but there were only three I could see: two with passengers, and the one who had bitten his thumb at me earlier. I tried waving surreptitiously, but there was no response. I waved again, and this time I was sure that he had seen me, but he chose to pretend he hadn't. He was moored alongside a great anchored barge and was eating a pie or something. Clearly, the man had such a small brain that he could not concentrate on his meal and a desperate passenger at the same time.

Glancing around towards the house, I could hear Gil arguing with his friend, but the words were lost in the swirl and slap of the water beneath me. A dead hound floated past, and I stared at it, wondering how long it would be before I was thrown into the water and floating away alongside him. He rolled over as he was caught by a current, and his paws waved at me as though in welcome.

At last the wherryman seemed to finish his meal and began to row towards me. I waited with bated breath, hoping that the fellow was coming to me at last, but before he reached the shore, I heard the voices grow louder. The waterman had his back to me now, pulling strongly for the shore, and although I waved and hissed frantically like an enraged swan, the black-hearted bastard didn't once turn around.

Steps were coming closer. In desperation I fled, hurrying along the wharf to the farther side of the house. From there I ran back to Trig Lane itself and stood for a moment, wondering what to do. There was the sound of shouting, and when I bent my attention back towards the river, I was sure that it was the wherryman bellowing insults at me for disappearing. No doubt by suppertime the fool would have persuaded himself that I was a ghost, and he would sink into his cups with the conviction that he had narrowly escaped the devil's wiles. These sailormen are notoriously superstitious.

There was no place of concealment here. I crossed over Trig Lane and into the yard of the house opposite. There I heard the mewling of a child and realized it was the very house where the incontinent maid had produced a bastard for her master of the house. She was there, in the yard, and I quickly darted inside. The child was in a small cot near the door. I hurried to it and was almost there before I realized the mother was only yards away.

She gave a start, plainly thinking me a thief, but I tried to convince her, by smiling and bobbing my head, that I knew how to soothe her babe. I took it up, holding it at arm's length, and studied it. It studied me. I essayed a small smile. It still studied me with intense seriousness. I smiled more broadly, and the child opened its mouth to its fullest extent and then let blast such a clarion call of horror that I all but dropped the brute. A hound began to bay, and the maid began to wail, and I hurriedly placed it back in its mother's arms and ran back the way I had come before the hound could find me.

I was in Trig Lane once more, and as I glanced back at the house, I saw the man with the broad-brimmed hat talking to Gil. But then I saw them turn, and all at once they saw me.

Gil shouted, and the man stared at me as Gil began to run after me. I waited no longer, but took to my heels.

I ran for a huge distance. At least six paces. Then I stopped.

In front of me was the Bear, the man I had seen in the tavern, and whose boot I could still feel on my arse. He smiled at me in the lazy way a snake would smile at its prey. There was no kindness or sympathy in that reptile's grin. He slowly pulled his cloak aside to display a long ballock knife, setting his hand to it and pulling it free.

Turning behind, I saw Gil laughing and the man with the black hat approaching. 'Don't do anything foolish,' he called.

I could understand that. With that man the size of a bear,

doing something foolish was likely to be suicidal. So instead I did something remarkably stupid.

The Bear was only three paces from me, and I had a sudden, clear memory of watching the bear pits in Southwark. So often you would see a huge bear with paws that could crush a cannonball, holding back in the face of mastiffs that sprang and leaped before it. Speed and aggression, when all was said and done, were the way to beat such brutes. Such was the idea in my head as I decided to force the issue. Without giving myself time to reconsider, I picked up some sand and rubbish from the road and sprang forward, flinging it as I went.

Now, I am not large; I am a man of average build, no more. But the sight of me jumping towards him must have made the Bear fear that I had lost my mind and was about to attack. He retreated half a pace, and that left me space to dart about him. He may have been bigger, but that meant I was faster, and I made full use of my skill in the poltroon's department of fleeing danger.

I took the narrower, winding alleys that ran parallel to the river, rather than the roads further to the north. It took me only a short while to make my way to the great bridge, and there I suddenly realized that my life was in danger again, for there on the bridge were many men in the city's livery or the queen's. This was no place for a wanted felon.

It was clear that I could not return to the house in Trig Lane. That was far too dangerous. The only place I could think of where I could be safe was on the other side of the river with Piers, but that involved crossing the river, and there was only the one bridge. Staring at it, I was all the while aware of the men holding their halberds with such apparent competence.

However, I had no choice. I set off, keeping my head low and hoping to avoid their attention, and, for once, all went as I hoped. The city's guards were infinitely more concerned with the thought of attack by Wyatt and his rebels than they were with checking everybody leaving the city. I could have stood and declared I was a notorious murderer from the rooftops, and I daresay I'd only have merited a shake of the head and an irritated 'Tsk'.

Not that I was going to put it to the test. I hooked my thumbs into my belt and continued over the bridge, past the great houses on either side, past the tower, over the drawbridge at the far side and thence into Southwark.

I had no desire to be captured, as you can imagine. Although I was outside the city gates, there were plenty of beadles and watchmen who would be happy to arrest me, drag me back and collect the reward that was no doubt offered for my head. It was not a happy thought, but it was a salutary one. I kept to narrower ways and alleys where I felt my face would not be immediately obvious to the casual onlooker.

Piers was an apple-squire. He'd once been a barber with a good business, but the drink had got to him, and over time he lost his wife, his shop and his livelihood. Now he plied his trade at the brothels down in Southwark because that way the strumpets didn't have to stray far from their hospitable homes. As the bawds knew, Piers was good with his fists when occasion demanded, and they were prepared to pay him not only in coin but in kind. It was not a post many men who were young and lusty would have turned down.

He stayed mostly at a house called the Cardinal's Hat, on Paris Street, and it was to there I repaired. I knew the Hat well enough. No, not as a client, but mainly because it was the cleanest-looking house in the whole of Southwark. As though to reassure clients that the services offered inside were as pure as the driven snow, it was painted in eyeball-aching whitewash. Usually when I came to this ward, I would be heading for the baiting pens, for I could not often afford the cost of a wench and wine. I've heard from Piers of men who paid forty shillings for a night with a whore in the Hat, because as soon as the poor fellow was cozened into cups of wine, it would flow faster and faster, and he would have no idea of the cost until he woke the next morning with a sore head and two bully-boys standing over him, looking speculative, while the mistress of the house berated him and demanded her reckoning.

Finding the Hat, I slipped inside quickly. Two painted harlots were standing at the door, and one took my hand and placed it on her breast while she reached up to kiss me, but I wasn't so foolish. I took the other's hand even as she tried to fondle my purse. 'Where's Piers?'

The first, a brazen strumpet with a bold eye and delicious pout to her lips, eyed me. 'He owe you money?'

'No, he's a friend.'

The other cackled. 'Any friend of his is safe with us, isn't he, Nan?' she said. 'Come, lad, you look half starved. You need some food inside you.'

'Piers – where is he?' I said again, determined not to be distracted. I know full well that a man entering a trugging house would be given food, but at a price that would make a banker blench. Piers told me that they had pies in the Hat that a man could buy for fourpence along the way, but the bawds would charge eighteen. It ruined my hunger to think of that kind of cost.

'Don't you like us?' the one called Nan asked, ducking her chin and looking up at me from soulful blue eyes as though offended. She couldn't quite conceal her lusty nature, though. Her tongue slipped out and licked her lips.

'Piers,' I said, although my voice had risen. I walked past them and went to look inside.

They allowed me to go, with throaty chuckles at my discomfort.

There was a door at the end of a short passageway, and here I entered and found myself in a chamber with five women: one redhead, a blond, the others brunette. None was wearing much, and what they were wearing wasn't hiding anything. I swallowed. The redhead and a brunette languidly rose from their seats, and I felt what it was like to be a stag held at bay by hounds. I knew there was no escape.

'Jack, what're you doing here?'

'Piers, thank the good Lord!' I said with rather more effusiveness than was strictly necessary.

He was a short fellow, with a scruffy mass of curling grey hair surrounding a pate as bald as a friar's. I never knew how old he was. His skin was grey from sleepless nights guarding his charges, and his flesh looked thin and unhealthy. Add to that his watery blue eyes and thin, colourless lips, and you have a vision of a man in his eighties or a thirty-year-old man who's had a seriously ill-spent youth. I lean towards the latter.

'Leave him, girls. He's with me,' Piers said, and led the way through a couple of doors to the rear of the house.

In a chamber that was almost as bare as my privy, and not a lot larger – and smelling about as fresh – he told me to sit on his little cot and fetched a large costrel of ale from a shelf. He took out the stopper, drank deeply and passed it to me.

'Come on, lad. What's this all about?'

I told him all about it: the dead man yesterday and my panicked run from the city today. It took a while, and he had to work at lighting tinder and gradually fiddling with it until he had a flame that could light the stub of a candle. Then he soon had a small fire burning and two other candles lit. The room began to feel a little more homely with the orange-yellow glow and the shadows moving, by the time I got to the thing I thought might be a coded message.

'Show me this parchment,' he said, and when I had passed it to him, he held it near his eyes, the candle-flame threatening his eyebrows as he stared at the symbols. 'I don't know what to do with something like this,' he admitted. 'There's one man could help.'

He passed the scrap back to me and took a long draught of ale, wiping his mouth and staring at me thoughtfully.

'There's a man comes in here sometimes. He's a clever bastard, really sharp, and got a mind like a knife. He thinks in squares and triangles all the time, and you can't get him to stop. He's a bit odd – he won't look you in the eye, and he gets quite . . . intense when he thinks you've given him something interesting to look at.'

'What do you mean, *intense*?'

'Just don't try to distract him when he's thinking about something. He gets irritable.'

I could cope with a degree of irritation, I thought. All I

wanted was some answers to the problems that were surely
multiplying all the time I was sitting here with Piers. 'Where
does he live?'

'You'll have to wait here a while. Until he comes in. He's
usually here on a Tuesday or Wednesday. So, you'd best just
settle in here,' Piers said.

'In here?'

'There are worse places.'

ELEVEN

His friend appeared early the next evening.

There are some men I've met who have instantly impressed me. Many were for the way that they cut out the light as they stood over me; a few had an impact because they looked so boldly dressed, with silks and velvets; only two ever had that effect on me because of the quality of their brains. One was this friend of Piers, a man called Mark Thomasson.

He was not impressive for his looks. It is an odd thing that I have come to notice: all too often a man's ability to dress well is directly opposed to his intelligence. I mean, if I see a man who is clad in the latest fashion, I can usually guarantee that he has very little between his ears, but show me a fellow with tatty clothes and hair all awry, not because he is poor but because he doesn't care what he looks like, and I'll watch myself. Those are the men who are dangerous. And Mark fitted that description perfectly.

Master Mark had a charmingly baffled expression when I met him. He was slim, with fine, aquiline features and a nose that could have been used to chop logs. His lips were thin as a razor, his hair a tawny mass of thick locks, and his eyes hazel in colour. He stood taller than me, but looked shorter because of his habit of sticking his head forward as if short-sighted. His eyes were perfect, I learned, but it was an affectation of his, as was his slow, stumbling speech. He would mutter and mumble with a frown on his brow, and then his eyes would clear and he would give a lucid commentary as though a spark of inspiration had just lanced into his mind. He was, in short, an astonishing fellow.

'Master, I would like you to meet a friend of mine,' Piers called when he appeared.

I was sitting chatting to one of the whores, who was less than keen to be talking to me, since I couldn't afford the price of a drink for her, and saw the lean shape of the man with Piers at the doorway. I rose and bowed as courteously as I might.

'Oh, um. Yes, I see,' Mark said.

He did not appear enthralled by my appearance. While Piers murmured a brief explanation, Mark was gazing lasciviously at a redhead who was feigning disinterest at the far end of the room. One of her poonts was protruding in an interesting manner, and Mark was gazing upon it like a knight who has at last found the Holy Grail after a decade's search.

'Yes, yes, um, fascinating,' he muttered, and tried to extricate himself.

'It's here,' I said, waving the parchment under his nose.

'Eh? Um, oh!' he said, and frowned at the shred of parchment without enthusiasm. He glanced up at the redhead again and then down at the parchment once more. His head tilted, and his mouth drew down at the corners, like a bow under tension, and he took the parchment from me without appearing to notice that I was still there.

'Can you decipher it?' I asked.

'Of course.'

His confidence shook me. I glanced up at Piers, but he shook his head as a sign that I should wait.

'There is no cipher or code invented by man that cannot be read with the requisite information. If there is a mere shifting of letters, transposition of numbers, new lettering designed to baffle the ignorant, each can be swiftly analysed and, given time, even the most abstruse of all forms can be, um, you know . . .'

His voice trailed off as he studied the parchment, and then he began to waft it about, as though he was warm and must fan himself. All interest in the woman had dissipated. He gazed at me. 'Where did you get this?'

Piers said, 'He found it in a purse lying on the street, didn't you, Jack?'

'Yes, that's right. I was walking along near St Paul's and saw it in the gutter,' I said.

'Was there any money in it?' Mark asked shrewdly.

I could answer that one easily enough. I held up my own purse. 'You can feel my purse if you want! No, I found this message stuck in the bottom, under a false base to the purse. It was well concealed, but someone else had taken the money.'

'I see,' he said. He wafted the parchment some more, frowning. 'I will need to take this to my office to consider it more deeply. You will meet me there tomorrow after noon.'

'No, I'll bring it to you,' I said. It was the only thing I had in the world that could be worth anything, and I wasn't going to wave it goodbye in the hands of a man I'd only just met.

'Are you really that stupid?' he said, peering at me like a physician eyeing a glass of discoloured urine. 'This scrap here could spell death to anyone who holds it, but you want to carry it on your person?'

'I don't want it; I only want to be able to guard it. I hardly know you.'

'You have Piers' word that I can be trusted, for else we would not be talking,' he said.

There was logic there, I'll grant.

Piers pulled at my arm. 'He's right, Jack. Leave it to him. He knows what he's doing.'

'That's more than I do,' I muttered. 'Where do I find you tomorrow?'

'I'll be at my house in Rose Lane,' he said. Then his attention returned to the scrap in his hand, and he left us.

'Who is he?' I demanded as soon as the door had closed behind him.

'Mark is a philosopher. He's interested in all kinds of things: how to make stronger bronze for guns, how to cast better cannonballs, how to make swords that hold their edge without shattering, how to write in a manner that no one else can understand – anything to do with learning is his sphere.'

'How did you get to meet him?'

'Oh, he's as interested in the tarts as anyone,' Piers said. 'Even the deepest philosopher likes a wench to snuggle up to on a cold evening.'

Wednesday 31st January

That night I must have been relieved to have given away the
parchment, for when Piers suggested that I should partake of
the sweetmeats available, I was anxious to agree. We spent
the evening with a brunette and redhead who were happy
enough to accommodate us, and thus that Wednesday morning
I felt more than a little under the weather as I left the brothel
and made my way to the shore, clad in some old hosen and
a leather jerkin that had seen better days. Or years. I had kept
my shirt. It was good linen, that shirt, and I wasn't going to
see it go to some vagrant.

I passed by the bear pits and stood at the shore. It was early,
my head was sore, my belly felt as though I'd drunk a quart
of sour wine, and I wasn't in the best of moods, but I was
keen to see Mark Thomasson.

I had already decided to make use of a wherry rather than
try to cross the bridge. There was likely to be more attention
paid to people coming towards the city today, and I wanted
little to do with the guards at the drawbridge. Instead, I had
borrowed some money from Piers, in the hope that the parchment might be worth coin to someone, and hailed a boat, glad
that it wasn't the man who had bitten his thumb at me on
Monday when I was attempting to escape Gil and his friends.

It was going to be good to talk to Thomasson. I was keen
to learn what this strip of parchment could mean. I had to
learn so that I could see whether it was worth any money to
me. I was in real need of money now. I swear, I never had
any desire to learn more about the dead man and the man who
killed him, and certainly nothing about the rebellion. But if
my wishes had any value, I wouldn't have been in such a mess
already.

The river was rough, and it was hard to see how to avoid
all the other boats and ships that were making their way,
tacking up the river or sweeping more swiftly down towards
the coast. I watched as the drawbridge rose to the sky to permit
a vessel to pass, and as soon as the ship was past, the bridge
was lowered once more, and instantly it was filled with peasants, traders and merchants with their clerks, some heading to

London itself, others passing in the opposite direction, a mass of mingled men, horses, donkeys and carts. The noise of the traffic and the shouts of hawkers came to me on the still air. Along with the reek of the city: middens, sewers, leather tanners, and all the other assorted foul stenches that the city held. Life at Whitstable had never seemed so appealing.

'You live in the city?' my oarsman said.

'Me? Well, most of the time, yes,' I said.

'What, been to the stews, have you?'

'Yes.'

He spat over the side. 'And now going back to your wife and children?'

'I don't have any.'

'You're lucky. Mine are seventeen, fifteen, fourteen, twelve, ten and eight. All boys. You wouldn't believe how much they eat. My wife works for a local merchant as cook, not that I see any of her food. It's always into the boys, and swyve me if there's a bite left for me by the time I get home. Me? I'm lucky to get a pie of gristle and bone from Mad Eric's on Fleet Street most days, I am. Sod that! My brother's no better, poor bastard. He married a shrew with the teeth of a rat. She sank 'em into him the first time they met, and she ain't let go her hold yet. But the first time he asked for food after a day's hard graft, she threw a trencher at him, told him to go and get something for hisself, if he was so hungry. Women, eh? Cheaper to buy 'em by the night.'

He set to gloomily hauling his oars. I eyed him with profound disgust. A man who couldn't order his own wife. Ridiculous.

My expression gave away my thoughts. He glowered.

'You'll marry one day. Find a pretty little face with a pair of bubbies like oranges and legs to her chin, you will, and you'll swear undying love for her to get between her thighs, and one day, you'll wake up when the wine's worn off and realize you've made a horrible mistake, while she batters you with her rolling pin, telling you to "Get out of bed, you lazy lummox" and "Haven't you got a boat to work?" and "Piss off out of here if you want anything to eat tonight." Never any bleeding peace once you've married.'

'Oh,' I said. It seemed something was expected of me.

It was a relief to get out of the boat and climb up the steps of the wharf. It was some way from our place, and I was early, so I decided to make my way back home and see if Moll was there. I tried to persuade myself I wanted to talk to Bill, but I wasn't very convincing.

I hadn't expected to find a body.

'Christ's bones, Gil!'

TWELVE

Gil had not died well. He was bound to a post at the side of the house, and his face was swollen and bloody. I felt his throat for a pulse, but I knew it was too late. I mean, all the blood on him and near him was congealed. When my finger touched his neck, it was cold as a stone – and about as soft. He'd just about frozen.

'Who did this, Gil?' I wondered aloud. I hunkered down in front of him, staring, as if he might be able to give me a clue. I heard once – in a tavern, I think – that a man's eye held the image of the last person he saw. If you could peer into his eye, you would see the man who killed him. Well, unless the victim was stabbed in the back, I suppose, in which case you'd get the image of some poor innocent bystander instead of his murderer. But that's by the by. I wasn't going to see the fellow here, because Gil had been given a real beating before he died. His eyes were swollen so badly that I doubt he could have opened them, and his nose was broken. When I looked at the ground, I saw two teeth in what looked like a frozen blood clot. It looked as if someone had hit him in the mouth so hard that his teeth had been broken free, and he had spat them out.

It made me feel sick.

Then I noticed something else. The purse was gone.

I left him there and made my way up the stairs to our house.

The inside had been trashed. Not that it was spotless before, of course, but now the decoration was modified by the addition of the straw from inside my palliasse, and the odds and ends of our belongings had been spread all over the place. My costrel had been slashed and torn open as though someone was looking inside it for a valuable . . .

I gaped. Someone had been in here and had torn the place apart looking for something, and since I had nothing of any value, the only thing that could have been the focus of the search must have been either the money, which Bill kept, or something else. In a flash, I saw again the face of Ann's friend, the black-hatted man, and the expression on Mark's face as he read my cipher. It must have been that damned note, I thought, and in an instant I bethought myself that a swift and lengthy vacation from London would be a good idea. The notion I had rejected a couple of days before when Bill suggested it now took on a more appealing aspect. I would have to flee.

It would be little effort to go to the river, take a boat over the Thames and then set off for Whitstable. How long would it take? No matter. Who cared, when the alternative was to end up looking like Gil? That was a thought that resonated. I didn't want to end up looking like him – a carcass left bound to a pole for the rats to feast on.

The door opened behind me and I yelped in fright.

'What in the devil's name are you doing back here?' Bill demanded, shutting the door quietly.

'I wanted to see how—'

'I told you to stay here, didn't I? And what do I find? I get back and you've pissed off!' he spat. 'I ought to stick you now!'

He had put his hand on his ballock knife, and I squeaked in alarm. 'What? Why? What have I done?'

'You saw what they did to Gil? We've had to bolt from here and find a new home because of you.'

'It wasn't me! Look at him! You think I could do that to Gil? He's twice my strength!'

'If not you directly, you brought this to him.'

'No, I didn't! You heard him talk about the man in the tavern who bought him drinks. Gil told you, and I said that was the same man who'd been in the tavern when the stranger was killed. But the day after, Gil brought that same man and his friend back here. I saw them. He was showing them the house and then they chased me. I had to run or they'd have done that to me! Anyway, they got what they wanted: they took the purse.'

'That purse? But there was no money in it,' Bill said.'

'You know that, and I know that, but maybe they didn't.'

'They killed him for an empty purse?' Bill said.

'Unless there was something in it that you and Gil didn't find,' I said evasively.

He didn't appear to notice my words. Walking to his own pallette, he kicked the straw aside and glowered down at it moodily. 'Nothing left here, is there?'

'What of the others?'

'They're all up the road. I found us a new billet at the back of Deneburgh Lane. Moll and the others are all there now.' He looked about him. 'There's nothing to rescue from this, is there?'

'No.'

'Come on, then. I'll take you there.'

I followed him down the stairs, and I couldn't help but glance towards Gil's body slumped by the post. He looked shrivelled, a smaller person than he had been in life. God knows, I'd no reason to like him, but seeing him there made him look so forlorn, like a discarded toy, that I wanted to go and report his murder.

'Report him? Who to? The beadle? You go. Do that. But don't forget they already have you marked as a murderer. It'll help the constable to know that you're responsible for a second dead man. They won't have to bother looking for another murderer, will they?'

I had to admit, he had a point. It made for a difficult series of thoughts. And then I had an idea.

The man who died: he had been arguing with his wife that day. Perhaps she could help. She was convinced he was spending money – there could be a clue there. Perhaps he was being threatened, perhaps blackmailed. If he didn't pay up, he might get himself killed.

I had to find his wife. But how?

Deneburgh Lane was a horrible, squalid little alleyway the width of a cart, with offal and waste making the cobbles slippery and dangerous. It was fairly steep in parts, and I slid three times until I was convinced I was going to end up in the Thames. The house Bill had found was a narrow building overlooking the river, with a shop beneath run by a wizened little man with a face like a short-nosed terrier, all wrinkles, eyes and skin as dark as a coalman's. There was a great thundering of hammers from the house next door, where a cooper kept up a brisk trade, but as the sun set and the cooper stopped work, it would grow moderately quiet, so Bill promised me.

I took in the room, which contained little more than a series of large palliasses stacked against a wall, a small table, a bench, and two stools that looked so old they could have been used by Cain and Abel. Moll stood in the corner. She had a more fretful look about her than I had seen in a while. Her eyes seemed to have grown to double their usual size with her alarm. She looked at Bill, then at me, and I could see she was nervous. It was hardly surprising. I had disappeared for a couple of days, and suddenly murder had visited the house. None of us was fond of Gil, but it's one thing not to like a man and another to see him slaughtered in that manner.

It felt as though Death was following me.

I began to walk to her, but she withdrew with an expression of real fear in her eyes.

That was when I realized: she actually thought *I* had done it, that *I* had murdered Gil.

She went to the fire, where a pot boiled, and knelt to stir it.

I was hurt. The idea that I would murder one of our fellows was really insulting to me. It offended my sense of justice. And then I realized that it meant she would never trust me. All visions of my sitting with her on my lap evaporated instantly. I'd never have her; that was certain. It wasn't fair!

Bill hadn't noticed. 'The men who did that to Gil, Jack. How many were there?'

'Three, but the other day here, when he brought them back, there were only the two that I saw. The man with the broad-brimmed hat and his sidekick, a huge man built like a bear. He scared the hell out of me, I don't mind telling you.'

'So you think Gil brought them here, eh?'

'Who else would have?'

Moll gave me a glance then, and I realized how her mind was working: I was so angry with Gil for bringing these men that I caught him and killed him later. The thought of pulling my knife and stabbing him was repugnant enough; the idea that I could have beaten him to a pulp like that was still worse. I turned my back on her. And then I realized that time was getting on. It was almost noon already. I should be at Mark's house.

I walked out, explaining I needed to keep my hand in. After all, we all needed some coin for food now. With Gil gone, we must all work that little bit harder.

And I would soon be working hardest of all. Mostly just to keep alive.

THIRTEEN

Mark's house was a small-fronted building. It was set back from the lane, and a small stream flowed down a gutter that was bridged by a large stone slab. I stood on the rock to knock at the door. A clatter from within told me that Mark was home. There was the sound of movement, and then the door opened a little, his wizened face appearing at the gap. 'Yes?'

'It's me. Piers' friend.'

'Oh, oh yes. Come in, please. Let me just move some of this . . . I usually tidy up in the afternoon, but I've been working . . . well, you know how it is. Come inside.'

All this was launched at me over his shoulder, while he proceeded further and further into the building.

I have seen sheds and workshops of all types in my life. I have seen smiths' forges that appeared to be formed from accretions of filth; I've seen brewers' shops where the floor could scarcely be seen for the mess of hops and grain; I've seen dressmakers' shops where the cloth lay all about like carpets; I've seen butchers' shops that had offal and bones lying all about – and yet I have never seen a sight to compare with Mark Thomasson's home.

There were, I think, tables. I assume that because there were apparently surfaces beneath all the scrolls, books and parchments. There was a great telescope on a tripod, and brass machines of various sizes to gauge the position of the sun or stars, and in one wall there was a pair of arrows protruding from a beam. A helm with a gross dint in it sat on a candlestick, and beside it a breastplate with two holes punched through it. I didn't like to think what had happened to the man wearing it. I saw a horse harness, bows, guns of great length and some with barrels of only six inches. There was a thick, weighty tome with rough page-edges, a pot of what looked like ink, with three quills sitting in it and a mass of fresh, untrimmed feathers beside it. And then I heard a rumble that appeared to pass towards me from the floor, and I shuddered at the horrible sound. A shape disconnected itself from the shadows near a fire, where a chair and a stool sat, and slowly paced towards me. It was an immense hound.

'Don't mind Peterkin,' Mark said as he walked to the chair. He sat in it and beckoned me.

'Peterkin?' I repeated dully. The brute licked his lips, clearly enjoying the sight of a human in terror.

'My little fellow? Yes. He is a handsome little thing, isn't he? I got him as a puppy, and I've been delighted to keep him by my side at all times, save when I seek some . . . er . . . more physical refreshment. Here, after all,' he said, waving a hand at the chaos that had engulfed his room, 'here I have more than enough stimuli for my brain. It is the needs of my heart that I seek from those ladies of Southwark.'

He navigated past a couple of tottering piles of paper, patting one as though it was a faithful and ancient pet, before seating himself. 'Come along, take your seat.'

I licked dry lips as he pointed across to the stool, and slowly and very cautiously moved past the hound. It's not that I'm nervous of all dogs. I'm only petrified of the ones that look as though they could take on a bull single-handed. This one had just that kind of look in his eye. As I passed by, I could feel the breath from his nostrils, like the breath from a demon's steed. A low rumble made the room vibrate once more.

'Calm down, Peterkin,' Mark said. He had pulled my strip of parchment from his scrip, and now sat studying it while I walked to the stool and sat. A growl made me leap to my feet, but Mark insisted that I be seated, and I sat. The hound sat painfully close to me. He stared at me fixedly. I was not comfortable.

'Now, you said you found this in the street. That was clearly untrue. It would not have been lost. In fact, I know of several men who are urgently seeking this already. One, I am sure, would kill for it, because it will mean the death warrant of a high-born noblewoman whom he detests; a second would kill because by finding it, and either preserving it safely or destroying it, he will save his mistress. The third is the intended recipient, and he would also kill to get it to protect his mistress.'

This was not good news. 'So, what should I do with it? Throw it on the fire?'

'You could do that. But, of course, if one of these fellows were to find you, how could you convince them that you had indeed burned it? They might believe that you were holding out for a better offer, and that might make them – ah – impatient, if you take my meaning.'

A picture of Gil's battered face rose in my mind. 'I see.'

'Your better route would be to keep it safe,' he said.

Safe! Where could I put something where it would be *safe*? The house with all the others? That hadn't been safe when the three thugs killed Gil and broke into the place, had it? Or when I had been there and had to run to Southwark to escape the Bear? That was hardly safe. I could find a merchant, but even if I persuaded one to put my parchment in his strongbox, how safe would it be?

'What is the message about?' I asked.

He leaned down and picked up the parchment from where it lay on a pile of papers.

╫╥ ▽∟ ⌀▽ℇ ⌐ ⍵ᗩ△ı℮ᴏℇ੧ ⌐ ᗩℇ⨍ıᶚᗩ∟ᴏℇᒋ▽⌀∧੧ ⌐ ╫╫ᗩη ı⁊ᗩ⨍
∟╪η▽ᒋℇ⍵ᴏℇ ⌐ ⫽ℂᗩℇᒋℇ▽6ꗟηᗩ∟ ℇ⍵ᗩ ⌐ ੧╫╫ı [ı∧੧∟ᗩ⌀⊖η
ᴏ⌀╫ᒋ ⫽ℂᗩℇ∟ ⌀▽ℇᒋ △ℂ⨍⫽ıℇ ⌐ ℇ▽ᒋ⫽ ꞩᗩ⨍ıᴏη ⌐ ∧▽⌀△▽⨍ℇ

Picking up a pen, he took a scrap of paper and wrote on it.

'This is what it says.'

I took the piece of paper and read aloud: '*Do not hesitate. Strike at once and deliver a blow that must topple the whole edifice. England must not have an Imperial consort.*'

'You see?' he said.

I smiled and nodded. 'Of course.'

He eyed me. 'No, you don't, do you? Jack, this is a note from someone in authority who is giving a vassal the command to topple the regime; to remove the queen. Our Queen Mary. There is little doubt that the line about not permitting an Imperial consort refers to the queen's infatuation with the son of the Emperor of Spain, is there?'

I began to understand. 'So this is a letter to someone to foment trouble in London?'

He looked at me as though I was not the village idiot but the city's. 'Not to "someone". It must have been intended for Wyatt. The man who is raising rebellion in Kent?' he added, seeing my expression.

'Oh!' That was not good news. Wyatt, the man who was marching on London. 'So who could this be from?'

'By the grace of God!' he sighed, resting his brow on his hand. I think he had a headache or something. Then he looked up. 'There are how many people who are in line to the throne of England?'

'I don't know.'

'Let me tell you, then,' he said heavily. 'There is Lady Jane Grey, who was, um, to be forced to the crown on the death of King Edward, but for the fact that Mary, our queen, and, after her, her half-sister Elizabeth, were already named in the will of Edward's father. Henry wanted Mary to rule if his son was to die. And so it came to pass. On the day that the, um, young King Edward succumbed to his disease, men were sent to capture Mary while others put Lady Jane Grey on the throne, but they set off too late and the princess was warned. She left her manor with a party of household knights, and rode far and wide until she had gathered about her a small army. When she came to London, the natural sense of English fair play and justice meant that all acknowledged her as queen. Lady Jane was arrested and thrown into the Tower, along with her husband and her father. She had enjoyed a nine-day reign, but England rejected her for Mary based on the ancient rights of inheritance. Yes?'

'Yes.'

'But now, with the queen's bold determination to marry a man of the Catholic faith, the support for her has faded. Yes?'

'Of course. We all know that.'

'So if Lady Jane Grey were to send a note to men who were rebelling against Queen Mary's rule, that would, um, perhaps make the queen angry, do you not think? Perhaps, if the messenger carrying this note to Wyatt, or to his supporters in London, were to be murdered in such a manner that the note he bore on his person could be discovered, Queen Mary would be pleased to have Lady Jane executed right speedily for treason, do you not think? The men who wanted to guard Queen Mary would naturally be glad to receive this note, and to see the messenger and any who gave him succour hanged and quartered, while those who sought to support the rebels in Kent might easily be persuaded to kill any man who held so dangerous a message?'

'So any could have killed the messenger?'

He sighed and looked at me with a kind of sad disappointment.

It suddenly came clear to me. I gaped, staring from him to the parchment. 'You mean, Queen Mary's friends *and* her enemies would both see *me* dead for this damned thing?'

Mark sighed with a contented smile. 'Ah! He appreciates at last!'

FOURTEEN

'But . . . but . . . what can I do? This is terrible!'

'It is for you, yes.'

'It's not so good for those who aided me, either. And those who have managed to translate the message could be considered as dangerous as me.'

His face fell. 'Ah! I had not, um, considered that eventuality.'

'Then start considering now, and quickly!'

'Perhaps this will, um, take a little time to think through,' he said, picking up a small brass bell. He rang it, and a man appeared in the doorway at the rear of the room. 'A jug of wine, Jonah.'

'We don't have any.'

'I'm sure I told you to order it?'

'That was a month ago. You've drunk it.' There was an expression of morose glee on the man's face as he spoke. He appeared to be older than Mark and was dressed in sober black, and though I was convinced he was a servant, his manner was more that of an irascible brother than a bottler.

'Then go and fetch some from the vintner,' Mark said with some heat.

'It'll take me a while.'

'Go!'

Mark scowled at the fire for a few moments after the door had closed. 'I don't know why I keep the fellow,' he muttered. 'He is more trouble than he is worth: he eats me out of house and home, and his rudeness is intolerable.'

'Why *do* you keep him, then?'

'I wish I knew,' Mark said, and then the keen look returned to his eyes. 'Very well, so we have the basic issue of what to do with the, um, parchment. We can guess who it came from, and to whom it was intended, as well as having a good idea what the result would be for us, were the note to be discovered.'

'Are you sure destroying it isn't the best solution?' I said, gazing at the fire.

'How long would they spend to make sure that you were not telling a lie? The rack is a fiendish machine and capable of utterly destroying your body. Then there are thumbscrews and other judicial devices that would make you really wish you had better news for your torturers.'

It was a good point. 'Then we have to keep quiet and hope that the rebellion will soon die away,' I said with conviction. 'What we don't want is to discover that they approach closer to the city so that the queen's men look for something to discredit her enemies.'

'If she becomes more powerful, that will mean her enemies will grow more alarmed at the risks to themselves,' Mark pointed out.

'Yes. But the queen has racks and torturers.'

'The others still have whips and steel bars,' Mark said.

That was fair. I didn't want to dwell on the fact that there was no safe option for us.

It was a while later that the miserable servant returned. He eyed us both, sniffed and went to the rear where there was a kitchen and buttery. A short while later, he returned and set a jug on the floor between us. He filled three large cups, two of which he passed to Mark and me, and then, to my astonishment, picked up the last and drank deeply, smacking his lips. Mark seemed in no manner upset at such familiarity from his manservant, but I was.

'Aye, ye'll want to know this,' Jonah said. He shook his head, staring at the fire.

'What?' Mark snapped.

'The first reports of the fighting against the rebels.'

'Were they beaten?' I asked. This could spell the beginning of the end of this appalling situation.

'Aye. They were soundly thrashed by all accounts. Aye, they were beaten thoroughly. So many went to the other side, ye see.'

'So the Whitecoats have saved the day!' I breathed.

'Eh? No, the whiteys ran to Wyatt, calling out "A Wyatt, a

Wyatt; we're all Englishmen!" and he took 'em in. Now he's marching on London with ten thousand, so they say. The few Whitecoats who made it back had lost their pikes and guns, and were all bedraggled, with their coats turned inside out to hide their royal insignia and badges. Aye, they were beaten sure enough.'

I could say nothing. I stared at him in mute horror.

When his morose servant had left us again, grimly delighted, I had no doubt, of the impact of his news, I looked at Mark.

'For now, our crucial difficulty lies in discovering our enemies,' he mused. 'The dead man is insignificant. He was a mere, um, messenger. It is said by all great warriors and leaders that the most important weapon is that of knowledge. A commander must know who his enemy is, where his enemy is, how large his enemy is, and what the territory is like where his enemy is. We know that we have an enemy, but little more.'

'I know who he is,' I said. 'He wears a broad-brimmed hat,' and I told Mark of the men I had seen in the tavern, how they had traced Gil and then killed him. If he was interested, he concealed it well.

'There was also the man with Ann,' I said. 'His name was Henry, apparently.'

'What did he look like? What form of clothing did he wear?'

I told him, sparing no detail that I could think of. I finished, 'One of those two must have murdered the messenger.'

'Aye. Perhaps one works for the queen, do you think?'

'I don't know.'

'Aye, that is a problem. Was the message stopped by, um, a queen's man, by a loyal servant of Lady Jane, or by someone else? How do we find out who this man Henry is, and then, when we know, how can we tell whether he is a fine gentleman or a knave?'

'He killed the messenger and Gil. He has to be a knave,' I said.

'Many a gentleman will kill to defend his faith or his mistress,' Mark said with a short burst of irascibility. 'And yet – you say his name was Henry, eh? Where does he live? Where does he frequent? You must find this woman Ann again, you poor cub, and this time make sure you learn all you can from her.'

'But she doesn't like me!'

'I have little doubt of that. She would be looking for a finer kind of gentleman, I am sure. But you will find her, and do all you can to learn what is needful.'

'I don't know.'

He peered at me. 'The rack is enormously persuasive.'

'Oh, very well.'

The meeting with Mark had not put me in a good mood. I was morose as I scuffed my boots outside his house and considered how to find Ann.

Like many a fresh courtesan, she tended to spend a lot of her day looking for work. I'd chatted to a tired whore once, who told me that she had to spend a third of her time walking and standing on street corners, trying to find an excuse to lie on her back the other two-thirds. It was understandable. In my case, I spent two-thirds of my time looking for a good mark, before dedicating the last third to getting to know them, robbing them blind, and running away fast. It wasn't always easy.

In the end, I decided to look for her around St Paul's again. It was her favourite hunting ground. The churchyard was always a good place for strumpets seeking gentlemen with money, and there was always the chance that I'd strike it lucky with another gull. I hoped that this time I would find a mark who wasn't about to expire and leave me with the embarrassment of his remains.

I made my way to the cathedral and bought an indifferent pie from a man on the street. The pastry was good enough, and the gravy tasted fine, but the meat was from a diseased or ancient bull, from the amount of gristle amid the stringy meat. I was tempted to go back and tell him exactly what I thought of his vittles, but reflected that it was more important for me to keep myself out of the eye. Mind you, from the quality of the man's pies, it would make him notice me all the more, were I *not* to complain and demand my money back.

The churchyard was a mass of people milling about as one service ended and others began. Horses were left cropping the grass while urchins stood with the reins in their hands, whores promenaded, and trendy, foppish men with the latest in tight hosen and jacks stood about chatting with supercilious sneers fixed to their faces. Any number of them appealed to me as potential targets, and I was keen to mix with a few of them, but each, I noticed, wore a short sword and a dagger of some sort. No matter how appealing their wallets looked, which usually was in inverse proportion to their intellect as far as I could tell, I did not like the odds of taking on any one of them.

Of course, there was one issue with approaching the churchyard that had not occurred to me. It was about to, with force.

'Hoi! You!'

It was this: I was close to the tavern behind which I had only recently been discovered with a dead man. I had forgotten that.

Yes, I know. You, sitting in your comfortable home with a fire before you and spiced ale at your side, reading this for your amusement at my predicament, will have observed my error in an instant. All I can say is that it is easy to be smug. I had experienced the unnerving sight of Gil's body, been chased by his murderer and a bear, I'd been scared half out of my wits by the thought that the queen's supporters and enemies both had the inclination to see my body dangling from a rope, and I was aware that the rebels were on their way to visit London, too. I was not having a good few days.

Which is why I had forgotten that I was a wanted man, and that here there were possibly fellows who would remember me, even in my new leather jerkin. One fellow I had not expected to see, however, was the young gull whose purse I had snatched. You'd forgotten? The fellow with the purse full of bone counters. He was there, and he was pointing at me. Why I had returned to only a short distance from the tavern where I had been accused of murder, I do not know. It was not intelligent, no.

I was aware that the man pointing at me was vaguely

familiar, but just at that moment I didn't recall him. However, I did recognize the kind of man who was with him. He was a large man, and while he was not in uniform, and did not hold a staff of office or badge of rank, he had the unmistakable look of an officer of the law. Although he wore only a shabby leather jerkin over a jack of some heavy wool, there was something in his belligerent stance that boded ill for the man he was pointing at. I turned to see whom he was indicating. Which goes to prove that a man of even moderately good intelligence can be a fool on occasion.

Before I knew what was happening, three toughs had grasped me by the arms and shoulders, and the hot-faced, official fellow trotted towards us like a pig seeing a tasty morsel in the gutter. He had a round face like that of a hog, and there was enough fat about his mouth to make me want to retreat. The men holding me tightened their grip.

'You!' he said again. 'I know your face. So does this gentleman.'

That was enough to make me blanch. I looked at the young gull, who now wore the sour smile of the victim who anticipates revenge, and realized I was in trouble.

'Me?' I said with an attempt at innocence.

'You were up here the other morning, when the man David Raleigh was slain!'

'What man?'

Suddenly, I felt a hammer blow on the top of my pate, and sparks and gleams of painfully bright light whirled and span about me. My legs wobbled and I toppled forwards, and just before the ground came up and struck me on the nose, I had time to think, 'Some bastard's hit me!' and feel a great sense of injustice, just as all went black.

FIFTEEN

I haven't woken too often in a prison cell. It's not a pastime I recommend to anyone generally, but if you do have a choice, I can recommend this one.

In the past, when arrested for being drunk, I had been woken by a bucket of cold, mostly fresh water being thrown over me. In the winter, having freezing water drench you is not a life-enhancing experience. However, it does have the merit of distracting from the acid in the stomach and the constant hammering of smiths in the skull that normally I associate with a sore head after an evening of riotous enjoyment.

Today I was not to feel the same relief, partly because I had not been uproariously drunk, and partly because there was no relief from the second blow to my head. I kept my eyes screwed tight for a while, as the dancing lights dissipated and stopped their whirling behind my eyelids, before I could even consider to venture to open one.

It was my right. I cautiously unlocked a lid and took in my surroundings.

The churchyard had disappeared. Instead, I was lying on a pallet on the floor in a gloomy chamber that had only one candle to illuminate it. Don't mistake me, one candle is significantly more than I had on waking in Newgate gaol. There, the only light came from the feeble sun trying to insinuate itself past the thick bars of the window high overhead. Here, the candle allowed me to see a number of chests with intriguing patterns that implied that they were full of rich and interesting items, and a sideboard with a selection of plates and goblets that would easily fit into a man's jack, so I felt. There was also a painting of a severe man who appeared to be suffering from an appalling form of constipation on the wall, staring down at me.

'So you are awake. Good.'

I turned on hearing that cool, calm voice, risking my skull

breaking open and spilling my brains all over the floor. Behind
me, I discovered, a man was seated on a stool.

'You will no doubt be wondering where you are,' the man
said. He had been reading a sheet of paper and now he set
this aside at a table near his right arm. He leaned forward. He
had a fleshy face, with a long nose and a small mouth that
made him look prim and disappointed. Slightly bulbous eyes
were framed by thick eyebrows above and weighty bruises
beneath. He was a man who needed more sleep, I thought.
He spoke in a precise, pedantic manner, holding my gaze all
the while. 'I am Stephen Gardiner, but you can call me "Lord
Bishop". I am Bishop of Winchester, and also the queen's
Lord High Chancellor.'

I took in the black cap on his head and the episcopal robe,
and instantly my heart fell.

Did I know of Gardiner? Yes. He was one of those who had
fallen out of favour during the reign of Edward VI. Something
to do with religion and the way the king was imposing new
rules, I think, but as soon as Edward died and Mary took the
throne, she released Gardiner, returned him to his bishopric
and elevated him as a trusted subject.

In other words, he was one of the most senior men in the
land.

'I should like to talk to you about the man who died in
the Black Boar three days ago. The man you killed.'

Those words froze me. He sat there, the candle making dark
pits of his eyes, and as it guttered, shadows flew across his
features like geese across a dying sun. I suppose he was
seventy years or so, but all I saw as I looked at him was a
keen intellect that was focused entirely upon me. The only
thing that looked hopeful was his eyes. Every so often I caught
a gleam, as though he was a sympathetic soul who felt for
my predicament, rather than a bureaucrat without compassion
who would sign my death warrant without compunction.

'Well?'

'I didn't kill him! I was out there, and a gate opened behind
me while I was there, and someone knocked me so hard on
the pate that he almost broke my head,' I protested. 'I was

only there for a piss, and the fellow came out after me. I don't even know who he was.'

'And yet you had been with him and drinking with him for the last hour or more.'

'No, I was in the tavern and met him when . . .'

'Be careful, my friend. You see, I know much of what you were doing that day. You were being watched.'

I felt as if there was molten lead in my bowels. If they had been watching me . . . but who had? I hadn't seen anyone.

'I did meet him before, I'm sorry, yes. My head . . . it makes it all confused. Your man hit me so hard, and on the same place I was injured before. It's made it all very difficult to remember now, and . . .'

'You must not think that I approve of torture,' he said, and although I didn't consider that his comment ran on logically from what I had been saying, I felt it would possibly be a good idea not to interrupt. 'I dislike the whole process – the concept – of torture. It means destroying someone. Breaking a body into its constituent parts is an act of horrific brutality.'

'Yes,' I said, trying to keep the relief from my voice.

'But sometimes a recalcitrant person must be prevailed upon to go against his natural inclination. Occasionally, if someone is seeking to endanger the throne or the realm, and wishes to conceal their part, torture becomes more acceptable. You do understand that, don't you?'

'Yes, of course, my Lord Bishop.'

'Good. Now, to start again. You were with the gentleman who died from the middle of the morning, roughly.'

'Um . . .' I racked my brains to recall. 'I think so.'

'Do be quite certain in your evidence,' he said.

'Yes, I think so.'

'That is a little better,' he said, and picked up the sheet of paper once more. He appeared to be reading and digesting certain facts, and then he put it down again. 'Now, when you entered the tavern, what happened?'

I tried to tell the story of bringing the messenger into the tavern without mentioning my intention of robbing him, and then I wondered about talking about the cutpurse and Ann. In the end, I decided I owed the man nothing.

'I wanted to help the young fellow,' I said. 'He was so clearly a stranger to the city, and I didn't want to see him robbed.'

Gardiner looked at me with a kind of world-weary disbelief, but I hurried on.

'I bought beers, and we went to sit at a bench. There were two others there already, and I think that they were cutpurses. These parasites do infest every part of our city, my Lord Bishop.'

'Yes. Indeed,' he said drily.

'So, a little while later, while talking to my new friend, I felt a hand tug at my coat, and then I felt something thrust into my hand. You cannot imagine my surprise when I realized it was my young friend's purse! I was astonished.'

'So much so that you hurried from the tavern to investigate the interior of the purse.'

'Yes, I . . . no! No, I was going out to see . . .'

'Yes. Precisely. What then?'

'I was outside and then the door to the alley opened, and someone caught me across the head with a hammer or club. I collapsed and knew no more.'

'Until?'

'Well, I came to a little later, to find the man who had filched the youngster's purse was standing there in the doorway to the tavern. He gave the alarm, and I suddenly realized that my companion was dead. I feared being unable to defend myself, so I fled.'

'Still holding the purse, naturally.'

'Well, yes.'

'Where is it?'

'The purse? I don't know.'

'I am sorry to hear that,' Gardiner said, and reached for a quill.

It was one of those moments when telling the truth can suddenly seem a very good idea.

'A fellow I know took it from me to use it himself,' I said quickly. 'But he was killed a couple of days ago, and I think the purse was stolen from him. He was horribly beaten and tortured before they killed him.'

'"They"? What makes you think there was more than one?'

'I saw them. You see, in the Black Boar I saw three men playing dice. One was a huge man, built like an ox, another was slim and fair-haired, and the last was clad all in black, with a broad-brimmed hat. I saw them in the tavern, but then I saw them again when I was at my home the next day. Gil had met them in a tavern and brought them home to meet me. I think he was wearing the purse and that gave them the idea. They went home with him, and when they couldn't find me, they slew Gil instead. But when we found his body, the purse was gone. It had been stolen from him.'

Gardiner eyed me for a long moment. 'Your tale is almost believable. It ties with much that we already know, certainly. However, there are some aspects I should like to consider. What happened to the contents of the purse?'

'My companions took the coins,' I said firmly.

'How many were there?'

'I don't know. It was full, but I never had the chance to add it all,' I said. 'My companions took it as soon as it was seen.'

'And there was nothing else in the purse? No charms, no buttons, no pieces of paper?'

'Paper?' I repeated, and then hurriedly added, 'Buttons and charms? Not that I saw, no.'

'These companions, are they loyal subjects of the queen?'

'I wouldn't live with them if they weren't!'

'But you would even though you knew that they were thieves and felons. An interesting distinction. Still, I am glad that you are a devoted servant of the queen.'

'I am! I'm a very keen supporter of Her Majesty.'

'Good. And so too are your friends?'

'Oh, yes!'

'So if they were to discover something that might be of harm to Her Majesty, they would clearly bring it to the attention of the proper authorities, just as you would?'

'Um . . . yes.'

'Good. Because that means I can safely rely on you to check with them whether they found a note in the purse, can't I? And since you are a loyal servant, you will naturally bring anything to me.'

'But, like I said, the purse was stolen. Gil was killed for it. After they killed him, they went through our belongings, too. They destroyed the place. I don't even have a penny. I've nothing with which to buy a loaf or pint of ale.'

He eyed me for a moment, then picked up a small leather purse. He weighed it in his hand and set it on the floor near me. 'You have some money now. That will help you question people, and will stop you starving. We have to hope that anything that was once in the purse is not lost, but that one of your light-fingered latch-lifters has it still. That way, you can bring it to me here, and have the threat of pain removed.'

'Threat?'

'We don't want to have to question you more invasively, do we?' All of a sudden, his kindly eyes didn't look so kindly after all. 'So let's hope you can find something.'

SIXTEEN

I was deposited outside. Rather to my surprise, I was not in Southwark, where the bishop had his great inn and hall, but still in Paternoster Row. The Lord Bishop must have a friend there near the cathedral, I supposed, who could provide a room when required. It was curious, the fact that the bishop had been happy to be alone in a chamber with me, but then I assumed he had other men listening and watching, ready to pounce on me if I showed myself as a danger to him. Not that I was, of course. The only threat I could offer was to his ears, if anyone tried to touch my sore head.

Looking about me, I realized I was just opposite the charnel chapel. I looked back at the house. It was well decorated and rich-looking. Perhaps the good bishop came here occasionally to see what sort of strumpet he could find? But the thought of wenches of variable value put me in mind of my original purpose in coming up here. The man who had accosted me in the churchyard was not to be seen, but as I gingerly felt the lump on my head, I decided on the spot to give up hunting for Ann. Instead, I walked away towards Bill's new home for us. I hoped that, with some luck, I could make my way there before my head tried to fall from my shoulders. I wasn't convinced, though.

It was a bright day, with the smoke from the fires making the sky look milky, but when I looked up at the sun through the veils and wisps of smoke, I saw only a hellish glow that seared my eyes and seemed to weld them to my skull. All I could do was grit my teeth, wince and carry on.

'Where have you been?' Bill demanded as I entered.

Moll was behind him, and she took one look at my face and rushed to me, all her earlier reticence gone. I gave her a smile of pathetic gratitude as she helped me to a stool and seated me with my back to the wall.

In truth, as she fussed about me, fetching wine and placing

a damp cloth on my swollen head, I could barely hear the angry drone of Bill's voice. He was telling me off, I think, for leaving and going back into town. For me, it was just a wash of noise in the background, rather like the Thames itself. It had no impact on me because I was incapable of listening.

Moll stood over me, her breasts only a few inches away. It would have been so easy to reach out to them. All I really wanted just now was to rest my head on them and . . . in my state, I was in no condition to try to fondle her, let alone fight Bill for her.

'Well? Where were you?' he said.

'I went to see if I could find Ann to learn who her man was – the man she was with in the tavern, I mean. And the Bishop of Winchester had me captured and taken to a house.' I told him all that the bishop had said to me. 'So, there you are.'

'A button, a token or a scrap of paper?' Bill repeated. 'Why would he think we'd have anything like that?'

'You will have to ask him that,' I said, closing my eyes gratefully. Moll left her cool hand on my brow, which was as near to heaven as I had ever been. I was fairly sure that she had smiled at me, too. This was very different from before. No withdrawing from me now.

'Didn't he tell you? He spent all that time telling you about what you had been doing, after all!'

'You need to ask him,' I said. I was falling into a doze already.

'There was nothing there, was there?' Moll said. 'No token or note in the purse Jack took?'

'No, of course not,' Bill said, but there was doubt in his tone.

I had the impression he must be eyeing me, as though suspecting me of having found something. Just at that moment, I couldn't remember what I had told him, and, in any case, I wasn't bothered. All I knew was that my head felt as if it might explode at any moment, and I wasn't keen to have any further discussions. 'If there was, the man in the hat took it when he killed Gil,' I said shortly.

'Well, then,' Moll said. 'Go on and leave him alone.'

Bill muttered something, but Moll was not going to listen

to him in her present mood, and the two began to shout at each other over my head until I put my hands over my ears. '*Stop!*'

Bill set his jaw. 'Are you ordering me around now?'

'Shut up, Bill! In the name of all that's holy, just piss off and do something useful! Find out who the man was in the tavern, find out who the man with the wide-brimmed hat was, find out *anything*, but stop shouting and screaming over my damned head!'

I must have used the correct manner of speech or inflexion, because, to my surprise, he went.

SEVENTEEN

don't know what happened after that. When I opened my eyes next, it was the middle of the night and a rushlight was burning in a holder at the wall. By its light I could see Wat and the large mass of Ham beside him, while Bill and Moll appeared to be lying farther off in the corner. Bill always picked a bed as far from the door as possible, just in case disaster might happen.

Tonight that was to be.

I had fallen into an unsettled dream, which appeared to involve me walking along Paternoster Row with men banging me on the head at regular intervals, when I was flung to the ground and began to fall into it as though I was lying on quicksands. I urgently tried to swim to hold myself above the mire, but nothing would prevail, and I felt the icy clutch of dead men's fingers grasping my ankles and pulling me down, until the filth was at my mouth and I felt the bog's waters lapping at my throat, and then . . .

The door burst open. I gave a yelp of fear and fell off my pallett, scrabbling about on the floor for my knife or a branch with which to defend myself, while men shouted and argued. Looking up, I saw Bill standing naked before a small, fierce little man. He looked like a robin redbreast defending his nest against a sparrowhawk, looking up at Bill and spitting angrily. Behind him were several men in drab clothing, ragged and weary-looking.

'What do you mean?'

The little man stared at Bill up and down. 'You haven't paid for the room! You bleeding swore I'd have the money yesterday, but I haven't seen a penny piece yet, and I don't know if I ever will at this rate. So either you lot can load your packs and march, or you can pay me now. If you can't pay, these lads have the room because they have money.'

'I rented this place for a fortnight, you thieving old scrote!'

'Did you? Show me your indenture, then, boy!'

'We shook hands on the deal!'

'Show me the paper where we agreed it!'

Bill and the man, who, I gathered, was the owner of this run-down little building, squared up to each other like game cocks. I looked over at the men at the doorway. 'Who are they?'

A man leaning against the doorway looked at me. His face was grey, and he had splatters of mud on his cheek and the breast of his coat. 'We are all that's left. Fifteen of us marched to meet the rebels to support the Whitecoats, but they went to join Wyatt and his men. When the fighting started, we were too few. We didn't stand a chance, not against so many.'

He looked as though he was ready to fall. The rest looked scarcely any better.

'Why do you want to stay here? Aren't you Londoners yourselves?'

'Nay. We're from north of the city. We had hoped to stay at an inn, but you try to find a place just now.'

'Why?' I asked. I was still feeling punch-drunk and light-headed from the blows to my head.

'Because it seems that all the rooms are taken. And the ones where there's space seem to cost more than they did three days ago,' he added, looking at the landlord.

'That's not my fault. It's just the way things are,' the fierce little man said.

Bill pushed him with both hands on his chest, and the irascible man took a couple of paces backwards. 'You try that, and you'll find yourself explaining yourself to the watch. I'm not scared of getting the watch in here!'

I was getting fed up. My head hurt, I was tired, and the last thing I wanted was a fight in my bedroom. 'Bill,' I said, 'why don't we let them come in? There's only a few, and look! There's not one of them who is capable of attacking us. They're all far too tired.'

'They're having the room whether you like it or not,' the landlord spat.

'You should be careful,' I said. 'After all, if you have a bawdy house here, you might get paraded to the stocks. Who was it? A man called Chekyn, wasn't it? He was accused of bawdry last year, you recall? He was living on the profit of his wife and carted to the pillory, wasn't he?'

'I haven't got a wife,' the little man said.

'No. Which is why it will be all the easier for men to understand that you wanted young Moll here. But when you tried to force her to become your whore, she grew so incensed that she had to report it.'

'What?' The man's face fell.

'That, at least, is how the magistrate will hear it. So, good master, be off and leave us to settle this among ourselves.'

'I want you lot out!'

'And it won't happen,' I said. 'In the name of God, go now, and you will get a fair share of the fee for the room, but if you stay, I swear I will have you in the pillory. I have friends who will help me.'

'Who?' the man sneered. 'I suppose you're a friend of the queen, are you?'

'No. But I dined today with her Lord High Chancellor, Bishop Gardiner, and he is powerful enough not only to have you carted but to confiscate every building you own. So be off with you and don't bother us again this night!' I said, and I backed up my words with a menacing step forward.

Perhaps it was the apparent determination, or maybe he believed my tale, I don't know, but he looked about him at all the men in that chamber, and clearly decided that there was no point in remaining to be battered and belaboured like a cat in a sack. He muttered something about expecting to see his money quickly, and then, as the soldiers eyed him with the casual interest of a man watching ants before standing on them, he bolted.

At last, I thought, and returned to my bed. But even then I was not to be allowed to sleep. Although I earnestly craved the chance to close my eyes, the newcomers entered like a whole company of plate makers, rattling and thumping their way to find unoccupied areas of the floor. In the end, I was forced to give up.

'Where are you lot from?' I asked their commander.

'I am called Atwood,' the grey-faced man said. 'The men call me "sir". You can call me Dick.'

He drew himself upright from the door frame like a man who had laboured hard, and entered the room with the rest of his men filing in after him. Although I earnestly craved the chance to close my eyes, the newcomers entered like a whole company of platemakers, rattling and thumping their way to find unoccupied areas of the floor. In the end, I was forced to give up. Atwood had said fifteen joined him, but there were only six with him now.

I have seen soldiers before. They tend to be loud, raucous fellows, often young and prone to squabbling, but these men were older and more serious. Or perhaps it was only their recent experiences that had made them appear so. This one looked familiar.

'We had heard that it went ill,' I said.

'It was worse than ill,' Dick said. He eased himself down at the wall and yawned. 'We reached them in the late morning with the Duke of Norfolk in command. Captain Bret was leading us, and we readied ourselves for a long fight. There was no lack of courage among my fellows. But then many of our companions threw in their lot with the rebels. We thought they were charging, but the traitors just ran to them, then turned and joined their ranks. We didn't have a hope after that. They had thousands of men before we arrived, and the turncoats gave them still more. The battle was short and went badly for us, so when we could, we had to disengage and come back.'

Disengage was a soft, gentle word for what they seemed to have gone through. At that time I had never been pushed and beaten into line. And, later, it was not to be an experience I would want to repeat. The thought of standing and waiting while an army marched at me, and then having to fight with sword or pike while others were shoving steel in my face or at my soft bits, left me feeling close to vomiting. It wasn't only the idea that a man might be attempting to inspect my liver with a halberd, but the idea of stabbing with a blade and seeing a man impaled on it. In my mind's eye, I could see a fellow like Wat, my sword entering below his breast and running in, or a youth like the young man who was killed at the Black Boar, standing and staring at me while I hacked at his neck . . . no, I don't think I could do it. If a man was trying to kill me, perhaps I could defend myself, but even then I'm not sure. Slashing and thrusting at a man is all very well as a concept when it is a matter of killing or being killed, but the trouble is, I feel sure that my own hands would disobey me, were I to try it.

Disengage, indeed. What he meant was that they had all had enough of terror: of the fear of death, of the sight of friends dying, of the rattle of steel on hauberks and breastplates, of the smell of bowels opened by steel, and the noise of men breathing their last while calling for Holy Mother Mary or their own mother. Who wouldn't be happy to escape that kind of hell?

'What next?' Bill asked.

'They'll be coming here, I think,' Dick said. 'What else would they do? They will be coming here to take the city. Who knows, they may have already set their accomplices in the city? It would only take a few apprentices shouting for their clubs to paralyse most of the folk in London.'

'There are many of us who're prepared to fight for our city,' Bill said warningly.

'Many, yes. But are there enough thousands? Look at the city's walls and ask yourself, how well would they hold up against a determined foe? Look at the bridge over the river, and consider how well that could be defended against four or five thousand. And don't forget that this Wyatt is no fool. There were rebels all over the country, and all have been quelled. But Wyatt has formed an army and expanded it, and still it grows as he marches towards us. He is a keen student of warfare, a skilful tactician and a shrewd strategist.'

I said, 'Do you think he can succeed, then?'

'He could. Whether he does will depend on the men here in the city,' Dick said, and his chin was almost on his breast as he spoke. Almost before he finished speaking, he was snoring.

Bill and I exchanged a glance, and then returned to our own palliasses. I think Bill was soon asleep, from the way his breathing altered, but for my part, I stayed awake a while, staring at the burning flame of the rushlight and thinking what hell it must be to be thrown into a battle.

It was lucky I could not see into the future.

Thursday 1st February

When I woke in the thin, wintry light that Thursday morning, I had no idea that I would witness one of the more momentous days of London's history. For me, it just seemed that the world was a very cold place. The room stank of soldiers, of rancid skin, sweat and privies. Someone had eaten something that didn't agree with them.

I was one of the last to rise from my sleeping mat. The soldiers were already gone, and Bill was outside. Moll was swearing at the tinder and trying to stir some life from the sparks she was showering liberally over the little hearth. I rose and found that my pack had been moved. Somebody had rifled through it. Probably a soldier, I thought. They were desperate enough to hope that even I might have something worth stealing. Luckily, the bishop's purse was securely placed inside my blankets as I slept.

Going to Moll, I tried to help her, but the effort made the bruises on my head pound still more painfully, and in the end I decided that I had done enough. The fire did not want to light. Wat ambled over, struck his flint once, and sat back smugly when a flame appeared almost immediately. From the gratitude that shone from Moll's eyes, I suddenly discovered I didn't like Wat. I left them to it.

Outside, I found Bill sitting on the wharf, his jack unbuttoned, staring moodily out across the river. 'Look! They've raised the drawbridge.'

I followed his pointing finger and, yes, there was no doubt of it.

'The wherrymen will be enjoying a feast day on the back of this lot,' he said. 'They can charge what they want.'

I nodded. 'I had best be off.'

'Where to?'

'I have to find this man. You can't help me with the bishop's questions. Perhaps the fellow who found me beside the youth in the tavern might be able to help. If I can only find out who he is, perhaps then I can take something of use to the bishop. He may allow me a little freedom, or even ignore me for the future.'

'You think so? Bishops don't think like that, Jack. Especially not the political ones like him. He's the Lord High Chancellor: he thinks only of what is good for the queen. Other mere mortals don't measure to him. Men are viewed through the window of his needs.'

'He seemed not too—'

'He threatened you with the rack.'

'Yes, but only because he thought it was necessary.'

'Just as he'd have your head cut off, if he thought it was necessary. Just think: Wolsey, Cromwell, and now Gardiner. Do you not see a theme with the sort of man who gets that position? They are all ruthless, mostly seeking to serve themselves, and the best way to do that is to give their masters what they want: heads. And right now, yours is moderately cheap and easy for him to procure. You'd do better to flee the city and make your way back to Whitstable.'

'With an army marching in our direction? No, I don't think so.'

He moodily picked up a pebble and flung it out into the water. The river flowed so swiftly that it barely caused a splash before it was washed away. 'I really think it would be better if you left, Jack. Stay here, and you'll be swallowed up by men like Gardiner.'

I didn't meet his eyes. 'What do you think will happen, Bill? Will the rebels break in?'

'If there are enough citizens in the city supporting them, yes. They could run to the river there, lower the drawbridge and let Wyatt and his men in. It's quite possible. And then God help anyone who's been serving Mary. Wyatt would have Lady Jane out of the Tower and on to the throne faster than you could say, "Ballocks to that!"'

I left him there, ruminatively hurling stones into the water, and I went up towards Ludgate and the Black Boar once more. I would see what I could learn with the bishop's purse.

Mostly, I learned the price of ales in different taverns.

EIGHTEEN

t was dark, with the reek of smoke wafting about, so that even the candles appeared with their own little haloes in the fumes. I sat at a table and was served with cold mutton chops, a quart of thin ale, and a half loaf of bread that had been fresh sometime in the last week. Still, after the last few days, it was a breakfast feast, and I consumed it quickly, before leaning back and belching with satisfaction.

However, as an occupation, while it was filling for my belly, it was not ideal in terms of finding either the man Henry or Ann. There was no sign of her again. I finished the ale, tipped the waitress with a casual wink, as though I was rich enough to feast in this manner regularly, and made my way outside. I was looking for the sort of man who would usually be Ann's target, but today I saw all too few. Instead, on a whim, I headed southwards towards the far side of the cathedral. I don't know what I was expecting to find, but suddenly there was a blaring of trumpets and horns, and then some muted cheering. Intrigued, I went on and craned my neck to see over the multitude waiting. I saw a small cavalcade, with a woman almost at the head.

She rode well, almost appearing to glide on her ambler. Its gentle motion, swaying from side to side as it lifted both left legs, then both right, was supposed to give a lady a comfortable ride. To me, it made her progress look regal, whereas all the knights and men about her seemed to jar with their lurching gait. Suddenly, a man cheered, and another bellowed out his support for the queen, and she turned to us and gave us a grave smile.

Very well, I confess, Queen Mary was not a jolly little strumpet like Moll on a good day, but I'll give her this: she knew how to play her part. She was in the presence of a crowd that could, in a moment, turn into a mob, yet she still carried herself as though never for one instant doubting that she would be honoured and protected by the citizens of this city. Of course, later we learned that she was as mad as a sackful of tomcats, but that morning, in the chilly air, with the steam rising from the horses and from every mouth, she was not only every inch a queen: she was *our* queen. She had an elegance and grace about her, riding along with all those guards in their armour. They would have gleamed, if the sun had been but a little brighter. She did not, though. The queen wore sombre colours, and her face, which could never be described as 'beautiful' in the best of circumstances, was grim. She knew that her reign hung by a slender thread, I thought. It was easy to remove a challenger to the throne, but I confess I had little idea just how easy it would be to remove an aspiring queen's head. That I would soon learn.

I was reflecting in this sombre manner, when I saw her: Ann.

She was over at the other side of the crowd as the parade rode past, and I could see that she was watching the crowds more than the queen and her men. Ann was surely looking for another mark, I thought at first, but then I saw that her appearance was not that of a confident floozy searching coquettishly for a helpful man to fund a new dress. She looked scared, as though seeking a threat.

It was impossible to push through the people, and even if I had, the road was blocked with horses and riders. Besides, any man darting into the road would be viewed, rightly, as a threat and cut down. Only a complete fool would try such a thing. So I bided my time, waiting until the way should become clear enough for me to shove the nearer men from my path and cross to the other side of the road.

She was already moving away. I could see her quite clearly at first, as she passed along the road, down towards Ludgate. She was working the crowds, I saw: smiling and ducking her head in the prettiest manner imaginable whenever she caught a man's eye. I know, because from where I was I could see the men giving her appraising looks in return or colouring slightly at being acknowledged. After all, when she wanted to look appealing, Ann was a thoroughly attractive woman.

At the edge of the old Blackfriars, where the Okebourne Inn stood, catering for all the visitors from the west, she turned south towards the river. There was little there, I knew, apart from Puddledock. I hurried down after her. There was a place there where the buildings overhead almost met and the sun was all but extinguished. It was like walking in the middle of a dark night. That was where I hurried my paces. At the last moment before I grabbed her arm, she realized I was following her, and she gave a squeal, whirling, her face a mask of utter terror. I'd never inspired such horror in anyone before. Most women considered me more a source of amusement than fear.

Perhaps that was it. As soon as she realized who I was, her face's panic turned into an expression of contempt. 'Oh, it's *you*,' she said, but I saw how she peered up the alleyway behind me.

'What is it? Has someone threatened you?' I asked.

'Just leave me alone!'

She was terrified. But it was not terror of me. It was another man.

She started to make her way down to the dock again, but I went to her side and joined her. 'I need to find out who was with you that day in the tavern.'

'Why?'

'Look, Ann, I'm in trouble. I think that fellow is involved in something. Yesterday the Bishop of Winchester had me knocked on the head and taken to see him. Look, do you want to feel the lumps on my pate? That's two now, and I'm getting fed up of being used as a target for every bully's cudgel. Just tell me who the man is, so I can go and speak to him.'

'I told you his name.'

'You said he was called Henry. What is his other name?'

'I don't know that I should tell you . . .'

'Ann!'

'Oh, very well. His name is Henry Roscard. He has a house on West Cheap near the conduit.'

'What does this house look like?' I asked.

She described in precise detail a narrow hall, recently built, with timbers that were still pale golden where the limewash

had not stained them. It was a two-level house, with an
overhung upper storey, with carvings on the timbers and wattle
and daub facing the road. I could recognize it by the larger,
brick-built hall next to it that was double the frontage on the
road.

'That's all I know,' she said when she was done.

'Why were you so scared when you heard me behind you?'
I persisted. There was something here. I could see it in her
eyes. She kept glancing behind us as though expecting someone
else to join us at any moment.

'It's nothing,' she said.

In fact, she said it several times, until in the end I grasped
her upper arm and pushed her against the wall. I don't usually
maltreat women, no, but this was a bit different. I was getting
worried that my life was in danger, after all.

'Ann, I have at least three men who are hunting me and
may well try to kill me; at the same time the bishop has
threatened me with torture. I don't know how much you know,
but in the name of all the saints, you must tell me! Please!'

'You are safe enough. No one knows your name. I kept that
from Henry and the others.'

'A man can kill a nameless stranger as easily as a man with
a title,' I pointed out. 'You know this man Henry, Ann!
Wouldn't you be anxious with him after you?'

She bared her lower teeth and bit at her upper lip with them,
holding my gaze for a while. Then, at last, she seemed to
come to a decision. 'Look, the man who was with me, he's a
spy, all right? I think he works for my Lord Edward Courtenay,
the Earl of Devon. Henry is a keen supporter of his master in
all things, and, right now, Earl Edward wants Queen Mary to
give up her infatuation with the Spanish emperor's son. Earl
Edward thinks *his* buttocks would suit the throne better than
those of a foreign man. *Now* do you understand?'

I shrugged. 'What has this to do with me?'

'Henry saw me two days ago. He wanted me to find you
and get you to talk about a small message that was inside
the purse you stole. That was what he was after: a small
message from someone who would help his master to prevent
the marriage. I don't know what it was, but it would help him,

apparently. He believes you have it, and that means he will do anything to force you to give it up.'

'Anything?' I said. I wanted to make sure I had heard her aright.

'Yes, Jack, *anything*! He's a competent man with a knife or a sword, and he likes to sit waiting for a man in dark alleyways and passages. Henry enjoys killing men – and women, too, I have no doubt.'

'You are scared, Ann. What is it?'

She was silent, staring at me for a moment, and then, 'I tried to blackmail him, Jack. I said I'd tell others what he's been up to, and now I think he'll kill me so I can't talk. I'm going. I'm leaving this shithole. There's always money for a woman with a brain, body and the inclination to use both. So leave me! Let me escape!'

'Where will you go?'

'I have my looks. I can find a man wherever I want. I always wanted to see Calais, and this is a good time to see it. You should do the same: you need to leave the city. Run away and hide, before he can get to you. Otherwise, you will end up in his webs or discarded.'

I knew what that meant. I had a mental vision of Gil's body as she spoke. 'Why me, though?'

'Because he thinks you found this message. And that makes you useful, if he can see the message – and dangerous, if you are thinking of sharing it.'

NINETEEN

Her words made a lump appear in my throat. Everything I learned or did just now seemed to result in more threats to me, more risks.

I saw little point in delaying here; I wasn't to know what dangers she faced. At the time, my sole concern was the effect that this was all going to have on my own life. Don't forget, I was still concerned after the sight of Gil's body. His murder, and the manner of his death, had a profound effect on me. I was, basically, terrified. I also had a lot to mull over. The bishop, Henry Roscard, my dead friend from the tavern.

She continued on her path. 'Where are you going?' I called, but she paid me no heed. In fact, I was about to return to Paternoster Lane, to see if I could find this man Henry Roscard, when I heard something. What? I don't know, really. Just a scattering of gravel, I thought, or the sound of leather rasping on a wall. Whatever it was, it was enough to catch at my attention. I stared back the way she had gone, but there was a bend in the alley, and she had disappeared around it.

I took a step, listening intently, then another. I thought I heard a thud, but I couldn't be sure. By now I was already anxious and approached the corner in the alley as timidly as any mouse approaching a sleeping cat. There was a sudden scuffle and clatter, and I turned with my hand on my knife, the blade half exposed, to see an enormous rat observing me from the top of a rainwater barrel.

It was such a relief that I thrust my blade back in the sheath and stepped onwards. In one pace, I found my foot ensnared, and I was tumbled to the ground. Ready to curse the fool who had left something out to trip me, I turned to find myself staring at Ann's face. She was deathly white, but that might have been because of the red beard of blood that encompassed the whole of her breast. Her mouth was moving, but without effect. The weapon that killed her had opened her throat entirely, and, even as I watched, her eyes rolled upwards into her skull and her head fell to the side. One shoe pattered against the other for a moment or two, and then she was still, while I sat before her, appalled.

This was not a good occupation. I quickly rose and, staring about me, hurried down in the direction that she had been taking. Any man doing this could not have gone north – that would mean passing by me – no, he must have come in this direction, towards the Thames.

There was a boat moored there. A scruffy shipman was sitting on the dock, his knife out, cutting strips from some dried meat. He eyed me, chewing, as I approached.

'Did a man come past here a few moments ago?' I asked somewhat breathlessly.

'Been several.'

'A man has just killed a woman up the alley – it was only very recently. Did you see anyone?'

'There was a man in black, wearing a fashionable cape and black hat,' he said. He had set aside his meat, and now he wiped his blade on his forearm and thrust it into his sheath. 'You say he did this?'

'It must have been him. She was talking to me a few moments before, and when she left me, I heard her attacked.'

'I didn't hear anything,' the man said. He had the face of a man who had seen too many storms.

'Where did he go?'

The sailor pointed eastwards, and I ran on, following the direction he indicated, but now I wasn't alone. Three sailors dropped their bales and packs and gave up their steve-doring duties to join the hue and cry. There was a mess of ropes and old broken spars and floats that I took in a single bound, and then I was pelting onwards. The buildings here were all low factories for fishermen and occasional boat-builders, and I stared into each building as I passed, then on to a collection of barrels. I was almost at it, when the topmost barrel wobbled alarmingly. I slowed, and then the whole mass of barrels tumbled and clattered and rolled towards me. I was forced to spring sideways to avoid two of the larger casks, and as I looked up, I saw him again.

It was Henry Roscard, the man from the tavern. Ann's man.

He snarled at me. If I had been alone, I think he would have set upon me. As it was, he hared off up a narrow passage as I stared, panting and trying to catch my breath, and then I was after him again, filled with a kind of irrational rage that lent power to my legs. This man had tried to see me captured for murder, had pursued me, I believed, for days, and now had murdered poor Ann for no reason, after slaughtering Gil for an empty purse. He had wanted me, and, if he could have done, would have seen me deposited with the bishop to have me tortured, and all for some ridiculous message that I had been unable to decipher without the aid of another man. It was not too much to say that I loathed this man. I hated him with all my heart.

He bounded off like a man possessed, and my posse and I chased behind like demons after a recalcitrant soul which now regretted the pact of a lifetime ago. We splashed through puddles, we beslubbered our legs with mud and ordure, we ducked under cables stretched across the alley, sprang over midden-heaps, and almost slid on our arses when we landed in one particularly foul pile of filth, but somehow we managed to recover. I almost fell headlong when I leaped a particularly nasty pile of sticks, and my foot caught the top, but although I landed badly, I carried on.

But that was the end of the race for me. My head was already pounding like a stone as the dresser chips away the rough edges, and after that slip, I suddenly found that my ankle was beginning to hurt. It started as a dull ache, but quickly it became a sharp, stabbing pain, and putting my weight on it grew harder and harder. Just as I saw Henry turn out of the alley and into a broader way that had to be West Cheap, I was forced to accept that my ankle wouldn't let me continue. I leaned against the wall and lifted my foot from the ground, staring at it with anger and frustration. I had been so close to him!

I hobbled onwards, but when I reached the road, he was nowhere to be seen. The sailors all stood with me, gazing about, but there was nothing we could do, and soon I left them to return to their portering duties. We had lost him.

But that did not matter. Ann had told me where to find him. I bent my steps towards West Cheap and the house near the conduit.

After my experience the day before at the bishop's house, I was prepared to exercise caution, especially since I had seen this fellow was capable of murder. I strode to the door with my anger at Ann's death being moderated by a sense of wariness. The house was quiet, and the noise of the street all about me was enough to persuade me that I was safe enough, for no man would want to commit murder here in the middle of the street, in full view of the whole of London. I was counting on that.

I hopped up the steps on my poor ankle and rapped smartly on the door. The solid timbers were clearly thick, and my knuckles bruised before I had finished. As the door opened, I suddenly wondered what I could do if he was there now. He could grab me and haul me inside, there to slay me. I would take the route of dissimulation, rather than run that risk, I decided. All the same, I let my hand rest near my dagger's hilt and fitted a stern expression to my face. I was feeling bolder than usual after seeing Ann die, but no matter how courageous I felt, this was a dangerous task. Still, I had been threatened with the rack the day before. There was little that the men in here could do to me that would be worse. That led me to feel a degree of bravado.

It was unnecessary. A mild-mannered servant stood gazing at me.

'Yes?'

The bottler was short and cheery-looking, with apple-red cheeks and a nose that would do service on a vintner's face after forty years at his trade. I peered behind him, looking for Henry, but he could, of course, have been hiding behind the door. 'I was wondering if your master was at home,' I said.

'Sir Peter? I'm afraid he's not in right now, but can I say who called for him?'

'Eh? Sir Peter? I thought this house was owned by a man called Henry,' I said.

'Henry? No, sir. It's the London home of Sir Peter Carew. But he isn't in the house right now. So if you could allow me to take a message, I shall see that he receives it as soon as he gets in.'

'No. No, that won't be . . .' I paused. There was a glint of anxiety in his eyes. 'Is Sir Peter this high? Broad shoulders, yellowish eyes, a beard and—'

'Oh, that would be Master Henry Roscard, sir. Henry is a friend of Sir Peter's, but he is not here just now either. Can I take a message for either of them?'

I left the house with a small feeling of satisfaction. Henry Roscard had killed Ann after she told me who he was. He must have thought she had outlived her usefulness, just as he had planned to kill me, no doubt. I had his name at last.

But who was this Carew? If Roscard lived at his house, was Carew also involved? I was beginning to feel that every stone I overturned merely exposed more stones.

Suddenly, a flock of pigeons scythed through the air just in front of my face, and I recoiled at the clatter of their wings. It was a near panic for me because it was so unexpected, and I felt my heart thundering in my breast as if it wanted to escape and follow the birds.

There was no safety for me. The bishop had told me as much. Somehow I had thought that if I discovered more about these men, I would learn something that could lift the bishop's threats, but that was ridiculous! The bishop was too powerful for me to be able to escape him. No, I would have to do as Bill had said: run away. Maybe do as Ann had attempted, and make my way abroad. There were others who had done it – taken a ship and crossed the Channel. It was not a pleasant thought. I grew seasick stepping over puddles, and the idea of spending hours on a rolling set of planks haphazardly nailed together was enough to make me want to spew right now. Still, it was less alarming than the thought of lying on my back with ropes attached to wrists and ankles while a friendly voice patiently asked me questions.

Yes. I would flee the city, I decided.

Yet another decision that was soon to be demonstrated to be pointless. I had as much control over my destiny as a bird quicklimed to a branch.

TWENTY

I set off to the house at Deneburgh Lane without any great enthusiasm, limping on my bad ankle. I was going to tell Bill that I was off, and then make my way to Southwark by boat before setting off to the coast to find a suitable vessel.

'Master Jack, I hope I see you well?'

I turned at the sound of a friendly voice, to see that the soldier from the night before was following me. He saw my puzzled expression and grinned widely.

'Master Atwood,' I said. 'You surprised me.'

'Call me Dick,' he said. 'Aye, well, I consider all the city is in a state of surprise now, wouldn't you?'

'Why?'

Captain Atwood gazed at me as though I had volunteered to dig the army's latrines. 'Because the rebels are nearly at the city walls. Had you not heard? They have already come to the outskirts of the south bank, and soon they must reach the city.'

I felt my heart plummet. It seemed to join the contents of my bowels, ready to embarrass me. After the soul-searching and decision to flee that I had taken only so recently, to hear now that flight was impossible seemed a cruel twist of fate. Not that I was unused to such bitter surprises after the last few days.

'Are you well, master?' Atwood asked, seeing my expression.

'I had hoped to leave London and go to see my father. He's on the coast,' I lied. I didn't like to lie to this kindly fellow, but it came so naturally to me. 'But that's in Kent.'

'Ah. Is he far? If it is a matter of a mile or a league, you could perhaps hurry there now and bring him back during the night?'

'He lives in Whitstable.'

Atwood pulled a face.

'You don't think . . .'

He shook his head. 'It will have been overrun already.'

I wanted to curse him then – and his cowardice. Although I had invented the desire to see my father, it did seem rich, this soldier, who had gone to defend the realm, gaily telling me that my father was already lost, more or less.

'If you want, you could join the city militia and help us ready the city for defence.'

'I am not made for fighting,' I said hurriedly. 'I've a poor ankle.'

'Oh, I wouldn't worry about that,' he smiled. 'The main thing is supporting those who will serve the walls and see to them in case of the rebels using artillery. If they cause a section of wall to collapse, we will need intelligent men to direct their repair. And men to help keep the arquebuses loaded and ready to fire, and men to loose arrows. There are many duties for the willing.'

I didn't like to point out that my only willingness would have been to ride a horse and remove one more mouth from a lengthy siege. 'I see.'

'I could ask that you remain with my force, if you wish. I could see to your safety,' he continued.

That made more sense. This man was experienced in fighting, as his speech last evening had shown. It was possible that he was a coward and poltroon, but even were that the case, he had demonstrated a propensity for survival that was, to me, inspiring. Perhaps I would be safer in his company than alone. I nodded. 'It's not my safety I'm thinking of, naturally,' I said, 'but how best I can serve the queen.'

'Oh, yes, of course,' he said. But there was a gleam in his eye that didn't convince me.

Saturday 3rd February

I was at the bridge with Dick Atwood for the next day, mostly helping manufacture barricades. It was hard work, lifting long baulks of timber and fetching and carrying stone to build into walls, and I was exhausted in the evening when I was permitted to go to my cot. It was not until the Saturday when Dick, whom I had to learn to call 'Captain', pointed to the first eddies of Wyatt's men appearing before us. It was a daunting sight.

They didn't come with all the folderol of military splendour I'd expected. There was none of the pageantry I'd seen with the marching Whitecoats when they left the city only six days before. There was only the slow, grumbling rumble at first, the clatter of approaching carts and wagons on the road, the creaking of leather, the rattle of cook pans and weaponry making a din that could be heard over the men on the bridge shouting, the hammering of pegs into the makeshift barricades.

'Aye, that's them,' Atwood said.

I heard a new note in his voice. It wasn't anger or fear, the Lord knows. I was coming to appreciate that Atwood was no coward. Yet there was a different tone. A blend of resignation, acceptance and – did I imagine it? – respect all commingled, like the elements used to make blackpowder – and, like that, all ready to accept the slightest spark to flare into noise and fury.

Then, about the corner of the road, far in the distance, a section of riders appeared. They were well mounted, and, from the gleams and sparkles, they were well covered at breast and arm, thigh and head. They trotted easily up the road, far out of reach of our grapeshot, and gradually I saw that behind them there moved a great mass of men and beasts. It was an incomprehensible sight. I had seen five hundred Whitecoats as they marched, and I had seen five hundred more men who had volunteered from the city itself, but five hundred is nothing when compared with thousands. The army of Wyatt moved at a steady pace, but it filled the road before the bridge.

I suddenly realized that all the noise about me had ceased. There was a knot of Whitecoats working at a gun, and a party of volunteers was trying to push a wagon into the road to block it still further, but just for a moment all had paused in their labours and were now staring down the road as though they were watching Death approach. Which, of course, they were.

'Load the guns,' Atwood commanded. 'Men, load your arquebuses.'

I had not received training in using these shoulder-weapons or the cannons, so I was relieved to have the opportunity to divert myself from the sight. In the name of Holy Mother Mary, there were *so* many of them! My teeth began to chatter. I have never known that before. In all the scrapes that I have survived more or less miraculously over time, I have never found my legs wobbling while my jaw resembles a handful of bone dice as a man shakes them before throwing them down. They did now, and nothing I could do would stop them.

More men poured into the road in front of me. It was like watching the slow, inexorable movement of a spider across the ceiling. Gradually, the men grew nearer, and their flags and banners became decipherable as crosses and urgings to join them against the tyranny of the queen, or so I thought. They were colourful, anyway, and as they approached, I became aware of troops of horses pulling heavier weapons. These were guns on wagons, and as I watched, there was a hold-up in their advance. Two men rode forward towards the bridge, but stopped when they saw that not only was the drawbridge up, but a span had been removed. They would not cross here unless they had access to wood and skilful carpenters to make good use of it.

The two had a muffled discussion, and while they spoke, I heard a man giving orders. All in an instant, I was engulfed by smoke and flame, which blasted for twenty yards, and I was choking and coughing, wondering what new evil weapon this was that they were using against us, that could have thrown such foul, sulphurous fumes. When I looked about me, seeking the poor, twisted bodies hit by Wyatt's cowardly weapon, I was shocked to see all the men moving about frantically, yet none seemed injured, while ahead of me there was a bloody gap in the marching men. Glancing to my left, I saw the men at the nearer gun swabbing and cleaning the barrel, then drying it with a sheepskin wrapped round a pole. They shovelled in powder, and I instinctively winced to see how they threw it in, ramming it home, and then pushed in a large bag with small balls, ramming that too, before quickly clearing the area and standing behind the gun as the gunner held his match up, his hand cupping the vent hole as he gazed about him to check all his own men were safely behind the firing line, and then stood back, setting his linstock to the touch hole.

There was a flash, a hiss of gas. A cone rose from the vent, and then there was a thunderous bellow as a roiling tongue of fire licked from the barrel, and the thick, greasy smoke coiled and blasted in the direction of the men. More were shattered and flung aside, some torn to pieces as they took the full brunt of the missiles.

It was a sight to thrill us, but it also appalled in equal measure. After all, I knew full well that they had their own artillery and would shortly be using it against us.

Atwood looked as though he had the same thought. He held up his hand. 'Stop firing now. We'll have time to warm the barrels another day.'

'They must see that they cannot attack us here,' I said hopefully.

'They may do, aye,' he said. 'But I've stood against Wyatt already. I wouldn't put anything past the bastard.'

The rest of the day there was spent in weary fetching and carrying. Rocks and timber had to be borne along the bridge and used to strengthen the defences, more cannon were shoved and hauled to the front, their massive barrels standing ready to bark defiance and deal death to the enemy. That was how the man next to me put it, anyway. Personally, I didn't want to be anywhere near those things when they went off again. The noise they gave made my head whirl, and the bruises on my skull thundered in sympathy, while the foul, cloying smoke made me choke uncontrollably. And it was made worse by the fact that the air was still and cold. In warmer weather, with a bit of a breeze, it would have been taken away, but here on the river, the fumes settled; just as the smoke from a house fire rose in a squat pillar and then sank over a house, these fumes loitered too, making breathing difficult.

I was pleased when I was told that I could take the afternoon off and rest. Atwood himself was to be relieved by another warrior, a happy-go-lucky fellow who went by the name of

Sergeant Dearing, but he had not yet arrived, and so I left
Atwood there and made my way into the city, taking the road
towards the cathedral as though my legs were bound by
magnets that dragged me.

Of course, I did not want to pass near to the inn and get
another lump on my pate. Instead, I turned from West Cheap
and continued down towards the cathedral, past the grand
houses of the canons, towards a little tavern called the Red
Dragon down at the south-east corner.

I was about to enter when a face caught my attention.
Close-set eyes, a narrow face, flaxen hair, the black of mourning
– it was the woman I had seen with the dead man that morning
outside the tavern. I slowed and watched her.

She clearly had no recollection of *my* face. As I stood, her
eyes passed over me without recognition, and then she walked
on past – not with the slow, heavy step of a woman struck
with the grim melancholy of sudden widowhood, but with
the urgent gait of a lady in a hurry. Perhaps she had been
to the church to organize the funeral of her man, I wondered,
but just then she turned into an alley between two canons'
houses. Without thinking, I followed her under a low arched
way and along a narrow passage. It was not a lonely, quiet
corridor like others I have known, but a busy thoroughfare
that had tranters and urchins barging into me every few paces.
At the farther end, the woman – what was her name? – took
a turn from that and into another, much broader lane, and here
I realized I knew where I was. It was a road some two hundred
yards from where I had first met her husband, a parallel street
with that of the tavern where David died.

I left her a moment, waiting to see if anyone was likely to
tap me on the skull again, and then nipped up the treads and
knocked boldly on her door.

TWENTY-ONE

Standing outside the place, I was struck by the contrast with Roscard's.

This was one of those places that a peasant could stare at without feeling jealousy. It was not a house to which any man would aspire. Only a stone's throw or two from the rich canons' houses it may be, but it was as different as a pigsty from a palace.

It was not huge, but everything about it looked dilapidated, scruffy and ill-kempt. It had glass in all the windows, but not a pane was clean; the timber frame had once all been lime-washed, and the daub between, and there were rich carvings on all the uprights, but the lime was worn and chipped as though it hadn't been decorated for three years or more. Just under the roof, where the gable faced the road, there had been painted a coat of arms, but that was so faint now that it was unrecognizable. This place was not owned by a man who worried about proclaiming his position in the world. It was strange. It did not seem to suit the fellow who had died in the tavern's yard that day. Was this really the home of David Raleigh?

I was soon confronted by a short, suspicious fellow, who looked me up and down with every sign of distaste. I could imagine him fondling the rosary at his belt in defence at any moment. 'Yes?'

'I would like to see the lady of the house.'

'She's not likely to want to see you. Piss off!'

He began to shut the door, but my boot moved faster. I smiled at him winningly, bringing the full power of my good looks to his attention. 'I've heard about her husband. I want to pay my respects and mention something to her that could be of interest. It will be worth her while.'

This servant wasn't in the service of the widow for no reason. I had a lot more persuading and cajoling to do before he finally agreed to speak with her, and then he closed the door and left me waiting on the doorstep while he went to consult the lady of the house. Meanwhile, I was subjected to a barrage of insults from the urchins who infested the lane. Wherever there is an inn, tavern or bawdy house, you get the little brutes. They stand about, hoping for a man on horseback to appear so that they can claim a fee for holding the reins while he goes to slake his thirst. As they wait, they are apt to amuse themselves by lobbing derogatory remarks to anyone who takes their fancy. This little band of degenerates was clearly out for amusement and would have taken any target. I happened to be convenient. Usually, I would have thrown myself into the fray with enthusiasm, but today I really craved peace. Nothing that attracted attention was welcome, so I resorted to ignoring them. That only gave them courage. One tow-haired brat was weighing a handful of horse dung and considering flinging it at me when the door was opened again, and I gratefully, and hurriedly, slid inside.

'She will give you time to drink one cup of wine,' he said gloomily, as though predicting the apocalypse, before leading me along a screens passage and into a hall.

I was not prepared for the size of the hall. It was small and not at all what I expected. The house was little more than a handful of small rooms. Not wide, the house stretched back from the lane one room deep. A fire flared fitfully in the hearth, and occasionally smoke billowed into the room. A pair of candles on iron pricks at either side of the fire dripped wax on the rushes.

Mistress Agnes Raleigh sat in a tall-backed, throne-like seat that had been pulled across the floor and installed a little before the fire. She was only average height, but from her deportment she could have been much taller. She had the appearance of a woman who had a pike staff for a back bone. Utterly unbending and upright in her seat, she had her chin raised and looked down her nose at me. Her hair was decorously hidden beneath her simple linen coif, and a black cap on top was the only concession to her mourning now that she had removed her black cloak. Mind you, her wine-red gown, richly decorated with coloured threads, made a nice contrast, I thought.

'Well?' she said. She had a goblet in her hand and now she pointedly sipped. Her eyes were a little too close together. It made her look shrewish and demanding. Thin lips, high cheekbones, a narrow face with piercing blue eyes. All in all, she wasn't my sort, but I was determined to make myself appealing to her.

I was about to bow, but then I knelt at her feet instead. 'Madam, I was so sad to hear of your husband's death.'

'Were you? Did you know him? You don't look like the sort of man with whom David would consort,' she said.

'He and I met only briefly, madam.'

'When?' she asked, sipping again. You will notice that she didn't offer me any wine.

'I knew your husband . . .'

'You think that will endear you to me? I knew my husband, too. A harsh man, prey to swift infatuations, and a spendthrift.'

'He was assuredly . . .' Her words suddenly battered at my brain. 'Eh?'

'He had worked his way through my dowry. Look at this house! It's falling apart. He was supposed to be my protector and support in this hard world, and instead he went off wenching and drinking, and now that he is dead, I am all but destitute. Look around you! I have not managed to have the hall whitewashed in years. Even my father's coat of arms is all but lost from the front. He was always so proud of that coat of arms, too.'

'Your father used to own this house?' I said, trying desperately to bring the galloping steed that was my brain back to the race course.

'Yes. Father was a goldsmith of renown. It was my marriage to this fool and wastrel that broke my father's heart, and now mine. All my dowry and inheritance, frittered away on foolishness.'

He hadn't looked like a man who would do that. 'When I saw him, his coat and hosen were not those of a man who spent unwisely,' I said tentatively.

'Do you say so?' she said with a pointed stare at my own clothing. It was not, apparently, up to her standard either.

She sipped more wine and I could see that the tide was

going down swiftly. Nothing ventured, I thought to myself. I couldn't see how to introduce this subject easily, so I decided I must leap in with both feet. I must learn all she could tell me, especially if she could help with the message in his purse. 'Madam, I was there. I saw him murdered.'

'You *what*?' she said, and suddenly the steel left her spine and she rocked backwards.

'Madam, I am sorry, but I don't see how else to say it. I saw him in the tavern, and then I saw him slain outside. It was a big man with a large black hat, but I didn't see the fellow's face.'

'I thought his killer was recognized. He was a man named Jack. A man just like you.'

TWENTY-TWO

Yes. She knew my name. That was enough to make me rock back on my heels, too. 'How did you know my name?'

She didn't answer immediately, but sipped again, peering at me over the rim of the goblet like a frog staring over a lily at a juicy fly while she savoured the flavour. 'I would think everyone in London knows your name now. You are famous. Murderers are.'

'I'm no murderer!' I said hotly. It was becoming a refrain.

'You say you saw him on the day he was killed. Did you go to the beadle?'

'I couldn't! The murderer was there, and I had to escape as quickly as I could before he killed me!'

'Really?'

'Madam, why was your husband there?'

'You think he would tell me?' she said, and now the bitterness that was poisoning her came out in a flurry. 'He told me *nothing* about his business, such as it was. All he wanted was to have me sit here like a caged bird, while he went out and about and enjoyed himself on my father's money. He thought himself so important and high in the esteem of the queen that he was safe to go and do anything! You know where he was on his last night? I do: at the home of his *whore*, all night. He was so keen to see her that he ignored me. You think I should speak kindly of the dead? He deliberately humiliated me all my married life. You think I should mourn him? I don't! I am pleased to be free of him!'

'I am sorry,' I mumbled. I was more than a little surprised at her outburst, as well I might be. A woman who has just been widowed would usually be a little more circumspect in her words.

'Don't be. I am not,' she said, and lifted the goblet once more. 'Look! My cup is empty. And I believe you were told that you had one cupful in which to entertain me. I thank you, Master Jack.'

I rose to my feet. There was little else. However, it was worth one more cast of the dice. 'Madam, do you know anything about a cipher he might have used?'

'A secret code? Him? If he had one, it would have been simple enough,' she said with disdain. 'He was strong, but not terribly clever.'

'I see.' Not that it mattered. If he was a messenger, as Mark Thomasson guessed, the code was not his own; it belonged to the couple who were using him to communicate. Could I ask her whether she knew anything of the parchment I had found? Surely that was pointless. She knew nothing, so she said, about his business. Raising the fact of his robbing another would hardly endear me to her. 'Are you sure of his whore?'

'Of course I am. She is Julia Hopwell, who lives on Fleet Street near St Bride's church. I'll bet her name was well earned, the amount of money my husband paid her!'

I was so taken with this news that I hardly heard the noises. It was only when the door slammed wide that I realized my error.

There was a crash at first, then shouting, and as I peered at the screens, I heard orders and saw a beadle appear.

It was enough for me. I was off, out through the back of the hall like a scalded cat, followed by the cackling laugh of Agnes Raleigh. There was a staircase up to the second floor, but, miracle of miracles, a low door through to a rear yard. I was off and through it almost before my thoughts had caught up with my legs. The yard was enclosed, but there was a gate at the far side. I ran to it, hurled myself at it and jumped for dear life, scrambling up the gate, then throwing myself over it.

Or I would have. You remember I said not to look behind while running? I didn't, but even as I was about to tumble over the other side, I felt the man's hand grab at my ankle. Only a judicious kick with my other boot freed me. Then I was over and running again. I had no idea where I was. Now, I think it was probably Honey Lane beside St Augustine's, and I was able to rush along it, out into Athelyng Street, and from there I took off through the crowds, hurtling past shocked dames and terrified urchins as I made my way to All Hallows'. There, I took a turn into the cemetery, almost running into a couple of horses that had been left to feed, past a pair of merchants haggling over the price of bales of cloth (I think), and back into Friday Street, from whence I made my way to the river.

There, I stopped and had to catch my breath.

I had seen the look of sheer cruel joy on Agnes Raleigh's face when the men arrived. She had not merely expected them, but she had kept me penned in her hall until they could arrive. I daresay one of the scruffy little rein-holders had been sent for the beadle by her steward as soon as I was enclosed with her. News of my supposed involvement with the death of her husband must have reached other ears. What a life! I was still no better off. I had learned that a wench who would haggle her virtue lived over near the Temple, and that she was a friend of the dead man. That was a lot of help. There were hundreds of women like that.

I was grimly slouching along the street when I heard a friendly voice.

'Hoi! Is that you, Jack?'

'Captain Atwood!'

It was a relief. His sober but amiable face was a pleasure to view just then, after my recent encounters.

'Come. Let's get some beer and food,' Atwood said. 'We're here to fight and defend the city; the least the city can do is ensure that we have full bellies for the task!'

I followed him along the streets.

There was rubble and mess everywhere, with citizens who had decided to flee the city dumping whatever they didn't need in the middle of the road. Atwood swore about their untidiness all the way, kicking discarded jugs and bottles from his path as we went.

I was glad of Atwood's company. He was stolid and reliable, and always seemed to pay attention when I talked to him. Now, as we reached the city itself and made our way towards the cathedral, I was struck by how little the city seemed aware of the approaching danger. The shops were still open, and those selling weaponry of all sorts were doing a roaring trade, but women paraded and children still played, dancing about in the streets as if nothing more alarming than a feast day was anticipated. Perhaps they were right. I mean, men like Atwood would fight and probably die in the attempt to defend the city, but men like me, who could fling off any uncomplimentary apparel that carried the wrong badges, and women, who could make an invading army feel welcome, would have less to fear. This wasn't Europe, after all. No English army would want to harm London. It was the source of the nation's wealth, and any venal, thieving, avaricious soldier or commander would have to contend with the still more fiendish and acquisitive people who populated this city. I wasn't sure that the army behind Wyatt would survive that contest.

'You look glum, Jack. Don't. Wyatt's men have to cross that river before they can get to us, and they won't find that easy with the only bridge taken from them.'

'There are a lot of them,' I said.

'There are plenty of us inside the city to defend it, too.'

'Yes,' I said. I didn't sound convincing to my own ears.

He looked at me with a frown. We were outside the Boar's Head in Candlewright Street, and he caught a serving wench who glared a moment and then seemed to take a fancy to the tall soldier. She grinned, and quickly went inside when he asked for beer. Soon she was back with a large leather jug and two mugs. He paid her and gave her a grave smile that seemed to set a fire in her heart. For the rest of the time we sat on the bench outside the tavern, she kept returning to serve us.

'You are worried about the citizens in the city? Do you not think they will rouse themselves to stop Wyatt?'

'I think there are some who try to manipulate the people,' I said. 'There are some who would willingly see the queen toppled and another put in her place.'

'Such as who?'

'I am not a politician – how should I know? All I know is, whoever they would place there would be unlikely to last very long. The kingdom is as safe as a building bonfire. While it's unlit and people are throwing boxes and trash on to it, making it grow, it is solid and sound. But once it is lighted, it is likely to topple. Our kingdom is the same. Right now, it is solid and safe, but the flames of rebellion are licking, and once they catch hold, the bonfire will fall.'

Atwood nodded as though I was a philosopher.

'Or something,' I added, and drank some more.

TWENTY-THREE

He sat without moving as he absorbed my words. 'Rebellion, you think?'

A man passed by, holding out his hand for alms, and Atwood impatiently waved the fellow on. Then, 'There are many who would have considered others as more suitable for the throne, but they are mistaken, I am sure. The country doesn't need more fighting. We need stability after King Edward's death.'

'Yes, I know.'

'But you fear that malcontents in the city could try to manipulate things to their own advantage?'

'You must have seen them yourself,' I said.

He shook his head. I drank my third tankard. I had been abstemious for the past few days, sticking to mild beers, but this was good, strong beer and it did go to my head a little.

Not that it affected me. I am used to good beers. The main thing was, Atwood was a good fellow. He had proved himself to be reasonable, avoiding a fight when he could, and showing himself keen to take me on when I was at a loss. I knew full well that, were a man to try to attack me, my captain would do all in his power to protect me. That was a reassuring thought as I downed my tankard. We spoke of the bridge and the defences, and we spoke of the enemy, and we talked about our past lives, our families, our lovers (that took me very little time, him quite a while), and the blackjack was emptied and we were forced to ask the maid for another, and I felt more and more that Atwood was reliable.

'We do have to be careful, though,' he said at one point. I don't entirely recall what we had been saying, but at this I nodded sagely and belched quietly. 'We should not talk of such things in front of the other men. They might get the wrong idea. They aren't all bright like you.'

I nodded again. 'They aren't men of the world like you and me.'

'No. I think you have faced many dangers compared with even our soldiers. Today, for example, you look very weary.'

'I am! I have faced dangers! I could have been executed, and a man tried to kill me – I have just been talking to his widow, but she thought I had killed her husband. Me! I ask you, sir, would anyone think me a murderer? I have been set up for a man's death, and even his widow thinks me guilty. She called the beadle to capture me.'

'Really? Were you arrested?'

'Not I! I managed to escape,' I said.

'Who was this man?'

'Well,' I said, staring down into my mug. 'He was called David Raleigh. I met him only briefly. And then I was knocked down when my back was turned, and a fellow killed him.'

'And this murderer – did you see him? Do you know what he looks like? We could find him, bring him to justice and renew your good name.'

'Nay. He was dressed in black, with a broad-brimmed hat. When I saw him, he was walking with two other men, one a smiling fair-haired man, the other a vast great man, huge in all proportion. He tried to kill me again, later, but I managed to escape. It was lucky, too, for they murdered my companion, Gil. That was why we moved out and took up the rooms where you found us.'

'Three of them?' Atwood said. He seemed struck by something I had said. I don't know why; I wasn't. 'Why would these three have been after you?'

'I don't know! I never harmed anyone,' I said, adding defensively, 'not with sword nor stick.'

'And you know no more?'

Even in my cups, I wasn't going to speak about the message. 'Not about why they should try to hurt me, no. It was a mystery to me. But they wanted to kill me, just like the other.'

'Which other?'

'Henry. The man who killed Ann.'

He raised his eyebrows. 'Ann?'

'She was his companion on the day David was killed,' I

said somewhat tersely. 'I saw the fellow in the alley, you see. He cut her throat. Right across, here to here,' I added, indicating with my forefinger. 'It was horrible, and I chased after him and saw him go up, and when I went to speak to him in his house, his servant told me he wasn't there, but I don't believe him. I'll bet he is involved in the bishop's plans.'

'Up? Up where? What bishop?' Atwood said, and when I looked at him, I saw that his face was a picture of confusion. He must have drunk more than I thought. He didn't seem able to follow even a simple story like this.

I sighed, and as the blackjack was refilled, I told him all about the events of the past week. It took me a while.

'So the bishop has interrogated you and wants the message, you say, and this fellow in dark clothing killed your friend Gil as well as this messenger?'

'Yes.'

'But Bishop Gardiner is the Lord High Chancellor under the queen, and this other man, Henry Roscard, what does he want? Why should he want to kill the woman Ann?'

'The servant told me that he was a friend of Peter Carew's,' I said.

'And he is the friend and ally of the Earl of Devon,' Atwood said. 'Edward Courtenay, the earl, is very powerful and viewed highly by Her Majesty, I'm told. You pick your enemies well, but that doesn't answer my question.'

'I don't pick enemies. This man Roscard picked *me*!'

'Why would he go and murder a woman from the streets, then?'

'I don't know!' I wailed, and then was quiet a moment or two while I tried to gather myself. 'Look, I saw that she was terrified of him, and soon after, she was murdered. I saw him running from me. It was surely him.'

'Roscard,' Atwood mused. 'If you are right, the man with the black hat killed the man you say was a messenger, he killed the man who took the purse, and now this Roscard has killed this woman Ann, too. That means the two have murdered all who knew of this message. If I were you, I would keep away from them both.'

'I intend to,' I said, and hiccupped.

'Meanwhile, you should try to find the message so you can give it to the bishop. But tell me when you think you have it. I will help and guard you. Because if this Roscard learns you have it, your life won't be worth that,' he said with a snap of his fingers.

It didn't make me feel reassured.

It was lucky. I had drunk more than enough by then, and told Atwood that I was going to return to the house and get some rest. I felt very tired after my efforts that morning. Atwood agreed, and I set off homewards, while he was busy, he said, checking with the city bailiffs about provisions for his men. At the time I thought nothing of it, but I was glad to be walking back. The light was fading gradually, and I wanted to get inside and in front of a warm fire.

I would have liked that.

However, I had wandered only a little way up Candlewright Street and taken the lane southwards towards our house when I felt a stone hit my back. A diversion, I thought, and set my hand on my purse. It was a common enough trick: get a small boy to lob a stone at a mark's back, then have another fellow run before him and grab the purse before both disappear and share their profits. Quick and easy for a foolish victim, but I was no fool, I thought. I span and glanced behind me, but instead of the small boy I expected, I was confronted by the Bear again. He smiled at me and held his arms outstretched. He was clearly not going to be fooled this time, and there was barely space for a man to pass another in this narrow lane.

It was enough to turn all the ale in my belly sour.

I turned, ready to bolt, but as I did so, there was the man in the broad-brimmed hat again.

Where did you spring from? I wondered, but kept my mouth shut. I had already received two too many blows to my head in recent days.

He stood casually enough, leaning his shoulder against a wall while studying a piece of wood in his hand. With a small knife, he was carving it into the shape of a sitting dog, I saw.

'You have been a sore trouble to me,' he said.

'Many people say that,' I said, attempting a little humour to conceal the terror that all but made me empty my bowels there and then. I could not take my eyes off that small blade and how its terrible, sharp edge took long, thin slivers of wood from the dog. I heard the Bear's steps behind me, but even his physical presence was not as scary as this quiet man with the knife.

'My name is John Blount. I have powerful reasons for speaking to you, master. I know you have formed an opinion of Henry Roscard, and I think if I know the man at all, your opinions are too kind.'

'He's a murderer and thief.'

'And spy, yes. And he works for Edward Courtenay. He and Roscard are dangerous men, both. You have bitten into a poisoned cake, my friend.'

'I don't know what you mean!'

'I was at the tavern, you recall. We saw your friend Henry take the purse, and then we saw you filch it from him. It was,' he said, looking over to me, 'as pretty a piece of thievery as I have ever seen. I salute you.'

'You want the purse.'

'Not really. That would be easy. No, I want what was inside it.'

'I don't have the money.'

'We both know I don't care about the money. I want the other thing.'

I could have dissembled, but after all that beer I only had two things on my mind: flight and a privy. 'Well?'

He sighed. He had a square face that would have appealed to many women, I thought. Dark hair, dark eyes set under low brows that gave him a curiously serious appearance. When he fixed those brown eyes on you, a fellow knew he was devoting his uttermost concentration.

'I want it.'

There was no time for me to speak. Suddenly, my legs were taken away by a blow from a plank behind the knees, and I collapsed and found myself staring up into the face of the fair-haired, grinning man. His hands passed quickly over my clothes and removed my dagger and eating knife, before he removed my purse and subjected it to the sort of investigation a pox-doctor would give a man's tarse. He had my coins out and sought any double stitching, but had to confess himself baffled. Then he took my jack and felt inside the seams while I was still wearing it. I was not happy, but then again I had sunk enough ale to stop even Hercules in his tracks. If I closed my eyes, I would doze, I thought. I closed them.

His hands went everywhere: round my breast and back, about the collar of my jack, down my legs, and then he removed my shoes and studied them for secret compartments, too, I have no doubt.

'Nothing.'

'Check his cods,' John said.

'Oi! No!' I said, but before I could scramble from his path, a massive booted foot landed on my chest, effectively holding me there. I looked up into the Bear's nostrils. It was like looking up a horse's nose.

'You have been dabbling in things you should have avoided,' John said. 'You're holding up affairs for the queen, for the bishop and for many others, including me. It's not a good position to be in. So, just give up the message and we'll let you go.'

But before the man could do anything, there was a sudden roar. I heard a solid thud, and the Bear's eyes rolled up into his head. I confess that sight brought a warm glow to my breast. Then I knew real terror.

He fell, and I would have whimpered as he collapsed on top of me, except I couldn't. I had no breath. It was like having Sisyphus's rock roll on to me: he was a ludicrous lump that I could by no means shift. I could hardly even breathe! I panted shallowly, like a broken donkey, desperate, while all about me I heard the sound of blows being struck. At last there was a shout, and finally someone came and pulled the Bear from me, and I gasped desperately, my lungs burning. I turned over on to all fours and tried to regain my natural state, but it wasn't easy.

'Come, man, get up, and be swift! They will be back at any moment!' It was Atwood, hissing at me urgently. He had three men with him, and one of his companions gripped a great

club in both hands and glared at the alley as though daring
all the thieves, draw-latches and demons to come and attack
him. The man in the hat had fled already, but he could soon
be back, this time with more men.

I allowed myself to be picked up and lurched after them as
they pulled me back towards the main roadway.

TWENTY-FOUR

I have no memory of the hurried scampering through alleys and lanes back to the rooms we had taken. Bill was there when we entered, and Atwood slammed the door and barred it with a show of haste that impressed even Bill himself.

'What is it now?'

'How much does he know?' Atwood asked me.

'Most of it. Not about Roscard, though,' I said.

Atwood made a good fist of telling Bill about the man called John Blount while Moll brought me a cloth and bowl of water. I had mud and . . . well, similar-coloured refuse, plastering my jack's breast.

'This Blount, this is the man who killed Gil?' Bill said at last.

'Yes. A nasty piece of knavery, if ever I saw one,' I said.

'We will need to put paid to his threats,' Bill said thoughtfully. 'I don't like the idea of a spy and scoundrel trying to disrupt the kingdom, but I like the idea of any man hurting or killing one of my own even less. I want his blood.'

That warmed me. It sounded as if he was talking about avenging the harm done to me. But then I realized he meant Gil. I was still unwanted.

'Who are these men?' Bill said. I was sinking another half quart of ale, and looked at Atwood hopefully.

'Some of the most dangerous men in the kingdom,' Atwood said. 'Now the rebellion is growing, those who would see the queen removed from her throne are growing bolder.'

'You say the man who did that to Gil is working for the Earl of Devon?'

Atwood nodded.

'But you say there is this other fellow? Roscard? Who is he?'

'I don't know,' I said. 'All I know is that he keeps appearing when I don't want him. And he knows much about me, it seems.'

'You know that, and still you come back here?' Bill said, his face darkening.

Atwood took up the story. 'There are others to consider. Gardiner, for example. Queen Mary has relied on him for years. It was he who crowned her, and he is her most trusted adviser, some reckon.'

Bill nodded, and I did, too. It was said that it was much to do with Gardiner, this plan on the queen being married, although many, like Wyatt and his rebels, didn't like the idea. Most folks had nothing against her particularly, but she was determined to marry a foreigner, and no good, true Englishman likes that sort of behaviour. Especially when the betrothed in question is a member of the Imperial family: Philip of Spain. That was enough to put up the backs of almost everyone.

'I would guess that Roscard and Blount have good reason for wanting to get the message and kill Jack here,' Atwood said.

'Why would they want to hurt Jack?' Moll asked.

'Yes! It was nothing to do with me!' I said. I was upset, I have to confess. It wasn't fair!

Atwood shrugged. 'They all seem to think you know where this message is.'

'But I want nothing to do with it!'

Bill sneered at me. 'You think anyone will give a tuppenny knee-trembler for what you think? You're not from London, you're not a rich merchant, you're not a local apprentice. You're just the son of a leather-worker from Surrey somewhere.'

'It's Whitstable! And it's in Kent!'

'So what? The fact is, Jack, these men are much bigger than you. They have money and power behind them. You have to keep out of things. Let us sort it out.'

'I'm not running from here!'

Atwood agreed, somewhat to my surprise. 'Let him stay. They won't want to do anything to him. Jack is nothing to them.'

'He's a loose end,' Bill said firmly. 'Jack, return to your

village. That way you may live yet awhile. Stay here, and you'll die.'

'But if I flee, they'll assume I'm guilty!'

He looked at me. 'If you don't, they'll assume you're guilty and they'll hang you. If you run, you may live!'

'You can't just make him run,' Moll protested. 'What will happen to him?'

Bill glared at her, and I realized he didn't care about me at all. He just wanted me gone.

'If he stays here, we're all at risk, aren't we? You as well, Moll,' he said roughly.

That was, I realized, a good point. 'I'd better take my share of the purse, then.'

'You had the purse and whatever was in it,' he said.

'But the money . . .'

'It's for the good of the gang. You're going, so you're not in the gang.'

I gaped. He stared back without expression. His eyes were dead and dangerous. He was already in that frame of mind that told him I was gone. He didn't care whether I hung around or left, but he wasn't going to share the money with me: that was clear. I could have fought him, of course. It would be like wrestling a charging bull in a dead-ended alleyway, but I was perfectly at liberty to try it.

No, I didn't. You think I'm stupid?

However, his words had made me think of something: I needed money to escape the city, and although I owned nothing, I did have that piece of paper from the stolen purse. Maybe there was something in there that could be worth some money? I could take it to the queen, or take it to someone else who would pay for it?

Yes. I know it wasn't the best of ideas, but I wasn't having a good day.

'I cannot help but think he really does not like you,' Atwood said a little later as we left the room and made our way through the dark streets.

I pulled my cloak about me, shivering at the icy blast.

There were times when I was with my father, when the

wind would whistle about our ears like demons, and the chill would make our flesh feel as though it was being scorched. Here in London, it was in the streets like this, which were aligned with the Thames, that the bitter wind worked its unholy worst. A man out without a hat or gloves would soon feel all sensation depart, and those who slept out in it were often found stiff as a board the following morning. I can bear any amount of heat, but God protect me from the cold. I hate it.

'I am sure of it,' I said. 'He fears me. I could bring a constable into his group at any time, and that could mean his end on a rope. But it is more because he fears that I would tempt his woman from him. He knows she can barely resist me.'

'Of course,' Atwood said with a chuckle. He was impressed by my confident manner.

He was quiet for quite some time as we walked along the street, heading towards the great bridge. Then he stopped, and a frown wiped his smile away. 'You know, Bill could have a point. You are not safe if any of those men decide to remove you. You are only a pawn in their game of chess.'

'I'm happier here than back in Whitstable. Have you ever been to Whitstable? No, well, you wouldn't understand, then,' I said. The mere idea of my father's leather-working shed made my flesh creep. I seemed to discern, as though from a great distance, the far-off, rancid odour of herrings drying in the sun, the sour smell of pitch and tanning leather. It made me shudder. 'But I do want to stop this man John Blount from attacking me again.'

'Well, if you don't have the message any more, you should be safe.'

'But I told him that in the alley this afternoon, and you saw how much he trusted me then! He was going to open me from crop to gizzard to check my insides.'

'Perhaps if you gave it to someone you trusted, though?'

'I already have.'

'Who?'

I was about to answer, but thought better of it. 'Never mind that. How can I have this John Blount arrested? Perhaps if I go to the bishop and tell him all about it . . .'

A vision rose in my mind of the patrician bishop staring at me and shaking his head in disappointment. After all, he had asked me to find the message for him. If I were to tell him that I'd given it to Mark Thomasson, he would probably grow very disappointed. Disappointed enough to make the rest of my life very painful. He would send me to the torturers: not because he thought I could give more useful information, but just for the appearance of things. If he didn't, he could be thought to be slacking. I didn't like that thought. I was fond of my arms and legs as they were, neatly articulated.

'No,' I said.

'I think you're right. You need to tell him something about this note,' Atwood said. 'Either that or find it and take it to him. Perhaps that's your best option, now. To retrieve the note and take it to him.'

'And be knocked on the head in the middle of the street so that anyone can steal it and take it to him? And then be stabbed, or captured and taken to the torturers at their leisure? I don't think so!'

'Ah. So you have a better plan,' he said. 'Good.'

'Yes,' I said as we trudged on. There was a distinct smell of iron in the air. I was sure it would snow before long.

'What is it?' he asked.

'Hmm?'

'Your plan. What is it?'

Thus it was that, as darkness was falling, I found myself outside Mark Thomasson's house again. Atwood himself remained outside, concealing himself as best he could in the shadows while I hammered gently on the door.

'What do you want?' Jonah demanded.

'I have business with your master.'

The servant peered at me with a lip curled in disdain as he took in my clothing. 'I doubt he would want to see you, nor you him.'

'Don't be a fool!' I said, and barged past him.

You know, it is a strange thing, but I've noticed that steel feels cold when it touches you. It doesn't matter where it touches you or what the temperature is, only that it is sharp.

There's something about, say, a sword with an edge like a razor that gives it a magisterial quality compared with a horse-shoe. And now, as I felt that metal touch the back of my neck, I felt as though my entire throat was closed up with ice. It was not a nice sensation. Nor was the urgent need to urinate.

'You, master, have given me a bastard run-around today,' the man called John Blount said.

TWENTY-FIVE

I was just preparing to say my prayers when he took his sword away and pushed me hard into the parlour. The enormous hound, Peterkin, was there again. I had assumed the brute would be dead, but as I walked in, he blearily lifted his head, smacked his chops a few times, the drool falling on the floor before him, and then let his head flop down. I suppose with Blount and his two companions in there, their weapons drawn, he didn't see the need to worry himself about me. He didn't mind *them*.

'Get in there and sit down!' Blount said.

'I said you wouldn't want to come inside,' the old servant chuckled, and walked out to the buttery.

I was determined to behave like a true-born Englishman. 'What do you want with me?' I growled.

Blount sat on a stool and waved a hand at Mark Thomasson. 'You tell him. The way he's squeaking, he's near to fainting.'

'I am not—'

'Shut up, sit down and listen carefully,' Blount said.

I did what he asked. As I did so, I saw the Bear kneel at the hound's side and tickle him under the ear. The hound rolled over, paws in the air, while the man rubbed his chest. Anything more ludicrous could not be imagined.

'Jack, I did try to warn you,' Mark said.

'What have you done?' I demanded. 'You've betrayed the message and betrayed me!'

'Now, now, Jack, don't you worry about that. The fact is, the message you found should not have been so easily discovered.'

'Why?'

Mark and Blount exchanged a look.

I saw at a glance what was happening. 'Mark, I can see that you have been cruelly treated by this felon,' I said. 'He has bullied you, but there is no need to fear him. You must do your duty as you see it,' I said, and winked, hoping he would realize that there was no need to divulge the import of the message.

'Mark, in God's name, give this fool the truth,' Blount said.

'Whose truth would that be? I saw you at the tavern. You ran along the alleyway and came upon me in the tavern's yard, didn't you? And you knew Gil had the purse so you killed him, too!'

'Who?' Blount asked, staring.

'He led you to me, down at Trig Lane, and you tried to catch me, but then you tortured him and left him there, bound to a post near the water. Why leave him there? Did you want to leave a message for me?'

'I have no idea what you are talking about. There was a man who took us back to your house, but he was well when we left him. And we left him shortly after you ran away, paying him for any more news he could bring of you.'

That gave me reason to think again. All at once I had a new perspective. It was like the cogs of a great clock slipping round a fresh turn, the teeth meshing in a new pattern. Rather than this man Blount, perhaps Roscard had murdered Gil? But who had murdered Raleigh? Was that Blount, as I had thought, or was that Roscard too?

Mark interrupted my train of thought. 'Jack, Master Blount here is in the service of important people. The message you intercepted should not have been sent. It was a great error. And Master Blount here has been trying to rectify that error for some days now, in order to protect his, um, lord. The message has become discovered, however. That makes matters . . . problematic.'

'Why?'

'Because,' Blount said, 'the message is no longer secret. Since you started blundering about, you have brought it to the attention of others.'

'I have been diligent in keeping it secret,' I protested.

'That is how the bishop came to hear of it? And the agent of the Spanish, Henry Roscard? And that turncoat rebel, Atwood?'

'Roscard is an agent of Spain? I thought he was in the pay

of the Earl of Devon?' Suddenly, his words struck home and I felt it like a sickening blow to the stomach. When I spoke, it was in a squeak. 'Atwood? A rebel?'

'It was astonishing that he managed to suddenly appear in the alleyway, wasn't it? We were trying to help you see what was happening, but he appeared with three bullies and forced us to leave. Poor Will here has a sore head because of Atwood's men.'

'They'll regret it when I meet them again,' the Bear said, sourly rubbing his skull.

'He's no turncoat,' I said. 'Why, he came here to protect me on the way back. He wanted to guard me.'

Mark sighed and rested his brow on a palm, shaking his head. He looked up at last. 'Jack, do you not understand anything? Atwood hopes to see the message delivered to Wyatt because it will support the rebels and give them the succour they need. But Atwood cannot afford to fail, because no matter what, if he does so, he will be dangling from a rope and then split four ways, while his head sits on a spike. He is a rebel, man! If this message fails and the rebels fail, his life will not be worth a feather!'

'He's expecting me to bring out the message when I leave here,' I said, and shivered. Not entirely from the cold.

'Then you shall do so,' Mark said. 'And then you will leave him urgently and look to your own safety. Do not stay with him; that way lies death for you.'

'But then the message will get out anyway,' I said.

'But you will be alive,' Blount reminded me.

It was good to know that someone seemed to value my life as much as me. 'I don't know. I'll still likely die tonight. I have nowhere to go and sleep.'

'Then, perhaps, if you give him the message and ask him to protect it as your commander,' Mark said thoughtfully, casting a sharp look at Blount, 'that would serve, would it not?'

'It would serve well. It should protect Jack here and give Atwood the opportunity he needs. All he must do is cross the river and deliver his note. Then events may take their course.'

I was floundering. 'I don't understand! What, then, of the message?'

'Nothing, man. You will be safe. If Atwood has it, he will be content and in far too much of a hurry to worry himself about you. He will take it and flee.'

'And my problems will at last be over?'

'Yes,' Blount said, and once more I saw a quick glance from him towards Mark.

Why didn't that register with me as suspicious?

'Well?'

Atwood was waiting exactly where he had promised he would. It was dark now, and I had to screw up my eyes to see him, standing all but hidden in the shadows.

'It wasn't easy to persuade Thomasson,' I said. 'He wanted to keep it, but in the end he agreed to let me have it.'

I passed the little scrap to Atwood, feeling doubt rise in my breast. It was hard to believe that this man would have slain me had I not given it to him, but the others swore that he was so determined that my life was meaningless to him.

'That is good!' Atwood said, lifting the scrap and staring at the symbols. 'What does this mean?'

'How should I know? Mark in there was going to try to decipher it, but he hasn't got round to it yet. I'm not surprised, either. Look at it! It makes no sense at all. Perhaps it was written by a fool without thinking.'

'So you have no knowledge of what it means?' Atwood said.

You know, he was smiling, but he just reminded me of a reptile. A lizard would do that, smiling with its mouth but with no humour ever touching its eyes. He was just putting on a show. I'm sure of it.

He wasn't the only one could do that. I smiled my widest and held my hands out. 'How could I? I'm a street-worker, not some college-trained expert in ciphers. If I knew what it said, would I have bothered to bring it here to be deciphered?'

'What will you do now?' he asked, his eyes straying to Mark's door.

'Me? Take it to the bishop, of course. If I could, I'd just burn it. It's brought me nothing but bad luck. I want nothing to do with it. If only I could get rid of it for ever and pretend I'd never seen it.'

'Let me take it, then. I will see it's delivered to the bishop. That way, you'll have nothing more to do with it, the bishop will be pleased, and he may even reward me a little.'

'You would do that? But what will he do to me?'

'I'll promise him that you'll never mention this to another man for the rest of your life,' Atwood said.

I had a sudden vision of my body lying here on the cobbles. A dead man tends to be very silent.

'Tell him that I don't know what it says and I'll soon move back to Whitstable – as soon as I can escape the city,' I said. 'I want nothing more to do with the damn thing.'

'I will tell him,' Atwood said. He stepped nearer to me, his eyes flicking left and right, and again I was reminded of a reptile. His hand was close to his dagger's hilt, I noticed.

And then there came a sudden shout. The sound of running boots, a clattering of old and rusty armour, and a force of city irregular volunteers came running down the road. Four carried torches; one had his lighted. One of the soldiers saw me and pointed. Atwood had already faded away, stepping back into the shadows once more. I was beginning to think they suited him.

'Hey, you!'

With relief, I recognized the voice of Sergeant Dearing. 'Sir!'

'Who was that with you?'

I was about to declare Atwood's presence, but then thought better of it. 'No one.'

'What are you doing out here in the middle of curfew?' he demanded, but then shrugged. 'Ballocks! Who cares? Come with us, Jack. We're being called to the bridge. Those bastard rebels are trying to force the gates. We have to get to it and stop them.'

TWENTY-SIX

Sunday 4th February

When we approached the gate, we could hear it. An attack was in full swing, and I felt my ballocks shrinking at the sounds.

Dearing shouted at me and motioned me forward. Well, that was fine, except I didn't want to go. He saw my reluctance and shoved a helmet on to my head, thrust a halberd into my hands and pushed me on.

It was an excursion into hell.

You haven't been in a battle? All I can say is, you don't want to. You have no idea what it's like until you are there. Imagine: standing behind barricades which should protect you from danger, and seeing the timbers less than a foot away suddenly turn to smoke, and all that is left behind is a pattern of holes where small shot has ripped through; seeing the man next to you torn apart, one arm taken off at the elbow and whirling away to strike another fellow across the face; another fellow patting with his hands, trying to cover five or six two-inch gashes in his torso; the sight of blood spraying from a hole in a man's thigh, pumping with every heartbeat; a man lying with his throat open, the cartilage of his windpipe showing bright and yellow in the mess of blood and muscle. Imagine: cracks and booms as cannons fire from our side, the smoke blowing into your face hot and foul as an exhalation from hell; fierce scorching in your throat as you inhale the disgusting brimstone reek; screams and screeches assailing your ears.

Imagine all that and you are partway there. Because there is also the disgusting mess that you must step in at every pace. Blood, shit and piss, all adding to the hellish nature of the scene. There is nothing proud or glorious about being on the front line of a battle, believe me. It was my first experience, and I fervently hoped it would be my last as well.

The men at the other side of the bridge were concealed in the buildings and behind low walls. Of course, the cannon were easy to see, because they flamed and gushed smoke as soon as they roared and hurled their stones at us. To know where they lay was one thing; to hit them with our own shot was another. I saw balls strike the roadway and bounce, skipping over the wall; others flew too high and struck buildings behind. Once, a ball whirled madly through a small company of men marching forward, flinging bodies and limbs in wild confusion, and the men on my side cheered and huzzahed, but only for a moment, because then three shots came in speedy retaliation and wreaked a dreadful carnage on us.

I said this was hell. It wasn't: it was worse than hell, because this was devastation wrought by men against men. And I wanted no part of it.

Atwood was nowhere to be seen, which was some relief. I saw a couple of his men about my company, but we were all too busy hiding beneath the cannonade to worry about our friends. The rebels had taken advantage of the darkness to fling great timbers across the gap in the bridge where the span had been removed, and now they were trying to dash over their makeshift causeway to attack us. That was when I felt most terrified, when I saw their white, screaming faces running at me. Men with fear but determination in every line of their features, pelting across a dangerous set of wooden planks just to reach me, to hack at me and kill me if they could.

That's what it felt like. All those shrieking lunatics were running straight at me, and me alone. I noticed that the man who had wielded the club against the Bear in the alley the day before was nearer me, and that was a relief. Another of Atwood's men was with him, and I felt the gratitude that all soldiers must feel to see friends from their company nearby. Shared terror is almost terror reduced. Actually, it was more the fear of injury that was shared in my case, as though the fact that there were others there meant that injuries would be shared by us all. If I were alone, I would take all the wounds, whereas with Atwood's men there, too, I would be taking only a part of the cuts and bruises.

A loud roar, a thunderous detonation, and I found I was flying through the air with the grace of a sparrow. It was a curious sensation, and it seemed to go on for a very long time, so that I could gaze about me with interest. I saw Atwood's men at the centre of an expanding rose, all pink and red, and very beautiful, until I realized it was their blood. And then I struck something, and I know that I smiled as I seemed to fall into a wide blanket of black fur, all warm, cosy and comfortable, and then someone closed the blanket over my head, and that was it for me.

There was a roaring in my ears. I must be beside the sea again. I could hear the metallic crunch of waves breaking on the shingle, and the steady hiss and suck of the water withdrawing from the stones. There was a howling gale, too, from the sound of it. I could hear it distinctly over the water exploding and crashing, the noise of the gulls in the air, screeching . . .

I opened my eyes and the peaceful scene by the sea at Whitstable was eradicated like a fog whipped away by a gale. I was on my back in a tangle of ropes and beams. None, by a miracle, had landed on me, so at least I was undamaged, but all around me it sounded as if that was the least of my concerns. I clambered to my feet and spent some time staring at the halberd. Where the metal reinforcings ran down the shaft, now there was a tangle of strips of steel and shattered splinters of wood. I also noticed that there was a pain in my flank, although I wasn't going to investigate that. I might discover something I didn't want to see. My arm was still attached, and my hand worked, and that was all I cared about at that moment.

'Jack? Get up, you lazy git!' Dearing shouted, and I found my hearing had returned, although there was a lot of hissing and popping going on.

The rebels had reached the barricades, and the fighting was ferocious there, but I could do little about it with my halberd. It was no more than a stick with a dangling head.

I took an experimental swing with it, and the head flew off, narrowly missing one of our Whitecoats and making him turn and glare at me. Giving an apologetic smile and shrug, I glanced at Dearing, who gave me a sour stare and pushed me towards a small pile of weapons on the ground. I took one up and nearly dropped it. They were all covered in a mess of once-human bodies, and the feel of the blood and little gritty bits of shattered bone and stuff was revolting. Still, I didn't get the feeling that my natural repulsion would win me any sympathy. I took it up gingerly and was shoved towards the barricades just as a fresh assault was forming. The cannons cracked and roared, and bloody slabs of meat were left lying where men had been standing only moments before, and then they were running at us. One gun fired, but the rest were silent, and I watched with the others as the men stormed towards us. I glanced over my neighbour and saw that the men at the gun were working furiously, ramming home the powder, shoving in a canvas sack of small shot, ramming that down as well, and finally standing well back as the gunner held out his linstock with the glowing match and shoved it into the touch hole. There was a sharp fizzing, a neat inverted cone of smoke, and then the gun bucked and a vast gout of flame spurted towards the rebels.

It was hideous. I happened to see them before the smoke mercifully obliterated the sight. In front, two men bore the brunt of the grapeshot, and it tore them to shreds at that range. Bits and pieces of them were flung back at the men behind, but they were struck by the shot in their turn, and another few men behind them, too. They couldn't hope to take our barricades under that storm. Those who could do so turned to flee back to their own lines. Two more shots were sent after them, but it was a pointless act. Most of the men were already injured, and much of the shot went into the men already lying at the bridge's roadway. Many of the injured stopped worrying about the pain after that.

That was their last attempt that day. I was tottering already, and when the last horn blast came to give us the stand-down, I sank back on the barricade with a grunt of relief. The thing I had most feared had not come to pass, thankfully. I had not

been forced to exchange blows with a hairy-arsed peasant from
the wilds of Kent. They were a fearsome lot, them. As bad,
in their own way, as the madmen from over the Scottish
Marches. I would never go up that way, and I didn't see why
these fellows were so determined to come here to London.
Not when I was in their way.

Atwood's men were all in a mess. One, the fellow who had
clubbed the Bear, was still alive – just. His eyelids fluttered
and he beckoned me – because there was no priest about, I
thought. I went to his side and took his hand, and began to
mutter the *pater noster* to calm him, because from the look
and smell of the wound in his guts, he wasn't going to be
around for long.

'Sorry,' he said. There was a lot of rattling going on in his
throat, but that was easy enough to understand.

I carried on reciting.

'He told us to. Wanted you dead.'

I found myself stumbling over the words at that point.
'What?'

'Atwood. Told us to kill you when the fight started. Said
you were a traitor and a danger.'

'Why would he think that? He's been my friend,' I said,
although suddenly I remembered that curious little glance that
had been exchanged between Blount and Mark Thomasson.
The *bastards*! They'd known Atwood would do something
like this! I could have gone after him right then and beaten
his face to a pulp, if I'd known where he was, or had any
idea how to fight like him. Sadly, the fact was, I'd have been
the injured one again.

'He's a good man. Good man. Just sometimes doesn't think,'
the fellow said, trying to excuse his master for trying to kill
me. It didn't work, as far as I was concerned. I'd get that
bastard. Perhaps, though, I'd get someone else to do the deed.

This man was no more risk to me, though. As I was thinking
how good it would be to see Atwood's face beaten by, say,
the Bear, I realized the fellow was not breathing any more. I
let go of his hand with a feeling of disgust and rose slowly
to my feet.

So, Atwood was gone, I was thrown from my own home

with Bill and the others, and now I was in this rag-tag army defending London, much against my will. It was not the sort of position I had expected when I walked into the tavern that day with my gull. David of Exeter, someone had said. What a name.

What a poor fool to end up here in the city, dead.

TWENTY-SEVEN

Monday 5th February

I have no idea what time it was, but when I woke, it was daylight again, and I rose stiffly, frozen to the core, my shoulder a throbbing concentration of pain. Someone had thrown a blanket over me, and at least lying where I had meant that I had been out of the worst of the wind. Now, as I stood and stared over the remains of the bridge, I could see that the enemy had gone. Only the bodies remained lying in the dirt, with many gouges to show where the cannons' shot had left their marks.

A physician was moving about the injured, averting his face from the more noisome wounds. He was used to a shilling a day in his expensive consulting rooms, I thought, and this was more a civic duty than a profitable task. Still, when he saw me, he came happily enough, thinking that at least I wouldn't spout blood at him. He passed his hands over my arms, which made me moan, and then touched my back, which made me whimper. I was one enormous bruise. However, it was when he put a hand to my shoulder that I yelped like an injured mastiff. He chuckled to himself, and I watched as he put his fingers on something. I could see it from the corner of my eye, but, I confess, terror had distracted me. Apparently, when I was flung through the air in the dark, I had been struck by a large splinter of wood, which had apparently punctured me as effectively as a poignard. He yanked it free and held it before me proudly. I took it and pushed it into my purse. It took a lot of effort. I was finding concentration difficult.

'Well, soldier. I do not blame you for wanting to keep that as a memento of your service this night,' he said with a big smile.

'Yes, I hrfurdle,' I said. I could have laughed at the sight of his suddenly perplexed expression, and as I wondered why on earth my tongue felt so large, I very slowly and gently collapsed at his feet.

I was taken away, apparently. The physician, for all his squeamishness in the presence of so much injury, was a good man, and had forged some close friendships with the fellows at St Bartholomew's Hospital. I was borne there on a carriage, I learned. Later, I would recall being rattled and jolted, along with five men who were likewise incapacitated, although by the time we arrived there we were only four. One poor fellow, who looked only about sixteen summers old, barely of an age to grow more than a puppy's down on his upper lip and chin, had expired on the way. I saw them lift him up and set him on the ground outside the main hospital next to seven other figures.

That was a salutary sight. I was determined at once that I would not be added to their number.

I was walked inside, and it was a relief to be installed on a pallet inside the main hall. After my experience of receiving cannon shot, I was given to musing about the weight of wood and rock above me. The ceiling was far overhead, and I thought to myself that the rafters looked dangerous there, and that if they were to fall on me, I would be squashed as flat as a mosquito when a hand catches it. There would be no need to worry about a splinter in the shoulder if that lot ended up on my head. And with that reassuring thought, I sank into the darkness again.

Later, I felt gentle hands washing my face and shoulder. A poultice of some sort was smothered over the wound at my shoulder, and a white-hot agony seemed to thrust into it like a lance, but it lasted only moments, and then I was able to breathe again. However, from that moment I have only fleeting memories of my stay in the hospital. I slept, I woke, I was washed and patted like a faithful hound, and then I slept again.

Pre-dawn Tuesday 6th

I finally woke in the night-time with a raging thirst and a hunger that was all-encompassing. In the previous day, I had eaten but a snack or two with the men, and a little light ale to wash it down. The periods between the attacks had been all too brief for more than that, and now I was desperate. A helpful passer-by saw my distress and fetched me a small bottle of ale and a hunk of bread with a little cold meat, which I wolfed down, and then lay back with a sigh of relief. I could feel the cold ale passing down my gullet and into my belly, where it sat like a lump of lead.

Patting myself, I soon determined that the only real injury was the hole in my shoulder. The rest of me was sore and bruised, but that was only to be expected after my unexpected flight through the air. I was fortunate to have landed on something fairly soft, I thought.

The fact that I was in the hospital was a relief, too. No matter who might be hunting for me, I was surely safe here, I thought. John Blount and his two companions were unlikely to think of looking for me here, and so too were the bishop and his companion. No, being here, in a bed, was a great method of concealment. All I needed to do was wait here, heal myself while all the dangerous fighting was going on, and then, when it was safe enough, flee the hospital and London together, and make my way to safety.

Whitstable. It wasn't the sort of place I would have looked upon as a haven at any other time. In fact, I had cordially detested it. The smells would stay with me forever, I knew – salted fish and the stench of the tannery, the odour of dogshit.

Then something happened to drive all thoughts of Whitstable from my mind. I heard tramping feet, and I looked up to find myself staring at Henry Roscard.

He was sauntering along between the beds, glancing at all the injured men with a half-smile on his face, rubbing one hand with the other like a man with an ache or the beginning of arthritis.

I looked away hurriedly and rolled uncomfortably from my bed. In Christ's name, that hurt! Every muscle, every tendon was complaining fit to hobble me. It shows how painful it was by the fact that I didn't think of the bruises on my head for once.

Roscard was looking for me, and I didn't want to see him. Not just now. I had a very unpleasant vision in my mind of the result of a talk with him. All I could see was two options: one in which I was being stretched on the rack; the second in which I was lying in a mess at the side of a road, with a puncture mark in my breast like the one that David from Exeter had won for himself. But David could have had no idea that Henry Roscard was going to find him and kill him.

The events of that day seemed clear enough to me now. I had thought it likely that John Blount had bludgeoned me at the gate, but he seemed to have no reason to hurt me. Instead, could it have been Henry? Ann had said she thought not, but could he have come along the alley and surprised me? He could have sprung out from the gate when I opened it, clubbed me, and then run to David and killed him. Poor fellow: David had only been a messenger. Perhaps even an unwitting one. Gardiner had given me a purse; what if the same had happened to poor David? He might have had no idea he was carrying a message, too. But perhaps not. His expression, on seeing his wife, seemed to show that he had urgent business.

Whether he had known or not, he died for bringing that silly scrap of parchment. Then Henry had gone to the tavern's door to make enough noise so that all would know he had been outside with me. By chance, I had woken and fled when he slammed the door. No doubt, if I had not woken, Henry would have told everyone that he saw me kill the lad, and then he knocked me down before calling the hue and cry. The posse would have seen me there with my dagger drawn and made the obvious connection: dead man on the floor, unknown purse-pilferer with knife in hand – easy. Thanks, Master Roscard, and goodbye, poor Jack.

Except they hadn't got me.

Then I guessed why he was rubbing his hand. I remembered Gil's body slumped at the post, and I could see clearly the white of his teeth gleaming in the pool of puke and blood. A man who punched a fellow's mouth and head hard enough to cause that much damage would surely hurt his own fist. Roscard had killed Gil. That explained Blount's surprise at my accusation!

It was all so clear now, in retrospect, that I was astonished I hadn't seen it all before. How on earth could I have thought that Blount wanted me dead? It was Roscard all along. He and his masters, the Spanish, wanted the note at all costs.

I rolled up the blanket in a hurry and threw it over my shoulder, pulling my sword's baldric over my head so it kept the blanket in place over my injured shoulder. Then I took a deep breath, grabbed a sleeping warrior's hat, and strode out while pulling it straight.

Outside, it was still dark, although I felt that it must soon be clearing. The sun was due over the horizon, and I was soon going to be conspicuous if I didn't move away. With no set destination in mind, I set off in the direction I was already pointing. Without thinking about it, I soon discovered that I was heading west, and I bent my steps towards Mark Thomasson's house again. He owed me, I felt.

Meanwhile, I was thinking quite hard. The knock on my head must have shaken something loose, because I was finding it easier to consider things. First was Roscard.

You see, I'd heard that he was supposed to be working with the Spanish. The bishop was working with the queen, and she was determined to marry the Spaniard; that should mean that Roscard and the Spanish must be working to the same goal, surely? Yet Roscard appeared more to be working on his own. If he was with the bishop, why wasn't he there when the prelate interrogated me? Perhaps he was, in the shadows behind, but I doubted it. No, it looked more and more to me as though the bishop and Roscard were working to different ends. Perhaps the Spaniards had offered him something – perhaps they didn't like the bishop? Could they be trying to do something on their own account, without telling the queen? Maybe they simply did not trust the bishop. After all, the bishop's authority would diminish considerably once the queen was married, so he might try to stop the wedding. And so they hired Roscard as a mercenary to spy on people. He wanted the message to incriminate the queen's enemies.

That was offensive, I thought. If they were trying to plot in the kingdom, they weren't the sort of people among whom she should marry. The sort of man who makes plans about his wife before he's even married her, that is not the sort of man I would want for any daughter of mine. Not that I was likely to have a daughter. Not that I admitted to, anyway.

I was at Mark's house, and I struck the door warily, like a beadle suspecting smugglers might be inside, keen to defend their brandy.

When it opened, I didn't thrust it wide like last time.

'Can I come in?' I said.

TWENTY-EIGHT

The miserable old servant motioned me inside with barely a snarl of greeting. As soon as I was in, Peterkin began to rumble deep in his throat and then lower his head and step towards me.

For once, I really felt nothing in the way of fear. I glared at him without blinking. 'What? If you want to end up looking like a mastiff who's run into a wall, just try your luck, you great lummock. Otherwise, belt up!'

'There is, um, no need to be like that. He's perfectly friendly,' Mark said, and passed me a jug and goblet.

I filled it. I had need of it.

'What can I do for you?' he asked.

'What was in the parchment you gave me for Atwood?'

Mark did me the honour of looking embarrassed. 'Ah, so you noticed?'

Jonah cackled in the background. 'Only a blind fool wouldn't have spotted your writing!'

'Be silent!' Mark said with a scowl. 'Go and clean the privy or something. It would make a change for you to actually *do* something in the house.'

'A fine thing for you to say. You realize that makes you the fool for keeping me on while you think I do nothing?'

'Just go, old fool!'

The door slammed, and Mark glared at his wine for a moment before tossing it down his neck. 'Blasted old stoat.'

'Why do you keep him?'

'He and I are accustomed to each other. When I was a captain in the king's army, twenty years ago, he saved me in a battle. It's hard to let a man like that go. But in God's name, I swear I wish I had done!'

'The message. What did it say?'

'What do you think it said?'

I racked my brains to remember it. The original had been

shorter, and there had been little to it. 'Suppose you tell me,' I said threateningly. 'It's probably my life you've put in danger, after all.'

'Not at all. With luck,' he added with a rare flash of honesty. He saw my expression and nodded. 'I made the same note, more or less, but addressed it to a different person. It was to be sent to Wyatt from a lady. I changed the lady.'

'What?'

'Try to keep up, boy,' he said testily. 'The message you brought me was addressed to Wyatt, the leader of the rebels, from a lady of rank in the country. If her part in this rebellion was ever to come to light, she would die. Master John Blount would be most disappointed if that were to happen. So, instead, I made it out to have been sent from another lady, whose life is forfeit anyway.'

'What?'

'Lady Jane Grey. Poor woman. I can feel a great deal of sorrow for her. She is such a lovely young thing, but desperately unlucky. She almost won the throne for herself, you know. That was the plot, when poor King Edward died: they were intending to arrest Mary and put Jane on the throne instead. With her English husband, that would have made everything so much easier. She would have maintained the standing of the new faith and the Church of England, and there would be no nonsense about a Spanish prince consort, the return of the old religion, ructions and rebellions, and so on. But now Mary has managed to upset all the vested interests in only a short period. And because of the attempt to give the kingdom to Lady Jane, she now languishes in the Tower. She will be executed anyway. So I made the note appear as though it had come from her.'

'But that's unfair!'

'Hmm? No, it's not fair. But it is good politics. Why, what's the matter with you? Do you like to see women executed? You would prefer to see a second woman beheaded along with Lady Jane, would you?'

'What? No, of course not!'

'Then don't be so foolish, man! Lady Jane's cause is already lost. I for one wouldn't seek to destroy a second. So I've done all I can to defend her.'

'And you were prepared to risk my life to achieve that?'

'I'd hardly risk my own, would I, eh? Um, if it makes you feel any happier, I did feel a qualm or two about that, but John Blount can be most persuasive on occasion.'

'Who is he?'

'He is the unofficial official for a lady of high standing,' Mark said.

'What does that mean?'

'Work it out for yourself. Now, is that all you wanted? You woke me at a damn silly hour of the morning to learn just that?'

'Eh?' I was still absorbing all that he had told me. 'Oh, no. I was in the hospital after the fight on London Bridge, when I saw Roscard searching for me. I only just escaped with my life.'

'That damned Spanish whore's son! I wish we could remove him as easily. If only a note could work to see him destroyed, too.'

I didn't feel comfortable in Mark's house. The old servant seemed to watch me in the same way that a beadle would, suspecting that at any moment a significant portion of Mark's property might disappear. Which was foolish. Nothing he had was all that portable, except for some cheap trinkets that I wouldn't have looked at, especially now I didn't know where to take them to fence them. Not since I couldn't go to Bill any more.

However, Bill might be interested to see me. Especially since I had my new wound. That would probably excite Moll as much as any other woman. They always like these proofs of courage and valour. I didn't necessarily need to tell her I'd been cowering behind a barricade at the time I was hit. And I could show her my splinter. I pulled it from my purse and studied it now.

It was a horrible piece of wood, about three inches long and almost triangular in section. The thing must have been ripped from the corner of a large baulk of wood. I moved my shoulder to remind myself of the injury, and I could feel the prickles of sweat starting as the pain stabbed again. There was a nasty suspicion at the back of my mind that the injury would not be sufficient to keep me from the barricades again, but I was determined to avoid them if at all possible. Standing there and waiting for other men to fire their guns at me was not my idea of a pleasant afternoon or evening. No, in preference I would keep my head down, well out of the way, and try to keep to the safer areas of the city. Not that many would be safe if the rebels broke in. That was not an event I was happy to consider. It would bode ill for any who had carried arms against them, and who might be considered to have injured or killed their companions.

No, I didn't like that thought at all.

Still, Moll might just look at me in a different light, now that I had this proof of my valour. If Bill didn't like it, well, I was coming to think I didn't like him much either. He was useful, but now, with luck, my life was in less peril than it had been. And Bill's churlish attitude towards me in my hour of need would affect Moll. I'd see that in her face.

I decided I would test her feelings.

I would go back.

TWENTY-NINE

It was the second hour of the morning by the time I reached the house, I'd guess. The sun was high enough to throw some of her light along the streets facing south, and I could feel a little of her insipid heat as I hurried down the alleys and lanes towards the place I had called home for such a short time.

I entered the chamber where Atwood and his men had appeared that fateful night, and there I found the place deserted. It was a relief, if I'm honest. If Bill had been there, I'm not sure what I would have had to say to him. As it was, I found myself in the chamber with a series of rolled-up palliasses and stored blankets, while my companions were all out, no doubt trying to win the purses of the panicky London mob. There were so many people there who would be carrying all their money on them, preparing for disaster and stocking up on essentials, that it was tempting to go out and try my own luck. However, the thought of bumping into Roscard again, or the bishop's men, or Blount – or, worse, Atwood – was enough to make me sit down on a stool. After the exertions of the day before last, the pain of my wound and the lack of sleep last night, I was exhausted, and I thought I would close my eyes for a moment.

When the door opened, it was already dusk, and the sudden noise startled me so much that I fell from the stool and knocked my head again. This time it was a knock on the same spot as that which I had earned in the tavern on the day David was murdered, and I rolled on the floor for a few moments, clutching my pate and pulling a grimace of anguish, while desperately holding back a number of the choicer curses that were vying for attention.

'What're you doing down there?' Moll asked. There was a hint of concern in her voice. Not, I should hasten to add, the

concern of a person for a friend's clear agony, but the concern
of a young woman who finds herself in the company of what
appears to be an escapee from the keepers at the Bethlem
madhouse. Even as I peered up at her, I saw her roll her eyes
and thrust her knife back in its sheath where she kept it, under
her blouse. 'Jack, in Christ's name, what are you doing back
here?'

'I came back to see you,' I said, with as much dignity as I
could muster. 'I've discovered what happened in the tavern
that day.'

She suddenly went quite still. 'You had best leave before
he gets back.'

'Who?'

'Bill! Who else?'

'There's no need for you to panic,' I said. Her anxiety was
natural enough, knowing Bill as I did. The man was insanely
jealous, after all. 'He'll be interested in this as well.'

'I'm worried for you, Jack. If he finds you here and thinks
you and I have been sleeping together, you know what he's
like. He'll beat me and kill you.'

'He won't do that. He'll be happy to learn that I think the
problems with the dead man at the tavern are all over.'

'They are?'

I explained about the parchment and the new message that
had been sent with Atwood. She didn't seem very
interested.

'These men have been hunting me down for the last week,'
I said, irritated by her indifference.

'So? We've all been chased at different times,' she said.

I didn't say anything about that. I don't recall whether I
mentioned it before, but she had been chased from her home
by an over-friendly stepfather. Our company was the only
security she knew. She reckoned that Bill had saved her, and
she owed him much for that.

I didn't want to remind her of what must have been an
unpleasant period in her life.

She must have seen how dumbfounded I looked, because
she smiled then. 'You're a poor fool, aren't you? Did you
come here to see him or me?'

I think my sudden flush must have been obvious, because she chuckled to herself and walked to me. I was nervous about touching her, but – to my astonishment – she placed her warm little hands on either side of my face and gave me a kiss that almost made my heart stop.

There were footsteps outside, and she moved away and busied herself making a fresh fire.

'What are you doing here again?' Bill demanded as he walked in, and his eyes flew to Moll, then back to my glowing face.

I don't know whether you have noticed, but men who can be prey to jealousy can also be very calm on occasion. It is as if they are listening and processing everything before flying off the handle like a badly fitted axe-head.

Bill was all smiles and kindness at the sight of me. He barely glanced at Moll, who fetched and carried for him when he called for ale and some bread, and she set a black-jack and cups on the bench near us, adding a half loaf that had hardly been a day from the oven. Bill broke the bread and gave me a hunk, dipping his own in his cup of ale and chewing with pleasure.

'A good day,' he said. 'I found a merchant who could hardly walk for the weight of gold he had in his purse. I think I saved him from great injury by liberating him from that.' He had more, too, finding a foolish old sot fresh from a tavern and persuading him to join him in a game of dice. Since the other player was Wat, the fellow had not a chance. What with that and a pair of kidskin gloves, the day had been successful already.

'My own day was less successful, although I am alive,' I said.

'Aye? Well, I didn't think you'd last above a day when you left here,' Bill said.

'You threw me out when I needed your support the most.'

'Yes. And I'll do it again. I won't have dangerous men in here. There are too many others here to put them at risk just to protect a wastrel, gangling fool like you,' he said, casting an eye at Moll.

I could see his point. It would be wrong to put Moll at risk of her life just so that I could find some fleeting, temporary security. She deserved better. 'I learned more about the note, though,' I said, and told him what Mark had said. Or I tried to. Bill put his hands over his ears as soon as I mentioned the Lady Jane.

'Stop! I won't listen to this, Jack! Are you mad? You can keep that sort of secret to yourself, lad, and don't share its like with me. If there's money in a tale, yes, I'll be keen to hear it, but if it's about politics and the conniving, thieving, rascally felons who infest government, you can keep that to yourself. I want nothing to do with traitors and other dangers, so help me I don't!'

'There is one piece of news you should like,' I said. 'Gil died because of a man called Roscard. He was the man who was working with Ann on the day the messenger was killed.'

'Why did Gil die?'

'I think because Roscard wanted me. He followed Blount, perhaps, and was led to Gil, so afterwards Roscard struck Gil down, tied him to a post, and then started punching and kicking him until he told Roscard what he needed to know.'

'Which was?'

'I assume he wanted to know where I was at that time. But Gil had no idea and couldn't answer, so he was killed. And then Roscard became determined to find me. Somehow he tracked me down to the hospital, and I think if he'd seen me asleep there, I wouldn't have woken.'

'You think he was there to kill you?' Moll said in a hushed voice. She looked at Bill with a strange look in her eye.

'I'm sure of it,' I said airily. 'But it takes more than an assassin to put paid to me.'

'It takes one inch of steel,' Bill said. There was something in his voice that chilled my blood.

'There is another thing, too. The captain of the soldiers who came here? He was not all he seemed either. He was determined to kill me. I barely escaped from him with my life. He's in with the rebels, apparently, and he has gone over to their side.'

'Him?' Bill said. 'How can you tell?'

'He was pretty unambiguous about it,' I said. 'He took the note from me to deliver to Wyatt himself, and then, when I went back to the barricades, he sent men after me to kill me. Can you believe that? A fellow who was fighting to protect the city, and he sent his henchmen to murder me! It was sheer good fortune that saved me. We were all knocked aside by a cannon. Look!' I said, and brought out the splinter. 'That's my blood, that is!'

'Where did it hit you?' Moll asked in a low, impressed voice.

I touched my sore shoulder briefly. 'That is why I was forced to go to the hospital. Any other man, they said, would have been killed by my experiences, but I am made of sterner stuff.'

'Cut the boasting, Jack,' Bill said. 'What are we going to do with you?'

That was not a question I had anticipated. 'Eh?'

'Well, I've already kicked you out of the company. What you wanted to come back for, I don't know, but I don't see that anything's changed. There's still danger for us all while you're here.'

His eyes went to Moll again, but she wasn't paying attention. She had set a pot on the fire and was stirring a thick pease pottage.

'Well, at least let me sleep here tonight,' I said. 'I don't have anywhere else to go.'

'No. You've stirred up so much trouble in such a short time that you're likely to bring danger to us. If they find you sleeping here, we'll be in trouble for harbouring a felon, so sod that. No. You can stay and have some pottage, but then you'll have to go. And this time, don't come back. Next time, I may hurt you to persuade you to sod off.'

THIRTY

There is one thing that I cannot argue with about Bill, and that is that he is a man of his word. No sooner was my bowl emptied of pease pudding than I was gently walked to the door and ejected into the evening darkness. I had my clothes, my cloak, a blanket, and little else. All I could think of doing was going back to the bridge, where I was likely to run the risk of another cannonade, I thought, and that was not appealing. However, it occurred to me that the other gates usually had a brazier for the men standing guard. Perhaps there I could find a little peace and quiet – and warmth – over the night?

It was the best idea I had. I strode off quickly, making my way to Ludgate and then down to the city walls. And luckily I was right. There was a small number of men there, standing in melancholy sympathy, staring at the flames.

That was one of the coldest nights of the winter, I've heard tell. The wind was not harsh, nothing like a gale, but it was steady, and every little draught seemed to strip another layer of clothing away, until all that was left was a man's body, shivering so violently that it was like suffering from the ague. I wrapped my cloak about me, and then pulled my blanket over my head and shoulders in an attempt to keep warm, but no matter how my face scorched, my back felt as chilled as ice. It was the most miserable night of my life.

You can tell how unhappy I was: I started chatting in a desultory fashion with the other men there.

One, a young, straw-headed boy, was an apprentice for a silversmith, and he was clearly disgruntled at being out there. When I asked, his evasive answers led me to believe that he had been found wanting in some fashion – his abilities didn't match the smith's expectations, or perhaps the smith had a pleasant daughter and the apprentice a wandering eye: such things happen – and he felt this was his punishment. If so, it was severe. There were five others about our brazier that evening, two of whom were grooms, one a servant from a large house, and a scruffy old thief I'd known before, called Rob of the Moor.

He was a shocking old man. To my knowledge, he had been accused of murder three times, and he had been convicted once, but had won a pardon from the old king, Henry VIII, before it could be put into force. I don't know how he escaped that one, but I suspect he was performing some kind of service for the king. Perhaps procuring girls for parties, or some such duty.

'What you doin' 'ere, lad?' he demanded.

He was a good-looking fellow. One eye was milky white, and a scar reached from his chin, down past his Adam's apple and on to his collar bone. His face could be politely described as possessing a 'lived-in' look, while the pepper-and-salt beard that never seemed to grow more than an eighth of an inch, and was never shaved to less, gave him a disreputable, shabby scruffiness that would have looked endearing in a man who possessed a less shrewd, sharp, acquisitive eye. As it was, when I shook hands with him, I made a careful investigation of my hand.

'Just counting my fingers, Rob,' I said when he asked.

'Garn!' he rasped, and spat a gobbet of thick, yellowish phlegm. 'You can go piss on yourself!'

'Even with my anatomical advantages, that would be difficult.'

He peered at me suspiciously. 'Eh?'

'What are you doing down here, Rob?'

He drew the corners of his mouth down and shook his head. 'Bastard beadle caught me trying to get a crumb or two. Found me with a small pie from Mrs Hoggins up on Smithfield's lane, and had me taken to the Newgate gaol. I was going to be up and accused next week, but I didn't reckon much to my chances if that happened, so when the turnkeys came round and started asking if anyone would volunteer to help defend the city, I thought that sounded a better idea. With luck, I'll win a pardon.'

'Good,' I said, but I kept my eyes on his fingers. Not that

I needed to worry. I had nothing of value that he could take.

'Aye, that's the truth. It was bad luck had me seen by the beadle, but now, well, looks like it was even worse luck to volunteer.'

'Why?'

'Christ's bones, boy, haven't you heard anything? This rebel, Tommy Wyatt, has gathered up all the peasants and yeomen of Kent. They say he has twenty or thirty thousand men under arms. What'll happen when an army that size gets to us here, eh? I'll tell you, boy, what'll happen is, they'll see my dust on that horizon over there,' he said, pointing, 'and they'll never see me in London again. Sod that! Think I'm going to hang around here, when there are thirty thousand hairy heathens from the wilds of Kent running at me with halberds? Ballocks to that!'

I mused over his words for a long while. The men I had seen running at me on the bridge had not been enormous, but had looked like ordinary lads. I doubted whether the fellows in the rest of the army were any more terrifying. Mind you, they had been terrifying when they got too close to me. That was the truth. However, the fact remained, if Rob was right and there were some thirty thousand of them, that was a large enough number to give all the soldiers and volunteers in London a run for their money.

'You know how many the city has recruited now?' he said.

'No.'

'Twenty thousand, they say. Twenty thousand. Think of that, eh?'

I did. And frowned.

'Yeah, twenty thousand? They wouldn't find twenty hundred in the city, I reckon,' he said. 'Even if they did, what sort of men would they be? Half of them would shout, "A Wyatt, a Wyatt!" and run to join them. The people don't like our queen, boy. They accepted her when her father died, but they won't be ruled by the wife of a bleeding Spaniard, and that's an end to it.'

'You think they'd give up the city to Wyatt?' I said. It wasn't something that I'd seriously considered, and the idea was appalling. That was the worst form of treachery, surely, when an entire city rejected its queen.

'What do you think?' Rob sneered.

I left him at the first opportunity and took to the wall, staring out over the suburbs as though I could see a safe passage away from the city, while I considered all that Rob had said. He had been depressingly convincing, I admit, but there was a small spark of resentment in me that refused to believe that all that many London or Kentish men would turn their coats. And a larger, more cynical part of me that was convinced that he was right.

But the key thing was, if Wyatt succeeded in his ambitions, then I was in real trouble. Because I had given Atwood the message that would later, presumably, be proved to be false. It was a forgery. So I really had to hope that the city stayed loyal to the queen. But that presupposed that the city winning was in my interests, too. And I wasn't sure of that. The bishop was an alarming character, after all, and he would be angry with me for not giving him the message, as he had demanded. He was the queen's most senior minister, so if he was cross, my life would be worth little. Then there was Roscard, who was apparently the servant of the Spanish. Certainly, he was likely to want my nuts in a bag after I'd chased after him on the day he killed Ann. And John Blount had sent me out with the forgery to give to Atwood – damn his black, demonic soul. He must have known I would be putting my life in danger doing that. I hoped he would soon go and join the devil for all the grief he had given me!

But that was no help to me just now. There had been a new moon at the beginning of the month, and tonight there were few clouds. Standing there, I stared out over the road and the low roofs of houses that stretched away in the silvery light of the moon, and pondered my predicament.

There was only one solution, I decided. I had to escape the city. I had to get far away, as quickly as possible.

I gazed at the road westwards with such longing that it was almost like love.

THIRTY-ONE

I woke to a cold, grey morning with a damp crust of ice sparkling on every surface. That was painful. My shoulder hurt like a bad burn when I stood and took stock.

Like the others, when my time on the walls was done, I had smothered myself in cloak and blanket as best I could, with my feet near the brazier, my back on a thick bale of cloth or something that had been left by the gate. It was almost comfortable. If I'd had another three or four hours' sleep, I would have been happy, but even as I scratched and yawned myself awake, the captain of the guard was running to and fro, shouting and making a general nuisance of himself.

'What's the matter?' the apprentice called blearily. 'Have they attacked?'

That raised a general chorus of chuckles. It was clear enough that all of us were still well, and there was no commotion at the gate. The timbers of the doors themselves were massive, and their vast weight caused the hinges to graunch alarmingly when swung open. With them and the six-feet-thick walls on either side, it would have taken a determined army to break through.

'No, you dull tarse-tugger, but they're moving this way.'

'Well, unless they're crossing the bridge, they won't get to us, will they, Captain!' the youngster called, and rolled over.

The captain walked to him and kicked him very precisely on the buttocks.

'You think there's only one bridge over the bleeding river? What if they get to Kingston and cross there? Stop choking your chicken and *get on your feet*! The rebels may not scare you, but if you're not up and ready by the time I get to you, you'll have reason to be bloody scared of *me*!'

There were more chuckles, but this time they were more

sporadic as his words sank in, and then, with many a muttered curse, we all climbed to our feet. Soon afterwards we were treated to a heavy downpour. The rain was set to continue all day long.

'Was he joking?' I asked Rob.

'I bleedin' doubt it. Didn't you see his face? I've seen happier faces on bulls in the baiting pits. Nah, today we're in for a fight, I'll tell you.'

There was a stolid certainty in his voice that brooked no argument. I felt a coldness forming in my bowels at the thought. It was like a lump of quicksilver, flowing and moving with me, but cold as steel and twice as heavy. This, I have come to learn, is what sheer terror feels like.

We were kept busy all that long morning, lugging defensive weaponry to the wall through the steady rain, fetching and carrying arrows, balls for the smaller guns that would be used up on the walls, and braziers and bowls. I think someone thought it would be a good idea to melt a load of oil and tip it on to the enemy, but all I can say is, if that's what they were thinking, they were welcome to try it. Personally, I planned to be nowhere near. I've seen what oil can do when someone's careless and it overheats. Rather them than me.

More men turned up through the day. It was mid-morning when I heard shouting and abuse, and turned to see that there was a party of men being marched towards us. These, I learned, were more recruits to help us defend the gate. It gave me no little pleasure to see Bill and Wat with them.

'Don't look so bleeding pleased,' Bill said. He had the grumpiest expression I'd yet seen on a man's face. I'd once seen a scent hound trying to find a trail, and failing, and his expression was rather similar to Bill's now.

I smiled broadly. 'Good to see you again.'

'Piss off!'

It was late in the morning when I heard horses riding towards us, and someone from the wall overhead (I was down by the fire again just then, warming my hands around a pottery mug of spiced ale) bellowed down to open the gates.

Bill, Rob and I were nearest, and we set our hands to the great baulks of timber that blocked the way. They slid back into the walls, and we struggled with them until the apprentice and one of the grooms came and helped us. At last the gates were free, and we could haul on the iron staples and pull the gates open.

Outside was a company of five armed men, led by a portly gentleman with a statute cap on his head but armour on his breast. He had sharp blue eyes and a goatee beard with moustache. I had no idea who he was, so I picked up the apprentice's halberd and stood barring the way with as ferocious an expression as I could manage. It was not so hard: the man was seventy if he was a day, and he didn't look as though he would be able to move too fast.

'Who are you?' I challenged.

'Sir John Gage, Lord Chamberlain and Captain of the Guard. Let me pass. I have to speak to your captain. Where is he?'

I pointed to where the captain was taking a morning ale, and Sir John and his small company rode on past, hoofs splashing in the puddles and splattering my legs, much to Bill's delight. I watched as they dismounted, Sir John taking the cup from the captain's hand and taking a long draught. They were engaged in a long conversation, and then Sir John rode back to the gate, the captain walking quickly behind him.

'Jack, Rob, Bill, Wat, you will be going back with Sir John in a little while. Gather your things. I'll collect up as many others as I can, Sir John,' he added, 'and have them with you at the palace as soon as I may.'

'That is good. Make sure to have them with me as quickly as possible.'

The knight nodded to the captain, and then rode on back along the road.

On hearing all this, you can guess how I felt. The cold quicksilver had returned to my bowels all over again. I had a horrible suspicion that I was about to be sent out to march to a battle. I didn't want to be in a fight, in Christ's name! I'd done enough already, what with the rebels firing at me and Atwood's men trying to kill me. 'What is this?'

I may have sounded a little petulant, but *really*! I was already injured, and I'd thought coming here to Ludgate would be safer. Instead, it looked very much as if I was going to be slung out of the city and sent to assail the rebels as they approached. I was already rehearsing *A Wyatt, a Wyatt!* in my mind as the captain sucked his teeth.

'It's like this, Jack. Sir John is in charge of the queen's safety. She's at White Hall, which is a good place to defend, and all should be well enough, but they lack men. Sir John has asked for some. So I am sending the ones I can afford to lose. That includes you, Jack. There'll be more to come. Don't worry: you won't be on your own!'

He chuckled at that, and walked away laughing, as though that was the funniest joke he had heard in a twelvemonth.

Bill spat a gobbet of yellowish phlegm into the road. 'Bastard.'

So I was marched to White Hall.

We were three-quarters of the way there when Rob and I exchanged a glance. It was plain enough that the thought in his mind was the same as that which was occupying mine: escaping from this new duty. At one point, one of our company stepped into what he thought was a puddle, but which was almost as deep as he was tall. It took three of us to haul him out, and then Rob and I stepped away carefully, waiting for our moment to flee. Bill saw, and joined us, but there was never time. Always someone had their eyes on us. It was infuriating to be confounded in such a manner!

Why? There are few tasks quite as dangerous as being told to guard a king or queen, of course! The men coming to attack us were rebels, men who had tossed aside the yoke of their masters in order to overthrow their queen. They each knew that, if they were to fail, the life expectancy of each man was reduced to about that of a gnat. No queen would allow such turbulent fellows to live, not once they had raised their banners against her. Wyatt would have a short wait for the axe, and the rest may escape back home for a week or two, but they would all be hunted down eventually. Most would not make it home, though. They would be cut down here, in White Hall, and their bodies thrown into the Thames, if they were lucky.

All of which meant that these poor fools had no reason to surrender. They were likely to fight on to the bitter end, and they would kill all in their path, because they had nothing to lose. They were lost already. And I was to be standing in their way, with Rob on one side, Bill on the other, and an apprentice behind, with a bloated old fool with a goatee and statute cap ordering us to fight to the last drop of our blood. Yes, he'd be the bold fellow standing well behind any danger.

I didn't want to die there.

There was no opportunity to flee. We were part of some fifty reinforcements who had been quickly scraped together, and now marched – almost in step – along the Strand. Out past the Temple Bar and up to Charing Cross, past the great houses and palaces that fronted the Thames, and thence down to White Hall itself.

Even in the heavy rain, we could see that White Hall was a massive place, but then all the houses down there were. You can see why the rich wanted more men to help defend them. For me, it was just a horrible walk. I should have enjoyed it, because every step took me away from the city, as I had planned, and since I had always enjoyed the country, it was good to be walking along and listening to the birdsong. At Charing Cross, we came to the new park of St James. It stank. The marshes here, where the Tyburn flowed, weren't as smelly as they would be in the high summer, but there was still the all-pervading stench of rotting vegetation, even now with the freezing weather. And then there was White Hall.

White Hall? I remember the first time I heard of it. An old soldier was talking about it. He had served in King Henry VIII's armies and helped acquire the place. Originally, it had been York Palace, back when Cardinal Wolsey owned it, but as he fell out of grace, Henry pinched it, renamed it, and started to convert it into a palace fit for a king. He bought up the swamps from Eton College at the same time, as a place where he could walk, hunt and relax, far away from the city and the troubles of ruling his kingdom. I daresay he planned on having the place drained and landscaped, the old fool. No one would be able to drain such a large area. The college must have had fits of laughter over that. I imagine they would have been trying to sell that land for years before they persuaded the gullible king to buy it.

White Hall, however, was a different matter. This was already growing into a palace to rival any. The great gatehouse itself was enough to make a man pause and stare: a massive block, with a gateway twenty-five feet wide and seven high, so two carts could pass beneath it in opposite directions. It was made of flint and stone, in squares and diamonds, and there were four great circular panels with paintings of faces set within. At either side, the gate had a tall eight-sided tower, all battlemented and very fierce-looking to a man with the intention of breaking in.

They called this the King's Gate. We soldiers called it the Cockpit Gate. As I looked up at the octagonal turret on the left, there was a sudden movement in the mullioned window, and as I glanced up, I felt my bowels turn to water.

Rob saw my look. 'See her? That's Queen Mary, that is,' he said, adding gloomily, 'She'll watch from there while we're all being paunched like coneys down here to protect her.' He spat into the roadside.

However, it wasn't the queen I was watching with such absorbed horror. It was the bishop who stood at her side: Stephen Gardiner.

THIRTY-TWO

I spent the rest of that day in a fever of anxiety, thinking up inventive methods of escaping the palace and running home to Whitstable, or perhaps finding a ship and leaving England for ever. There were rumours of new lands somewhere that the Spaniards were farming to their great advantage. Perhaps they would have space for a lone Englishman. Or I could just cross the water and go to the English port of Calais and start a new life there.

Who was I fooling? There was no likelihood of my escaping this. If I went back to the city, I would be accused of cowardice or treachery; if I were to try the other direction, I would meet with Wyatt's men, and very likely Atwood as well. That wouldn't bode well for my long-term future either. That supposed I wasn't going to fall into a pothole like our poor, half-drowned colleague on the way here. The roads about the town were appalling.

I worked hard with the rest of the men, building ramparts where none had existed before, fetching and carrying baulks of timber to reinforce the gates, collecting sheaves of arrows and bow staves for the men on the walls to use, for while everyone liked the noise and display of a hand gonne or cannon, when a man needed to actually hit a target at distance, there was little better than a longbow.

I was morosely setting out wicker quivers of arrows on the parapet of the Cockpit Gate when the bishop called to me.

'Master Jack. I am glad to see you looking so well. I trust you will remain in the best of health?'

'My Lord Bishop,' I said, and almost slipped from the damp wooden walkway as I jumped, startled.

'No need to throw yourself at my feet,' the bishop observed as I picked myself up again. 'I seem to recall that I asked you to perform a small service for me. Yet you did not return to me with the information I require.'

'I tried to, your honour . . .'

'You can call me "my Lord". I am no justice. Continue.'

'The truth is, I was attacked, my Lord. A man called Atwood tried to have me killed, and he stole the message from me.'

'Why?'

I blinked. 'I don't know. I don't even know what the message said!'

'Who is this Atwood?'

'He was a captain in the guard at the bridge, and I fought alongside him after I had fetched the note, but then' – inspiration struck: best to tell a version of the truth, because that way I couldn't forget it – 'then he disappeared with it, and I was left fighting at the gate under Sergeant Dearing, and I was badly injured. Look!' I fumbled for the splinter, which I held up for him to see. He was most understanding, too, when I pulled aside my shirt to display the pad of linen that covered the injury. He prodded it with a reluctant finger and made me squeal.

'I must have my physician look at that and make sure it's a genuine wound from that splinter,' he said.

'And then a ball killed Atwood's men who were with me, and one told me with his dying breath that he was ordered to kill me. All because of that note!'

'And where is it now?'

'Atwood took it, like I said, and he was keen to fight with the rebels. I think he took it to Wyatt.'

'So you have failed me,' the bishop sighed.

'No! I did what you wanted, but I was set upon, and I've been injured in trying to provide you with all you needed,' I protested.

'But still, you failed to bring me the note, and it would seem you have allowed it to fall into the hands of the enemy.'

I was about ready to push him off the top of that tower when I heard him say that. If it wasn't for the sentry on top of the nearer octagonal turret, I might have done so, too. This oleaginous old bastard was likely to see me slaughtered, if I wasn't careful.

He stared at me grimly for a long time, and then shook his head. 'I shall have to consider whether you could be of use to me in another way,' he said musingly. 'Else, it might be better for you to be made an example of.'

I knew what that meant: a period in the stocks or pillory at the least, locked in place so that the populace could come and hurl invective or other things at me. In villages up and down the country, a day in the pillory would mean people flinging rotten vegetables or dung at a man. I know that was the case in Whitstable. Here, about London, you would be lucky to have something so soft thrown at you. A man was more likely to have a cobble or rock chucked at him. A lot of men died from their injuries.

He shook his head as he made his way back to the door in the tower, the hypocritical old git. He left me staring out over the landscape and thinking I could possibly make it to those woods up in the far north on a hill. It shouldn't take me long to get there, and then, well, perhaps go east to the coast.

Anything, rather than stay here and wait to be told how I was going to be tormented.

I was still standing there, longingly gazing at that far-distant wood, when I happened to glance down and saw the familiar figure of Roscard.

It really did feel as though God had something against me that day.

The encounter with the bishop had unsettled me, I confess, but seeing the man who had murdered Ann, and who had tried to have me convicted of murder as well, lent a new terror to my position.

Yes, if I could have escaped, I would have done, but the sad fact was that the gates were routinely closed and barred now, with the portcullis dropped as well. I mean, there isn't much a man can do to escape a palace when it's shut up against invaders. Sir John Gage was here, there and every-where, a large pewter cup in his hand all the while as he ordered men hither and thither, a steward behind him refilling his cup at intervals. Which seemed all very sensible, but the man was in his seventies, and by mid-afternoon his temper was up. He was slurring and dribbling so much that it was well-nigh impossible to understand what he was saying, and soldiers standing and looking baffled did not improve his choleric mood. In the end, his steward poured faster, and Gage was led away, chortling to himself over something his esquire had told him. We didn't see him again.

Which should have been a relief, except now the sergeants were in command, and under their sober eyes there was nothing I could attempt in the way of an escape.

I was in the hall late that afternoon, eating in a mess with Bill, Rob, the apprentice and a loon by the name of Cedric, when an exquisite servant in particoloured hosen appeared in the doorway and stared about him at all the soldiers slurping and burping their way through their rations for the evening. It was plainly a sight that distressed him, and he spoke to one of the servants before making his way over to me.

'I understand you are Jack of Whitstable?' he said.

I felt Bill's eye on me as I nodded.

'Come with me.'

'What about my meal?'

'It's up to you, but if you don't come now, the bishop will be most discommoded.'

That didn't worry me. Mainly because I didn't know what he meant, but it sounded as though I was going to be in trouble if I didn't obey the summons, so I reluctantly gave my bowl a careful wipe with a hunk of bread, and rose from the table to follow him.

'Be careful,' Rob said. 'That arsewipe looks the sort who'd stick a man so he could steal his apple.'

I knew what he meant. As I followed him up a winding staircase, along a passageway, out into another hall, down a stair, and back along to a small door, I noticed that the messenger didn't once look to see that I was still with him, let alone make any conversation. As far as he was concerned, I was one of the unwashed thousands who laboured so that he could enjoy a peaceful and comfortable life. Clearly, he expected me to be one of the poor, downtrodden masses who would willingly give up my life for him.

'What's this all about?' I asked.

There was no answer. He opened the door and stood back.

I looked from him to the doorway, wondering whether this was some sort of trick. I recalled only too well how I had stepped into Mark Thomasson's house only to have Blount's blade at my back. I didn't fancy a repeat.

I had an easy solution to my doubts. Grabbing the exquisite by the shoulder, I leaned to the side. My momentum would jerk him from the wall, and then it would be a simple matter to shove him into the room. Once he was there, hopefully on his face on the floor, I would be able to saunter in after him, once I knew it was safe.

It didn't go quite as I planned. I grasped him by the collar, but he swiftly lifted both forearms, breaking my hold. His left hand took my upper arm, his right leg was outthrust, his right hand took my below the armpit, and suddenly I was flying through the air again, through the open doorway.

There was just time to think that this was not going to end well when the floor came up and slammed the air from my lungs. My back, which was already so badly bruised from my last excursion through the air, struck the solid stone slabs with a concussion that went through my entire body, as though I had been laid across an anvil and struck with a giant's hammer. My head crashed back, and I saw an interesting display of shining, whirling stars overhead.

'Hello again,' John Blount said.

'I dare wager you are surprised to find me here,' John Blount said.

I shook my head. A few of the stars popped and were extinguished. I tried to sit up, and three of them appeared to combine and whack me hard on the head, making me wince. I pressed a hand against my brow, where the thundering pain appeared to be worst.

'I thought you would be. So, can I take it that you tried to put the drop on young Walter here? He's really rather a vicious little savage, as you will have noticed. How is the head, by the way?'

'Sore. But so is my whole back, and my shoulder in particular. What is the meaning of this assault?' I said with as much dignity as I could manage.

'Never mind that for now,' he said. 'We have more important matters to discuss.'

'You may,' I said, and this time, with the help of his hand, I managed to get up. There was a stool to one side of a broad table, and I sat at it, resting my head on my hand and peering up at him from narrowed eyes. 'I have nothing I want to talk about with you.'

'Oh, I think you do. You see, the bishop is a keen believer in discipline and in the merits of examples. So, since he has no idea what you may or may not know, he will prefer to err on the side of caution. That means that all the while you are here your life is in danger.'

'I know that already. Especially since Henry Roscard is here as well.'

That shook him, I could see. 'Roscard is here? Are you sure?'

'Of course I'm damn sure! He's been hunting me ever since he killed David of Exeter at the tavern!'

'That could work to your advantage, then,' Blount said. He waved his bully away and I heard the door close quietly behind him. 'You need to protect yourself from him.'

'And how do I do that?'

'Kill him before he kills you, I would say. You will achieve two things in that way. First, you will make your life that bit safer; but, second, you will have performed a service for the good bishop. He knows Roscard is a danger, because Roscard is a trusted emissary of the Spanish.'

'But you said he is a friend to Courtenay, Earl of Devon. I thought the bishop trusted him!'

'Yes. The bishop did trust him until two days ago, when he discovered that Roscard was more determined to serve the Spanish than Mary.'

'I don't . . .'

'No, I don't suppose you do,' Blount said, the patronizing bastard. 'Let me put it as simply as possible for you: the man Roscard and the Spanish ambassador were working together to try to bring about the queen's wishes: she wants to marry the Spaniard. However, the bishop is less wedded to that since the rebellion, because he can see that the kingdom is in a ferment about it and he knows that worse may ensue if the marriage goes ahead. Roscard, on the other hand, has taken Spanish gold to push the marriage on. He is determined to see the wedding go ahead, because afterwards he will have more power and money than he could have dreamed of. And if he is shrewd – and Roscard is *very* shrewd – he will be able to drop in a few words of poison into the queen's ear, which will deprive Gardiner of his posts in government. Gardiner is working against the queen's stated ambition.'

'But I thought he was working to her advantage?' I said. My head was hurting again.

Blount looked at me and sighed. 'You have a very small brain, don't you? No, don't start moaning again. Whose house was it where Roscard was staying?'

'I told you, at the house of Peter Carew!'

'And who, or *what*, is Carew?'

'I don't *know*!'

'He is the man who was plotting with the rebels in Kent. Carew worked with Edward Courtenay, the Earl of Devon, to have an uprising in the west at the same time as others would rise in the midlands and Wyatt would foment trouble in the south. All were to work in synchronization to bring about the end of all plans for a Spanish marriage, and, more specifically, to end the reign of Queen Mary. Most of them hoped to remove her and install Lady Jane Grey upon the throne. It is sad.'

'I know. Your forged note means she will be blamed for the rebellion.' My mind was whirling now. Carew was with the rebels? And Courtenay?

Blount eyed me with little enthusiasm. 'Mark has been talking, I see.'

'He didn't have to! I would have worked it out for myself!'

'No, I doubt that.'

'I don't know how to kill a man,' I said, returning to the matter of my assignment.

'You had best learn, then. I confess, if you find Walter such a difficult man to overcome, you are unlikely to succeed against Roscord unless he is already stupefied or asleep. Even then, I'm not sure I would wager much on your behalf.'

'I don't want to kill anyone.'

'Then prepare to die, man,' Blount said, and this time his voice lost all its humour. 'There are men here who will cut your throat without thinking. If you are not prepared to do the same to them, you will not live to see the spring.'

He left me then, and I sat staring bleakly at the walls, wondering what to do for the best. There was one thing I was certain of, and that was that I was not capable of killing a man in cold blood. Especially, I should add, a man who was built like Roscard, and who would have put the fear of God into a Goliath, let alone me. David might have been bold enough to slay his giant, but I had no slingshot. All I possessed were my wits, such as they were, and my looks. I did not think they would serve against a man as capable and fierce as Roscard. After all, he had killed David, Gil and Ann to my knowledge. One more man to him would be more or less irrelevant.

I wandered back to the hall where I had been eating, only to find that my companions were already finished and had left. Now it was the turn of the servants who had brought us our food, and they looked at me in a surly manner, as though I was a greedy thief who, having eaten my fill, now wanted to eat their portions as well.

Leaving them to their food, I went to the chamber where I and the others had been given a room. Bill eyed me up and down as I entered. 'You look like you've been offered a choice between a hanging or the rack.'

'It feels much the same,' I muttered as I sank to the floor not far from Rob. I didn't want to sit too close, because that would have involved inhaling his unwholesome reek, but politeness dictated that I could not sit too far away. Bill eyed me bleakly.

'What is it, youngster?' Rob asked.

All right, I admit it. I was tired, I was cold, I was friendless, I was battered and bruised, I had a hole in my shoulder, and I was, basically, lonely. His voice sounded sympathetic, as though he was genuinely interested. It was the sort of voice an older brother might use, or even Bill. Well, Bill before he threw me out, anyway.

I told him of my meeting with Blount, and then I started telling him about the bishop, about Roscard, and even about Atwood. I felt so lonely that I would take any comfort I could.

He listened carefully to all I had to say, and for a long pause afterwards he sat staring at me. Then he slowly puffed out his cheeks and exchanged a look with Bill. 'You know how to make friends, don't you, eh?'

That night, the first of the sentries sent up to the walls were our friend the apprentice and two men who smelled like fishmongers. During the second shift, I was due to go up with one of the guards from the palace itself. However, when Bill stood and volunteered to take his duty, the soldier accepted with alacrity. Bill and I walked out to the walls and began our slow pacing across the battlements, occasionally staring out over the moonlit waste towards the north and west.

'I'll do him for you, if you want,' Bill said.

'Eh?'

'This man who's so keen on the Spaniards. I'll kill him for you.'

'You can't do that!'

'Why? You pay me, I kill him, all are happy. That's the way the world works, isn't it?'

'But you'd do that for me?'

'No, I'd do it for the money,' he said patiently. 'And since you know what I can do, you will pay me on time, too, won't you?'

'Um, yes,' I said. After all, it would mean that I had time to live a little longer and collect some cash for him. There were more than enough richly filled purses about the palace, I told myself. Getting my hands on a purse or two wouldn't be too much of a problem.

We were about to talk further, when the bells began to ring out.

THIRTY-THREE

It was ironic that all the while we were trying to plan the murder of Roscard, the rebels were approaching. Later, I heard that they had crossed the Thames the day before, after a hideous slog through mud and mire in that driving rain. Once they reached the other side of the river, their efforts had to be redoubled, for now they were splashing through the marshes of Knightsbridge and making heavy weather of it. It was said that they had poorly built carriages for the guns, and some cannons fell from their moorings and had to be man-handled back, with several men being crushed when the barrels rolled over. It must have been hellish in the freezing cold and the driving rain, with fingers thick and fumbling, heads muzzy with tiredness, legs weary from trudging in the filth and mud. I felt bad enough just walking about on the walls with my fingers locked in an icy rigor mortis grip about my halberd's shaft. Although I was chilled to the core, at least I had only rain landing on me. The rebels had the full gamut of rain, mud, shit and occasionally a bronze cannon.

Apparently, they were nearly at us when we heard the bells ringing in London. That was a warning signal and gave the alert to the city's yeomen and guards to gather up their arms and march to meet the enemy at Charing Cross.

Not us, thank God. If we'd been out there, we could have been caught, and I wouldn't want to be marching along when Wyatt's savages came upon us. Instead, we had the moderately safer task of protecting the queen here at White Hall. Moderately? Yes, because White Hall was not that well defended. It had grown up with additional buildings and bits and pieces of wall thrown together haphazardly over the years. At several places in the walls a cannon would have been able to batter the stones into submission faster than the sea washing away a sandcastle. It was not a thrilling idea.

'We'll talk later,' Bill said, and slipped away.

I hurried to the corner of the battlement and peered over into the main courtyard. There I saw old Sir John Gage, red-faced and bleary, bellowing at the top of his voice, 'Damned sword, damn my eyes! Where is it?' while men bustled and ran to their positions, some buckling on armour as they came, others settling swords and daggers and guns about them. Servants scurried, soldiers marched, and in a short time there were some one thousand men gathered in the courtyard behind the gatehouse. I stared as the men were given their disposi-tions. A half of them were sent out to the woodyard at the rear with Sir Richard Southwell, a good number of men left at the hall to cover the main defences, and Sir John Gage had the portcullis raised and the gates opened, and he marched out to the front of the Cockpit Gate with two hundred or more. And there he stood with them, all waiting for whatever might come to pass, before he marched back inside.

Me? I stayed up on the wall. I wasn't going to go down there to engage in hand-to-hand fighting. I'd had a bellyfull of that the other day. There was no hurry in any case. We were then to wait for five hours before anything remotely exciting was to happen.

Mind you, it was more farce than excitement.

The first we knew of it was a screamed warning, and then the bellows and cries of orders. And the worst of it? I was in the middle of it all.

It happened like this.

While the sun was up, the rain continued falling. We were all drenched, and that, together with the cold, made all of us slow, I think. I was hungry, apart from anything else, and would have murdered a score of Roscards for the thought of a hot pie in my belly and a cup of spiced wine.

Be that as it may, I was in the happy position of standing up there on the walls, looking down, and there were orders, and the rest of my companions were all pulled away and shouted at to go to different positions. I was happy enough to be left alone up there on the wall. After all, I had no wish to be hurled into another battle. My bruises were still all too painful a reminder that warfare was a hazardous pastime.

So I remained on the walls, and, peering down, I saw the yeomen of Queen Mary's guard out in the great court, and Sir John with his fellows out at the front, and then I saw the first of the mob coming up the street from Westminster.

You get to appreciate the size of an enemy when you've stood in a line to repel their assaults. My experiences were too fresh for me to wish to look at an attacking army again. However, I suddenly discovered an incentive to remove myself from the walls.

There was a clatter and the slam of a door, and I looked up to see Roscard smiling at me, higher up on the roof. He had his sword in his hand, a long-bladed dagger in the other, and his leer told me that he had recovered from his earlier fear of me, when he had run away after murdering poor Ann. On the other hand, my attitude had changed as well. Mainly because Roscard had two men with him, both with weapons. Odds of one against one do not appeal to me; odds of three to one in my favour are much more acceptable; three men against me is not a wager I would ever consider accepting. I stared at Roscard, and then, as he pointed at me, I ran.

It was a good twenty feet to the guardroom door in the tower, but I made it like a champion greyhound, opening the door and flinging myself inside. There was a bolt, and I shoved it over, and then hurtled across the room, and into the doorway at the farther side of the chamber. It gave out on to a winding stair, which I went down, constantly at risk of breaking my neck, until I reached the bottom. This was down in the main gateway itself. I pelted through the last door and found myself surrounded by men.

'Damme me! What do you want?' Sir John Gage demanded.

'The . . .' I couldn't think straight. My eyes were attracted to the door at the other side of the gateway, where Roscard had appeared. He stood nonchalantly, his men at his side, smiling in a very unpleasant fashion. 'The mob! The rebels are coming up from Westminster, sir!'

His eyes reminded me of poorly poached eggs: large and protruberant. He stared at me, sucked up something from a metal goblet, and then strode out to the roadway. 'Rebels? Where?'

It was no surprise he couldn't see them. St James's Park was walled all about, you see, and there was not a straight line. My view from the tower was over the roofs, but from here, at ground level, there was a slight dog-leg that concealed them.

'They wouldn't come here; they'd make their way straight to the city, you halfwit. Are you drunk?' the old fool demanded.

Later, I heard that when the rebels reached St James's Park, some went about the top to come at Charing Cross from the north, while more under Sir Thomas Cobham came around the southern tip and marched up King Street towards us. They were split by the narrow roads.

And then I saw them. There were a lot of them. An awful lot. I saw them marching in their ranks, Sir Thomas to the fore, with sodden banners hanging soggily from their poles. For all that they were as wet and as miserable as men could be, they were game enough, because, when they saw the guards before the gate, they gave a loud roar and began to trot.

For their part, the men and Sir John did not at first see their danger. I stood and pointed, but I had all but lost the power of speech. My legs, usually so reliable, seemed to have frozen to the ground, and my bowels felt as though they were about to empty, and all I could do was whimper incoherently as what looked like the entire rebel army descended the street towards us.

They gave a roar as they began to run, and my legs turned to jelly even as my bowels turned to water. I was petrified with terror.

The noise of bellowing rebels even made it through Sir John's alcoholic daze, and he paused in his drinking, a frown on his face. He was glaring up the road, but not towards Westminster. He was gazing with narrowed eyes towards the city, as though thinking the sound was coming to him from Charing Cross.

Not all the men under his command were so foolish. Someone saw my shaking finger, and shouting, 'Treachery, treachery!' he dropped his weapon and bolted for the gate.

Others looked around to see what had alarmed him, and fled
after him. Almost all his command had disappeared before Sir
John's servant threw down his jug of wine and bawled in his
master's ear, upon which Sir John turned his glowering face
in the direction of the enemy. Seeing Sir Thomas riding at
him, he stood stupefied. His jaw dropped and, turning ashen,
he dropped his cup before himself making a dash for the gate,
his servant grasping my shoulder and pulling me with them.

I was nothing loath. The man's hand on my jerkin seemed
to wake me from my stunned nightmare, and I raced along
like a hare. Before I had covered more than a few paces,
however, there was a clatter as the old fool tripped headlong
in the shit and dirt before the gate, right in my path. I had to
stop. His servant had paused to help him up, and the two
were in my path. To hurry them, I grasped Sir John's arm
and helped him up, spitting and cursing, and between us, his
servant and I, we bundled Sir John through the gates even as
they slammed and the portcullis was dropped, and then there
was a sudden calm for an instant.

Moments later, the first thunderous crashes were heard
against the gates. These were answered by a mad panic in the
great court, and men pelted across it in their terror, pounding
at the door of the great hall of White Hall, which was held
against them, rightly, by those of the yeomen who had been
commanded to hold it against the queen's enemies. Meanwhile,
I had seen Roscard and his two companions standing at a door
to the hall, and I was determined to avoid them. I suggested
that I should help Sir John's servant and the old knight up to
a safer chamber. I wanted to be in a place with other men,
and nowhere near Roscard and his friends.

I was taken across the courtyard, and the servant dismissed
me at the door to another spiral staircase. There would not,
he said, be space for him and me to help the old man. I
walked behind them, thinking that at least Roscard would not
risk following Sir John Gage into his private chambers. As
the servant turned off into a brightly lit room, I continued up
to the roof once more. Once there, I peered down into the
court: Roscard was still there. I had a few moments of peace,
I thought.

Looking out over the road, I saw that the rebels had grown bored with pounding on the gates. Sir Thomas Cobham had occupied his men by having them loose a number of arrows into the great court, but after that they seemed to be in as much of a quandary about how to continue as we were inside. Without heavy artillery, they would not break into the tower, so after hurling little more than verbal insults, while the guards inside were running, screaming, to the water gates and rear of the palace in desperation, trying to find somewhere safe to hide, Cobham had his men form up again and march off towards the city.

That was when I judged it prudent to go down to the court. I was on my way down the rear stairs when Sir John's servant came from a side door and, seeing me, called me to him.

I was not content to be called in this manner, but I was a great deal less happy when I finally obliged him and entered, only to find myself confronted by the haughty, somewhat dumpy figure of Queen Mary herself.

THIRTY-FOUR

'Guard,' she said, and I bent my knee quickly, averting my eyes in case I might irritate. It's best not to annoy a monarch who holds power of life and death. Besides, I didn't know if the bishop had spoken to her.

'Brave fellow,' she murmured. 'Do not fear me.'

She was not tall, and although she was not massive, there was a heaviness about her chin and face that made her look more weighty than perhaps was the case. Her face was pale, with watery blue eyes and reddish golden hair, and although she had a way of smiling, her head tilted down, so that she was looking up at a man in a most appealing manner, I didn't like it. She looked like a woman who was deliberately using a childish affectation to get her own way. I didn't trust that from a woman who could have my head on a spike by dinner time. Sir John Gage was standing behind her, with a sort of goggle-eyed, red-faced, horror-struck appearance that made me feel a foot taller and younger and bolder than I ever had before. The old fool took a long pull at his goblet, and I suspected that he was halfway to perdition on brandy.

'I saw you earlier, I think,' the queen said. 'You have the look of a bold yeoman, and I have need of such a man.'

I suddenly had a vision of being knighted by her, of Bill and the others looking on as the queen's latest knight received the honour; in the background was Blount, his face hidden beneath that wide-brimmed hat, and, beyond him, the damned inscrutable features of Roscard, standing close to Gardiner. It was a delightful idea. They would find it more problematic to make my life hard if I were a knight of the realm.

'I am your . . .' I was about to declare my adoration of her, and my undying loyalty as her servant, when she smiled at me and continued speaking. It was enough to make me come to a faltering halt. 'Your Majesty?'

'I said that I have need of a man to take a message to the

city, so that my loyal subjects know I am safe and have not
been captured. So many of my gentlemen here are too elderly
to make the journey, but you, sir, you are youthful and full
of fire and courage. I wish you to carry my message to the
city.'

Fire and courage? She hadn't been watching me, then.

She carried on, 'I saw your courageous defence of dear
Sir John here, and wanted to thank you personally. As well
as to tell you that your bravery will not go forgotten.' She
motioned to a flunkey, and suddenly I found a small, elegant
pigskin purse being pushed into my hand. It had a pleasantly
weighty feel to it. Before I could pull at the laces and get
to see inside, though, the queen started talking again. 'Your
message must be taken to Lord Pembroke or the Lord
Admiral, so that they know I am perfectly safe here with
my brave guards.'

Here, I saw her cast a glance at the goggle-eyed knight
behind her. There didn't seem to be too much respect for that
particular 'brave guard' in her cool appraisal.

'Your Majesty, I would be honoured, but I fear that I may
be no good as your emissary,' I tried. 'I was wounded in the
fighting at the bridge, and I cannot ride as swiftly as others.'

'I am sure you will ride all the fleeter for knowing you have
been specifically chosen by me,' she said. 'And now you may
depart. Please do not delay.'

And that was that. The old bitch had me hustled out, down
the stairs and to the stables almost before I'd known what was
happening. And then I was on a horse and being propelled
towards the gate, which most inconveniently opened.

There was no one outside when I peered anxiously up and
down the street. I had the choice of riding right, which would
mean riding into the skirts of the rebel army, or turning left
and riding as far and as fast as I could. That was appealing,
but although I liked the idea, I was horribly aware that there
was a negative aspect to such a journey, which was the fact
that as soon as the Queen realized I had fled the scene, she
would have me hunted down and captured.

Reluctantly, I set off at a trot towards the city. And if you
ask whether I spent the whole journey cursing the queen, I

will not answer. But my thoughts were not kindly disposed towards royalty at that time.

I rode along in a grim and morose temper until I came to a line of barricades. There were soldiers on my side of these recently erected barriers, and I sat on my horse, frowning at them for a while, until my brow cleared. These must have been set up to block any retreat by the rebels, I reasoned, and I was about to ride back when a grizzled old warrior, with armour that must have seen two decades of service, called out to challenge me.

'I am a messenger for the queen,' I called. 'She wanted me to go to Ludgate, but I see that the way is blocked.'

'Aye, right enough. We have been told to put up whatever we can to prevent their retreat this way,' the old man said. 'So, you need to get to the city?'

'I did, but clearly that's not possible, so—'

'You can still get by, man. Don't be so negative. There are alleys and lanes that the rebels won't have found yet, with luck.'

'Luck?' I was reluctant to put my safety on a throw of the dice again.

'You need to ride towards the river. Either take a boat and take the river, or just stay in the narrower ways. The soldiers won't take them. They want roads where they can get their men concentrated quickly. They seem to have held together so far. Besides, these are good Englishmen. They don't want to fight other Englishmen. They are determined on capturing the gate to the city.'

'How can I possibly get past them? There are thousands of them,' I said.

'As I said, take the river if you're concerned. You have the queen's authority. Take a boat.'

Since he was holding on to my bridle at this point, I didn't feel I had much chance of winning an argument. 'I think I should surely tell the queen,' I said.

He snorted. 'You reckon? I've heard she can be impatient with men who don't obey her commands. Still, it's up to you.' He grinned up at me evilly.

Which is how I came to be sidling carefully along a narrow alleyway between two great houses towards the river, hoping to find a small boat of some sort.

The only good thing, I thought to myself, was that Roscard was back there at the queen's tower.

It is never a good idea to count your blessings.

'Hello, Jack,' he said.

Roscard stood there staring at me, his sword unsheathed already, and gave one of those slow grins that would have suited a snake. 'Did you think you'd given me the slip? Sorry to disabuse you, but I was watching carefully.'

'But how did you get away?'

He shrugged. 'The queen was keen to leave the tower and show that she was safe in her own kingdom, so she had her most loyal guards go into the road and make sure all was secure. I was one of the first volunteers, of course, and since I had seen where you went, I merely followed your path and asked the first sergeant at a barricade where you had gone. You know, he didn't seem surprised to think that you were a potential traitor.'

'Me? I have actually fought for the queen!'

'Perhaps. But when I'm finished with you, your reputation won't sound so glorious,' he said. 'Now, if you wish, I can make this easy – or make it difficult.'

'Why? What do you have to kill me for?'

'Mainly because I really dislike you. You got in my way in the tavern, you took the purse that I had managed to cut from that young fool, and then you took the message that would have guaranteed me a rich reward. Why would I not want to kill you?'

There was no answer to that. 'It won't win you the message back.'

'I don't care. All I want is to see you silenced. So, which will it be? Painful because you fight, or shall I make it good, clean and quick?'

'Quick like Gil, you mean?' I said. I think I might have sneered a bit.

'Who?' He looked perplexed.

'Gil, my friend. You killed him and tied him to a post at the harbour—'

'I don't have time for this,' he said, clenching and unclenching his fist. He began to move towards me.

'How did you hurt your hand, then, if it wasn't when you broke his jaw?' I said.

'This?' he glanced down. 'I burned it at Carew's house. A candle.'

I wasn't sure, but he didn't seem to be lying. He looked genuinely surprised. I didn't know what to think. 'You didn't kill Gil?'

'I don't even know who Gil is!' He shook his head as though to clear it of an irritating fly. 'Do you want it easy or hard? It's up to you.'

I didn't know whether he had killed Gil, but I did know he had killed Ann. 'Why did you kill Ann?'

He paused. 'She knew a bit too much about my activities and tried to blackmail me. I wasn't going to have my affairs bruited about the city.'

As he finished, he took another pace forward, and I stared at his weapon. I didn't like the blade in his hand. It looked well used, and he was proficient with it. He blocked the alley before me; behind me, I had the whole length of the alley leading to the river. I considered my options, turned and bolted.

It would have been good if I hadn't tripped. There was a load of trash in the alley's side, and my foot went into it in the dark. The first I knew, I thought Roscard had grabbed my foot, and I squeaked as I discovered that my forward progress was halted. With my boot gripped by someone or something, I found myself plummeting to the ground. I landed in something that squelched unpleasantly, and closed my eyes just before I hit the mud. With the panic of a small animal expecting a hawk, I scrabbled and scraped wildly with my hands, trying to get away from Roscard and his shining steel, but even as I tried, a boot suddenly landed on the small of my back.

'So, it'll be slow and painful, then. I'm glad,' he said.

What an epitaph, I thought, and tried to roll over to dislodge him. My simple ruse surprised him, and he fell backwards against the alley's wall. I scrambled to my feet, and with my bare fists I battered at him, fighting with the strength of simple terror. One wild swing seemed to knock him senseless, for as my knuckle struck his chin, his head span around, and there was a thud as his skull slammed against the timbers of the wall. His eyes rolled into his head as he began to slide down the wall, and I leaped to my feet, hands clubbed. His sword clattered to the ground, and he continued his slow progress until his head was resting almost on a pair of boots.

Bill looked down at Roscard. 'He was getting a bit cocky, weren't he?'

I looked from Bill to the bloody sword in his hand. 'You killed him!'

'What, you wanted me to wait a bit?'

'But . . .'

'Just don't forget: you owe me,' he said, and shoved me from his path to hurry past.

THIRTY-FIVE

The rest of my journey was a blur. I ran as fast as I could from that damned body, and came out near Ludgate. There was a large gathering there. Later, I heard that Wyatt had been there, banging on the door like a debt collector. All I knew, as I warily stepped out into the street, was that there was no apparent fighting. There were some men milling about, and the guards at the gate itself were shouting insults at the men who were grumpily standing and calling back in a similar vein, with one or two throwing stones, but there was no actual fighting that I could see.

However, there was an increasing noise coming from along the road towards Westminster. It seemed to me that there was some sort of a riot up there. No cannons or the multiple rattle of an arquebus volley, but bellowing and screaming, and occasionally a whinny from a horse, I thought.

'I didn't think you had it in you,' I heard from behind me, and almost jumped out of my skin.

It was John Blount. He and his two companions had followed me and now stood cautiously peering out. I was about to protest, when Blount and the Bear caught me by an arm each and took me pelting over the street to a coaching house called La Belle Sauvage. It stood on the corner just outside the gate, with a narrow lane between it and the city walls, and Blount and the others pulled me inside.

'What are you doing?' I demanded. 'Leave me alone!'

The Bear chuckled as he wiped at a grimy window and peered out, while Blount unhurriedly took off his hat, wiped his brow and called to a young serving maid for ales. While I sat fuming, the trio stared out into the road.

'What,' I said with remarkable forbearance, 'is going on?'

'I'd say we have the best seats to see what happens when Wyatt and his men come to break into the city,' Blount said. 'And I was very impressed with your actions in the alleyway.'

'What actions?'

'Killing Roscard. He was a very unpleasant man, after all. You did well, though. I'd never have thought you would have managed to kill him. To stab him in the back . . . Although he clearly tossed you through a couple of barrels of mud on the way. At least, I trust some of it was mud,' he added with a slight curl of his lip.

'I have killed no one,' I declared. They were not going to accuse me of something like that and leave me to stew.

'No, of course not. A solid denial is always a good idea,' Blount said airily. 'But it was a good effort, nonetheless. Did he not even mark you? You must have caught him entirely by surprise. Was there a distraction?'

'They're coming!' the Bear said.

There was the sound of galloping, and a roaring and shouting, and a large party of men came bowling into the space before Ludgate, all bedraggled in the rain, many injured, some commanders on great horses, one a black stallion with a rent in his shoulder that was running with blood. From all the men there came a steady roaring of 'A Wyatt, a Wyatt! Wyatt for the City!' as though they expected the gates to spring wide.

'Poor bastards,' the fair-haired man beside the Bear murmured.

Blount patted his shoulder. 'It was bound to happen,' he said.

I was utterly confused now. 'What is going on?'

'Those men out there are the last of Wyatt's army,' Blount said. 'They were tempted to head this way, towards the city, but the queen's men blocked off all their escape routes along the way and erected barricades behind them, and then, close by Charing Cross, heavy cavalry attacked them in flank and cut them in half. The queen's archers did their bit, too. Since most of the commanders and cavalry were at the rear of their column, they were held back while the main part of their army was cut to pieces. Now, this is the remains of Wyatt's great army. That's him, the fellow in the pale brown jack and helmet.'

I saw a tall man, grimy from days of marching and hours of fighting, who wearily climbed from the black stallion and patted its flank with affection. Then he pulled off deerskin gauntlets and walked to Ludgate. Standing before it, he looked

up at the jeering men above him. 'Are you with me?' he cried
out, but the only response was a series of jeers and anatomic-
ally unlikely suggestions. He was stock-still for a few moments
as though at a loss, but then I saw him reach forward and
touch the ancient timbers of the gate, pressing the palm of his
hand against it, his head bowed. Then he stiffened his back
and strode back to his men.

'Shit!' Blount said, and for the first time I saw him look
alarmed. It was really very pleasing to see.

'What?' I said, and then, as Blount and the others pulled
away and ran for the rear of the inn, I saw.

Wyatt and all his companions were marching to the coaching
house where we stood.

We hurriedly made our way to the rear of the inn, where there
was a wide courtyard and two floors of rooms. While I stood
there, staring about us, wondering where the best place might
be to hide, Blount and the others ran across the yard to a
staircase that gave out to the upper storey.

Why didn't I follow them? I really don't know, except that
I'd already seen enough fighting that day, and running had got
me nowhere, only from one battle to another. I was tired, and
I felt that the man I'd just seen at the gate was as tired as me.
Wyatt had looked like a fellow who had just exhausted his
last reserves of energy in reaching that gate. He had no more
to give, I thought. The likelihood of his trying to kill me was
remote.

I walked to a bench near a well and sat down, nursing my
ale. My back was aching badly after my exertions. The fall
when Roscard had chased me had wrenched it, as had the
fight with him, and my legs were worn out. No: *I* was worn
out. I was more tired than I've ever felt, and I was fed up of
seeing dead men.

'You! Get up!'

It was the first of the men to enter the yard. All had heavy
sabres in their fists, and one was pointing his at me now. I
lifted my ale and shook my head. 'I deserve this. I won't
trouble you, but I've had enough of fighting and dispute for
the day already. No, I've had enough for the year.'

The man stood there, bemused, as though he could not quite believe that I would ignore his command, but then another, slighter figure pushed him aside and I heard him laugh.

'Jack, by all that's holy. I didn't expect to see you again.'

It was bloody Atwood again.

'You bastard! You tried to have me killed!' I declared. For all my weariness, I would have been at his throat, were it not for all the other men about him.

'Yes, my apologies for that. However, it was urgent that I took the message – and I really didn't want news of it getting about. Why did my fellows fail to remove you?'

'Your friends here fired a cannon ball into their midst, and they were all struck down at the same time.'

'All killed?' he looked crestfallen for a moment and then shook his head. 'Ah, well, that is the fortune of war, I suppose.'

'You know this fellow?'

'Yes, you can leave him. He's nobody,' Atwood said dismissively, in what I thought to be a rather hurtful tone.

The man in the pale jack who had touched the gates sent one of his men to demand wine and joined us. 'You are privileged,' he said heavily. 'You see us at the moment of our destruction.'

I looked at them. There were some forty men now, all downcast. Some few had walked to benches or stools and now slumped. One had pulled off his helmet and sat with his face in his hands, his shoulders shaking – whether from the result of his exertions or from tears, I could not tell. Others stood, but their faces were deathly pale. These men had seen too much. They had risked all, and now they would lose everything. A queen who has been threatened by rebels would be unlikely to be forgiving.

'What did you expect?' I said. 'Did you think the city would throw its gates wide?'

'Yes,' Wyatt said simply. 'That was what we expected.'

'It's what the note said,' Atwood shrugged. 'It assured us that the London mob would be on our side. That was why I couldn't let you live. But you saw it, of course.'

Luckily, at that point the maid appeared with cups and a

pair of large jugs of wine. The men grabbed it and set to pouring, which was a distraction to the whole company.

Me? I felt as though the whole of my world had suddenly collapsed. My belly lurched, and I could taste the ale trying to rise up and throttle me, and I teetered as if about to fall. My eyes went up to the balcony, searching for bloody Blount, but I couldn't see him. I took a long draught of ale and managed a weak, 'Oh.'

'What has happened?' Wyatt asked plaintively. 'We did all we were asked. We brought the men, we had them trained ready to fight, but the city betrayed us. I held to my side of the bargain. Where is Courtenay? He was supposed to bring the city with him.'

'I think he changed his mind, Sir Thomas,' Atwood said.

Wyatt nodded. He looked more exhausted than me. I suppose raising an army in a week, marching a hundred miles or more, and failing to force his queen to surrender, meaning his life was likely to be brief and painful, was enough to make any man weary. He slumped on the bench beside me.

'What did you say when you touched the gate? Were you praying?' I asked.

Wyatt glanced at me, but his eyes didn't seem to see me. They saw something or someone a long way away. 'I was just saying, "I have kept faith." I did what I swore to do. The failure or cowardice here was not mine. Bloody Courtenay! I hope someone will make the Earl suffer for his bad faith today. I damn him!'

'Sir Thomas!' a man called. 'We cannot wait here!'

'Nay, you are right.' He stood and drained his cup, then held his hand to me. 'Sir, I am your servant.'

I shook it with a feeling of sadness, and soon I was alone. There was the sound of orders being given, and then I heard hoofs clattering on the mud and stones of the roadway, making their way back towards Charing Cross.

'You bastard!'

'I know you may be a bit—'

'You and Mark together, you both convinced me, didn't you?'

'Jack, just take a moment to—'

'Damn you! You didn't mind me putting my neck on the block, oh no, and then you did that knowing that you'd lied to me as well, didn't you?'

'Jack, come on, now!'

I had climbed up the staircase taking the steps two at a time to find Blount and the others standing and looking mildly embarrassed.

'You let me think you were just changing the address on that note, when in fact you were making it an invitation to Wyatt and his men to come here and walk into a trap, weren't you?'

'Jack, you really do have to lower that sword. Blades make me nervous, and I'm liable to get all fighty,' Blount said.

I looked down. I hadn't even realized I'd drawn my weapon, but there it was in my hand, and it was pointing towards Blount's throat. It seemed a perfectly good place to leave it. I made a little jab with it.

Suddenly, I was on my back. I'm not absolutely sure how that happened. I vaguely remember the Bear stepping forward, knocking my blade aside with his forearm, and gripping the hilt of my sword, and then seeing his fist moving forward as though it was about to hit my nose. Actually, I think it did. There was an awful lot of blood on my shirt when I looked down, and I have to admit that if there's one thing I really hate to see, it's my own blood. I burped and brought up a little dribble of thin vomit. It didn't make me feel any better.

Blount crouched at my side and peered down at me thought-fully. 'You know, if you were not such an incompetent fool, you would make a very good ally. I like the way you killed Roscard. That showed real skill. However, I truly dislike seeing knives or swords pointing at me.'

'Why? Eh? Why did you let me think that message was going to—'

He held up his finger. 'Hush. No names, I think. One never can be sure who is listening. But as to the message we let you give to Atwood, why, I would have thought that was obvious. We wanted Wyatt to come here with all his men so that he could be crushed. You see, we Catholics have to club together to ensure that the queen survives.'

'No matter who dies, you mean!' I said, and I meant it to bite. I was being harsh, I know, but I was offended. Who wouldn't be?

His eyes hardened. 'England just now is a powder barrel sitting atop a fire. Soon it will grow too hot. My job is to keep moving it about so that the heat never gets so severe that the barrel explodes. Where tempers are fraying, I move the barrel: a man tries to incite rebellion, I destroy him; a mob attempts to riot against the queen, I inspire them to attack where I know the army is strongest; France tries to upset the queen's plans to marry, I find proof of French bad faith. In short, whatever our Catholic queen requires, I will seek to accommodate her. Yes, occasionally it means convicts, felons and otherwise disreputable fellows who live by thieving the purses from the innocent may be thrown into the fire, but better that than see the entire powder keg explode. And you are one of those, like me, who is fortunate enough to have been placed here at the right time to save our queen.'

I was almost convinced. But then I caught a glimpse of the Bear's grin, and suddenly any conviction I had held dissipated. No, I didn't believe him. Not a word.

Blount continued, head on one side, eyeing me slyly. 'However, I wonder whether you are a mere pawn in this game, or whether I may have a greater use for you.'

'Me?' I would have squeaked, but with the blood blocking my nose so severely, I couldn't do more than mumble.

'I had no idea you were quite such a competent assassin,' he said. He gave me a smile and a salute. 'I think my master and I may have a use for you.'

THIRTY-SIX

t was almost dark by the time I left the inn and made my way up the road to Bill's house.

My mood was not sunny. It had taken me an age to persuade the guards at Ludgate to open the postern door for me, because the fools were convinced that there would be another rebel army behind me. Perhaps they thought I was a one-man forlorn hope, determined to sacrifice myself in the aim of opening the gate to my comrades. It took a lot of shouting and several insults before I managed to speak to my captain – who was still there and hadn't managed to stir himself to put his own neck in danger, as he had with Rob, Bill and me – and finally persuaded him to have the gate opened.

'Not that you're the sort of man the city wants in any case,' he grunted as he finally let me in.

I made my way slightly haphazardly from the gate to the Black Boar, where the ale was moderately unwatered, but the serving wenches were better-looking than the whores in Piers's stews, and a lot cheaper. I had a half gallon of ale, and from there made my way towards Deneburgh Lane.

On the way, I saw a happy-looking maid. Not, perhaps, a young maid, but a young woman, anyway, a flaxen-haired wench with sharp features, who was walking arm in arm with a brash-looking fellow in velvet. Their smiles were enchanting as they stared into each other's eyes as though no one else in London mattered. So many would be relieved at the news of the broken rebellion, and I thought jealously to myself that there would be more than a few babies created this evening.

Yes, I was cheerfully drunk when I got to Deneburgh Lane. The ales had been strong, my belly was full, and I was comfortable after a portion of beef pie from the Boar and a snatched kiss from a young, buxom blonde, who slapped my face after

I kissed her, complaining about the blood on my face and my unwanted attentions. Still, it was worth the slap.

I climbed the stairs, knocked at the door and almost fell inside. Bill would probably tell me to piss off out of it, but tonight, if he tried it, I would tell him to . . . well, go away. I was tired, battered, bruised, worn out and fed up with being evicted. I wanted the company of friends again. Failing that, Bill and the others would have to do. And Moll, of course. Lovely Moll. She didn't deserve to be latched on to Bill. Or have Bill latched on to her, more like.

Actually, I thought, as I sat down and pulled the stopper from my costrel to take a long draught of refreshing ale, it was rather like a marriage. I had always seen things from the one perspective – that of Moll's being scared of Bill, and having to obey his every command; yet when I was with the queen, it was clear that all the men about her were petrified of upsetting her, and I suddenly had a strange insight: when I had watched the two together, it was almost as though Bill was more anxious of Moll than she was of him. But that was mad, because she was only a woman, when all was said and done. It wasn't as if she was as powerful and wilful as a queen! The plain truth was, Bill was worried that he might lose her, and that was why he was so pissed off with me. He knew that she adored me. It was there in her eyes, right enough. He could see it, too. She would be likely to throw him over to get her hands on me.

You know, I had always had a thing for Moll, but even after the ales, even now, sitting cross-legged on the floor in that cold building, I had a sense that my reasoning might not be a hundred per cent. There was a thought tapping at the back of my mind and waving heartily to try to attract my attention, but I wasn't paying much attention to it just now.

Moll appeared first, and when I grinned and waved to her, she seemed surprised to see me. 'What . . . why are you here? Bill will go absolutely mad if he finds you here!'

'He'll be fine, and besides, I'm past caring. I've had a miserable last few days, and I just need somewhere to sleep.'

Her eyes went from me to move about the rest of the room, and she gave a little half smile. I was sure I understood her thinking: here, she thought, was a man on whom she could rely. She knew I would always love her, and would never bully or denigrate her. In my ale-filled state, I thought I could see into her mind like a physician peering into a sample of piss, and I liked what I saw. She was desperate for companionship and a man who would give her the affection and security she craved. I knew that. It seemed only sensible to let her know.

'I love you, Moll. You know that. I've always loved you,' I said. 'All I want is for you to be happy. So, you come with me and I'll make you happy.'

'Just like that?' she murmured, and went to the fire. She began to prepare it, breaking twigs and scraping tinder into a pile. She had a collection of herbs and leaves in a cloth and she set these beside her fire. 'I think you should go now.'

There are times when I discover hidden reserves of real stupidity, and this was one of them. 'I'll not go without you, Moll.'

She looked at me then, with a strange stillness about her as she stared deep into my eyes. It made a shiver run up and down my spine, like the claws of a rat hunting for food, and rather than a frisson of sexual excitement, it repelled me. There was no reciprocal love in her face, only a cold calculation that made me feel that she was assessing me compared with Bill. It was as hard as a slap in the face. Colder than the slap I'd received in the Boar. And I'd deserved that.

'You won't join me?'

'Grow up, Jack.'

I rose, tottering slightly, trying – probably not terribly successfully – to maintain a certain dignity. She said nothing as I walked out and into the dark evening. She came to help me when I stumbled, but I turned and waved her away with such anger and despair that she didn't come nearer.

Miserable, desperate, I walked from the house.

All right, I thought, *so where now?*

My feet had already pulled me towards the home of Mark Thomasson, and I stood outside his door for a while, staring up at it. I disliked the cantankerous old man, but there was no denying he had some skills in deciphering codes, and appeared to have a good understanding of Blount and others. He was a man of the world, a man of experience, and that was something I needed badly just now. I climbed the steps and knocked.

'Oh, so you lived, then,' Mark said. He was seated, almost enveloped by a thick cloak of red velvet, so that little could be seen of him but his nose and glittering eyes. Peterkin rose and growled at me, but I glared back at the hound. The drinks through the afternoon had left me truculent, and he apparently reconsidered trying his luck. He lay before the fire again, occasionally casting a sulky glance in my direction.

'Yes, I live. So far. At least one of my enemies will not trouble me any more.'

'Roscard, you mean? That was a brave job, trapping him and killing him. And a good idea. He was a bold assassin, and he would have been a difficult opponent in a . . . fair fight.'

'How did you hear of it?'

'Our friend Master Blount told me. He was most impressed, I have to say. He said he didn't think you had it in you, and I wasn't convinced myself. You generally seem so . . .' His voice trailed away as he caught sight of my expression. Perhaps my new fearsome reputation was enough to make him rethink his words.

'I want to know who killed David Raleigh and tried to kill me.'

'I'm sure that—'

'No, it wasn't Roscard. He did not kill David or Gil. I don't think he had time to get to the alleyway to knock me down in the time it took for me to run from the tavern. Blount didn't seem to have the time, either. I left him inside the tavern, and while I think him devious, dishonest and capable of murder and worse, I don't think he killed David. So, who did?'

'Tell me of the day. What happened to you?'

I closed my eyes. The ales and wine were having their soporific effect. I told him again of the visit to the tavern with David, of the mistaken pass of the purse to me, of my attempt at flight, the gate, the strike on my head, and waking up later.

'Wait!' he said. 'The purse? You say it was still with you?'

'Yes. Why?'

He glowered at me, without speaking, and then at the fire. 'If the purse was left behind, then surely the murder was less likely to be for that. A man who found time to knock you down and then stab your companion would surely have made time to search both of you for the purse?'

'Blount or another would have searched David,' I said. 'Why me?'

'Because you have a common fame, Jack. Anyone would assume you had the purse – unless they were not looking for the purse.'

That was when I remembered the flaxen-haired, happy young woman. With a lurch in my belly, I thought of the harpie shouting at David in the street.

'His wife. We saw her in the street before we entered the tavern,' I said. 'She accused him of seeing a whore.'

'He was a man,' Mark shrugged.

'No, she said that he was visiting a wench called Julia Hopwell, that he was frittering away her dowry on this Julia, and that it was ruining their marriage.'

'Julia is no tart,' Mark said. 'She is an honourable lady.'

'Why does she need money, then?'

Mark peered at me. 'David was a messenger. He had brought news to London. He delivered that news to Mistress Hopwell, and collected a fresh note from her which he was to deliver to Wyatt.'

'What?'

'You will need to speak with Blount. I can say no more. Suffice it to say that the money has gone to aid a lady.'

'But Mistress Raleigh thought her husband was conducting an affair, and she was clearly most angry about it.'

'Then I would think you have your murderer.'

THIRTY-SEVEN

I t took me little time to climb Ludgate Hill to the narrow street north of the cathedral. There, I stared across Canons' Row towards the house where Gardiner had interrogated me. It left me feeling even more chilled and insecure than Mark's words had done. I hunched my shoulders and crossed my arms, waiting near the great square mass of the cathedral, with its massive spire pointing like a lance to the sky. I always loved the sight of that great building. It soothed me. And not only because so many purses inside there had enriched me over the years.

There were prayers being said, and then a chorus of voices. Of course, this was still the happy time when we were all learning the new services, free of the Roman style that had held men in its grasp so long, and there was a hesitancy in the responses. I listened with a growing sadness. I had no one to call my friend. I had lost all. I had no idea where I could go. I would be better back with the yeoman guards or serving the queen, I thought. At least then I would have access to a fire and food. I would have companionship. I even found myself feeling a nostalgic sadness to have lost Atwood.

The thought that had been demanding attention while I spoke to Moll was still rattling at my skull as I watched the church. The people were coming out. It must have been a thanksgiving service for the queen's (or, more likely, the city's) deliverance from the rebels, but that was not in my mind at that moment. With a final rap at my skull, the thought seemed to direct my eyes away from the first people, and instead towards a small group to the left.

It was the flaxen-haired woman, now clad once more in sombre black, as a widow in mourning should be. She was the woman I had seen in the Boar, but this time she was without her lover. And then I recalled her: David's widow, Agnes Raleigh, the woman who had accosted David before we entered the tavern; the widow whom I had followed and questioned and who had set the local watchmen on to me. The widow of the messenger. I hadn't recognized that happy face earlier in the day because she was not in black, and seeing her with a stranger made for a good disguise which I had not seen through. And then I had a strange feeling. Her flagrant behaviour with the other man today seemed rather disgraceful.

I began to follow her. She was not alone. With her walked two servants, neither of whom was the man I had seen with her earlier that day. She took me up a road away from Paternoster Row, and suddenly I realized that she was leading me towards the place where I had met her husband that day.

It seemed so long ago. Roscard, Ann, Gil, and since their deaths the madness of the rebellion, and, of course, my own eviction from Bill and Moll's company. I was forced to stifle a sniff at the thought of lovely little Moll and her tightly muscled legs, her taut little stomach, soft breasts, plump lips . . . Aye, it was a shame. I had thought she felt the same about me as I for her, but it was all foolishness. She saw me as nothing more than a distraction. That was all I was to her.

I stopped. Mistress Raleigh had halted outside a house. There were three steps leading up to her door, and as I stared, I felt a sudden shock: I recognized that place. It was the house where I had seen Bill that fateful day.

She was disposing of her two men. They tugged their forelocks and began to walk away and, as they passed me, I hailed them. 'Good sirs, that lady, I am sure I know her. Surely, she is the widow of David Raleigh from Exeter?'

'Aye,' one said. He was a pleasant enough man, with the look of a fellow who has a mild suspicion of being halted in the street, but he smiled. 'David, the servant of the Earl of Devon, Sir Edward Courtenay. Why, do you know her?'

'I knew her husband,' I said. 'A good man, and a sad loss.' The two nodded, and we passed with mutual good wishes.

I stood there, rooted as a young oak to its soil, and little thoughts, random at first, and then piling on top of one another like the bricks of a child's plaything, began to form a great steeple that seemed as tall as that of St Paul's behind me.

That day when I had met David, I had seen Bill standing here, before this house, searching about the roadway; meeting David of Exeter over there, and then being accosted by David's wife; the woman disappearing, even as Bill did; my going to the tavern, rising with David's purse in my fist, attempting to leave, but turning at the sight of Blount in my path. I ran out, to the gate, pulled it open as David appeared behind me, and I was clubbed. But would there have been time for Blount to run out, along the alley beside the tavern and out to the back, down that alley, too, in order to club me as I opened the gate? It seemed unlikely. I had thought it must have been Roscard, but he had gone outside the tavern with Ann, so she said, before running back inside.

But if it was not Blount or Roscard, who else could have beaten me and murdered David? There was only one man I knew who was there: Bill. Bill, who was always so anxious about Moll leaving him to keep my bed warm. I'd seen that in his eyes. Damn me, but he had made it so plain he wanted me far away from him after that first day, telling me I would have to keep my head down. He had kept me in the house at Trig Lane: surely he wanted to come and kill me when all the others were already gone. He must have hoped to have slain me in the tavern, but my hard head saved me. Or maybe he hoped that I would be captured and punished for the murder of David in his place.

It did at least answer the question of why I was left with the purse still on my person. That had surprised me afterwards. It made no sense for Roscard or Blount to have struck me down and forgone the opportunity to win back their key prize.

But there was still one question: what business did Bill have with the widow?

I had no home. I had no friends. I could have marched from there and left the city as the gates opened in the morning, but if I am honest, I confess that my interest was piqued. More than that, my anger was kindled. Bill had tried to kill me – either directly by breaking my head or indirectly by putting a rope round my neck – and this woman had something to do with it. I was going to find out why, I decided.

Striding towards the house, I climbed the steps and rapped smartly on the door.

The bottler was a short, cheery fellow with a broad Devonian accent that was so slow and odd I could barely understand a word he spoke, but we managed to come to an arrangement, and he took me inside. I was unpleasantly reminded of the last time I met with the lady of the house. That servant in the other house was as much of a contrast to this one as that house was to this.

I was taken through to a pleasant, warm, wide hall, in which a fire was burning merrily. Whereas the fire in the last house had been spitting and smokey, made from poorly dried logs, this was clearly built of good, well-cured wood. The chamber was well lime-washed, too, and the walls were bright with patterns painted in reds and golds, as befitted a man of some wealth.

'You wanted to see me?'

She was not so confident this time. I could see that at once. She entered haughtily enough, but when she saw me, I could tell that her back became less stiff. With a jerk of her head, she sent her bottler from the room, and then walked to a small stool near the fire.

'So, madam, you have returned to your real home,' I guessed. 'It is more sumptuous than the last place where we met.'

'This is my home, yes. You followed me to a place that I have occasionally had use of,' she said with a brittle calmness. I had the feeling she could shatter like a pane of glass at any moment.

'To meet with your lover?' I guessed.

'What is it to you? My husband deserted me for his trollop.'

'Mistress Julia Hopwell? I remember you spat her name out before.'

'Yes. I am not ashamed of it. My husband treated me abominably. I sought love in my marriage and found only desertion.'

'So you took your own course.'

'I have a good friend. But he's powerful, Master Blackjack.'

'Yes, you know my name. You attempted to have me arrested

for your husband's murder. At the time it struck me as odd
that you should have already become aware of my name.'

'Your name was bruited about after my husband's murder.'

I remembered Ann's assurance just before she died. 'No.
Yet *you* knew it.'

'I learned it from my servants.'

'Here? Or at the other house?'

'I don't know,' she said and, rising, walked to the sideboard. There were some pewter goblets and a jug of
wine. She poured for herself and drank quickly, before
refilling the cup.

Her discourtesy annoyed me, but with the ale still fizzing
in my veins after my afternoon at the Boar, I felt no need to
demand wine. 'I think you know perfectly well where you
learned my name. I saw your husband's assassin here, on the
day your man died. I was out there in the street, and looked
over here and happened to see—'

'You accuse me? You were only there because you wished
to rob him!'

That was not something I could happily deny. 'You took in
his killer, didn't you? And that's how you learned my name.
You spoke to the murderer of your husband to pay for that
service and discovered my name at the same time! You paid
an assassin to kill him. You wanted to remove the impediment
to a happier life with your lover!'

She drained her cup again and reached for the jug. I was
suddenly aware that I was short of breath. I felt slightly sickly.
Anxious that she would empty the jug before I had any, I
took it from her and filled another goblet, drinking it off and
refilling my own before replenishing hers. It was a good,
strong wine, and I felt it sparkle in my veins immediately.

'Well?' I demanded.

She had tears in her eyes, but she held her chin up defiantly.
'Why should I not merely call for the watchman to come and
arrest you? I could have you captured and held and hanged.
My companion is son to an important family.'

'No. I have had the joy of serving Queen Mary,' I said. 'She
has given me her blessing. And besides, if I were to tell her
that this house was the home of rebels, I wouldn't like your

chances. You look at me with contempt, madam, but how long will you survive, if you are flung from this place, with it confiscated by the queen? All your nice belongings taken by her whom you tried to see ruined,' I added, studying the pewter in my hand.

'No! I beg you!' she burst out, and threw herself at my feet. 'It wasn't me, it was David, and he was a terrible man to me. He never cared for me, and threw away all my dowry without asking me! There was no love between us. He wanted my money – that was all. My father wanted a good marriage for me, and David came of good stock. That was all there was between us.'

'So you spoke to your lover and arranged for your husband's murder. You were happy to see him dead, rather than remain in a loveless marriage. And you negotiated with a murderer to achieve that end.'

She bent her head. And then she said something that made the entire room rock around me.

THIRTY-EIGHT

I lurched from the house, and it was not only because of the wine and ale.

On my walk to her house, I had barely noticed where I was going. On the way back, I saw the roads and knew exactly the path I must take, but I swear, when I reached the door, I could not have said how I got there. All was obliterated from my mind.

I raised the latch quietly and pushed the door wide. Bill was in his seat near the fire, slurping his pottage loudly from a wooden bowl. Wat was cross-legged on the floor near him, chewing bread; Ham stood at the wall eating with a wooden spoon. Moll was behind Bill.

'I didn't think you would throw me from the place,' I said. 'It didn't occur to me you'd do that, Bill. After the first time, I thought I would have a bed here again as soon as things blew over, but it didn't come to mind that you meant it.'

'Shut the door behind you when you go,' he said, and turned away from me.

'I've been a fool long enough,' I said. 'I thought one of the queen's agents or one of her enemies' agents must have tried to kill me, but it wasn't them at all. I saw you the day David was killed and I was knocked down, but it didn't make sense until today. I didn't think.'

'If you stay here, I'll have Ham break your head,' he said, and his voice was low and mean.

'No. I doubt that Ham will do that, nor Wat neither. They're still friends. As are you, Bill. I had thought you wanted me out of here because you wanted to leave the blame pointing at me. At first I thought you feared I would bring the constables to your door, and wanted me to go somewhere else, but then I realized you really didn't want me to stay here in case I was hurt. And I believed that I was knocked down by a man who sought to steal the note from the purse. I thought I was just unlucky to have happened upon a spy and rebel, and I paid with my skull. But today I realized my mistake. I understand now. David Raleigh didn't die because of his support of the rebels, but because his wife wanted him dead, and she was prepared to pay an assassin to kill him.'

'You say I'm an assassin just because I helped you?' he sneered.

'No. You were there, but at first I thought you were looking for me, and then I wondered whether you sought David. Perhaps his wife said she would point him out to you? I don't know how these things work. I was sure you considered me a danger to the company after David's murder, and then I thought you wanted me gone because you saw that Moll and I were too friendly. I was a fool, right enough.'

'You should go now,' Moll said.

'It was only just now that I realized you wanted to protect *me*,' I said.

Wat and Ham turned to Bill enquiringly.

'You wanted to protect me from Moll, didn't you?' I said. 'That's what David's widow just told me. The murderer she paid to kill her husband wasn't you: it was another woman. And she described *you*, Moll.'

'I should have struck harder when you pulled the gate open,' she said.

It was plain enough. She had been to David's wife to have the husband pointed out, and as soon as she saw me, she followed us. Seeing us enter the tavern, she had guessed that I would try to get him drunk, and she took up her place at the rear of the tavern, watching through a window where she could see us both. When I rose to leave, she guessed my reasons, and saw the suspicious David hurry after me. She was at the gate in moments, opened it in time to see me, tried to break my head, and then went to her victim and murdered him. I daresay she told him I had robbed him, and when he bent to search me, she stabbed him with my dagger, thrust it into my hand and fled.

Quick, easy and straightforward for her. Any problems would be mine. Who would suspect a frail young woman, compared with a hulking fool like me?

'He has you there, Moll,' Bill said.

'Will you let him accuse me like that?' she said.

'Moll here is a good little wench,' Bill said. 'She killed her first man when she was young. That was why she fled her home: she murdered her stepfather. Oh, he was a nasty brute, I have no doubt. I daresay he deserved his end. Not that I'd like to be in receipt of little Moll's vengeance. I don't think that would be nice.'

'What now, Jack?' Moll said. 'You asked me to run away with you today. Have you changed your mind now?'

'What did you do to Gil?' I asked.

'He knew where you were. I knocked him down with a club, bound him to the pole, and when he woke, I beat him to persuade him to tell me where you were. But he wouldn't. In the end, I had to kill him.'

'You did that?' I said, staring at her slim shoulders and thin arms. I had not realized how strong she was. I recalled the sight of his teeth on the ground. It made the ale bubble sourly in my belly.

'I wanted to find you,' she said, but there was no coquettishness about her as she spoke.

'You wanted to kill me or make sure that I was captured and slain for David's murder,' I said. I felt a real coolness towards her now. You know, I could suddenly see a range of imperfections in her skin, and her eyes were a bit harsh, now I came to think of it. She wasn't as alluring as I had thought. Odd how your views on people can change.

'I didn't want you bringing the beadle to us,' she said.

'To *you*, you mean,' I clarified. 'You never cared about Bill, Wat, Ham, Gil or me. You were only ever looking out for yourself.' I stood. 'I'll be off. Sleep well, Bill. I hope you wake up, too.'

THIRTY-NINE

I spent that night walking about the streets. There was much to think about, after all. My adoration of Moll was completely gone, as you might expect, and my respect for Bill was severely eroded. The one thing I was convinced about was that I could never sleep in the same room as Moll. She was too dangerous, especially for me, now that I had exposed her as the murderer of Gil, and as the person who had tried to have me arrested for the death of David. So I walked about, and eventually ended up at London Bridge. It was cold, very cold, and I was glad to find myself with a number of soldiers at a brazier. Their companionship was refreshing. They didn't care about my reputation or my past. They were intrigued by my shoulder wound, and when I brought out my splinter, there was much sucking of teeth and shaking of heads. I rapidly gained the impression that I was accepted into their group when a small barrel of ale appeared and I was invited to share in their booty.

It was strange to stand there and watch as the barricades were removed, and most of the wood used to build a bonfire to celebrate the great victory over the rebels. I stood there a long while, staring along the line of the bridge to where the span was demolished, remembering the shock of my first battle, watching the lines of men marching towards me, only to be broken apart, the bodies flung through the air, and the sight of Atwood's men turned into shattered ruins even as they were planning to kill me.

I'd heard that the men who rode back with Wyatt were captured somewhere near Charing Cross, and the majority were probably in gaol already. Wyatt was in the Tower, although he was unlikely to live there for long; his men would no doubt be used to decorate gibbets up and down the country. Atwood was surely killed while trying to fight his way free, or was even now waiting in Newgate gaol for his own special

noose. To my surprise, I found myself feeling almost sorry
for him. He was a rogue, but at least he was moderately honest,
and he had been good company.

I remained there all night, and if I recall friendship and
much good humour and singing of ribald songs, it is no
surprise. The bonfire was large enough to keep half of
London warmed, so it seemed to me, and the sight of the
flames shooting up into the sky, sparks curling and whirling
above it, was warming more to my heart than my hands. It
seemed like a sign of survival. And when the women
appeared, and we all began dancing to celebrate, with
couples occasionally disappearing into the dark to enjoy
their own horizontal parties, I watched, but for once I wasn't
interested in the idea of a woman. I kept seeing Moll in
my mind's eye, a club in her hand as she slipped through
the gate, and that was enough to put me off wenches for
the evening.

Thursday 8th February

Next morning, I awoke to pulled muscles in my neck and
back. My thighs were stiff, and I had a cramp in my calf, but
I was, as I noted to myself, alive. I climbed up, and stood,
pulling a face while I tried to make my leg work. It was
damned painful, but eventually it began to move again.

My friends of the night before had all left me, and I was
alone by the warm embers. I stretched, swore at the pain in
my back and shoulder, and made my way back towards the
city. There were three guards standing blearily at the bridge's
gatehouse, and I nodded to them, continuing up the street to
fetch a meat pie, and it was while I was there that I saw Blount
leaning against the wall opposite.

I followed him up to Paternoster Lane, and waited there
while he walked to the door and knocked loudly. When it
opened, Blount beckoned me. I took a moment to think about
it, but I had little choice. I went inside after him.

'Ah, Master Jack. The assassin with so many colourful
names. I hope I see you well?'

The man speaking was a tall fellow, with a broad smile

on his fat face. He had the appearance of a rich merchant, but his accent was pure Welsh, which was rare enough in London.

He was standing beside a knuckle chair at a large trestle table, a black hat on his head, and a thick coat over his shoulders. As I walked in, he sat down, rubbing his hands. There was good reason. The fire had done nothing as yet to warm the room, and it felt colder in there than outside. Blount stood leaning against the wall near the window. He was a born leaner, I decided.

I bowed stiffly. 'With whom do I have the honour of speaking?'

His smile broadened. 'I am Thomas Parry, Master Jack. And I hope you and I will be able to serve each other.'

'For my part, I have no home, no friends and no occupation. All I possess in the world is the coin that the queen graciously gave me as a reward yesterday. I'm destroyed because David Raleigh took it into his head to bring a message to someone, and Blount here chose to have me risk my life passing it on to another fellow.'

'Do you mean to complain that your occupation as a felon has been curtailed without any punishment?' Parry asked. He had a deceptively mild tone of voice, but I quickly snapped my mouth shut. To confess to felonies such as cutting purses free from their owners' belts was to invite a remonstration that would be painful, if brief. He continued, 'I see you are reconsidering your complaints. Good. Then you do have your wits still. I have, in my brief life, been forced to make some unpleasant decisions. All too often they have resulted in painful consequences for other people. However, I have always been fortunate to have been served by my good friend here, Master Blount.'

He rose and crossed the floor to me, studying me closely. 'I see no guile in your face, which is surely a miracle, for one with so black a soul. However, Master Blount assures me that you are most competent. Will you accept my command?'

'I don't know what—'

'Master Blount will make all clear. I find such discussions distasteful. However, needs must, and in politics it is often necessary to accept that unpleasant behaviour is occasionally essential. I am prepared to provide you with a house, with an income commensurate with your position, and a fresh suit of clothing each year. Will such satisfy you?'

'What sort of house?' I hazarded.

'You need not worry. I have several, and all are in good repair. Well?'

What was I going to say? Other than that I had no idea what I was being offered and could scarcely make a rational decision, of course.

'Yes,' I said.

Blount and I stood outside the house and set off in step towards a tavern.

'He is impressed with you, I can tell. It's always hard to see how a fellow like you can earn a living. At least this way, though, you will be able to live as you have always wanted. You will be a gentleman, Jack. A new name for you, eh? Gentleman Jack!'

'But what does he want me to do? Spy on people?'

'Hardly. No. But we have a need of men like you. Men who are prepared to kill. I saw your face after you killed Roscard. You enjoyed it, didn't you? And we know how fast you are. That was an impressive killing. I could not have done better myself.'

'That wasn't me! That was . . .' I stopped. I had caught a glimpse of his expression. There was a cynical tilt to his eyebrow, and his grin proved that he was paying no attention to my words. And then, I thought, well, why not? There was money, there was a house, there were new clothes – what more had I always fought for? I wanted a roof, dear God, more than ever now that Bill wouldn't have me near, and even if he would be prepared to let me in, I wouldn't dare go to sleep in a room where Moll had access to a knife. That would be far too dangerous. And Blount didn't believe my protestations of innocence, so what would be the point of denying it?

I stopped and looked back at the house where Parry was installed, then gave Blount a careful look. 'How much money are we talking about?'

*   *   *

It was a good house, too. I was promised a series of rigorous training sessions with quarter staff, lance, sword, dagger and even my bare hands, and, after a suitable time, I would be given my first orders. I was a professional assassin. Well, that should be easy enough. I would become a professional who would take all the money and possessions with me as I bolted for the coast and fled to France, or maybe took ship to Spain or the New World. One thing I was certain of, and that was that I was most assuredly not an assassin.

This may be a surprise to anyone who knows of London in those riotous, murderous days. It sometimes seemed as though every other man was a gentleman who would be prepared to run you through just to see the colour of your blood. Well, Bill was of that breed, and Blount, too, but not I. I always preferred the comforts of life to the risks of death. And while I was being paid to behave like a gentleman, I was more than content. Besides, rumours of my new occupation began to spread, as these things will, and I discovered that I was looked upon differently by people who had once thought they knew me. Now, several of them looked at me in a new light, as if they saw not me, but some devil in human disguise, who could breathe brimstone over them and suffocate them on a whim.

Not that anyone knew much. I know that, because *I* didn't. Who was employing me? Well, I can make a guess as well as the next man. I was being instructed by Parry, and he was no doubt employed by the queen. Who else could have instructed him? So I was to be the queen's assassin. I mentioned that to Blount once, mind you, and he laughed fit to burst, so I could be wrong, but I doubt it. I worked for the most important woman in the realm, and that for me was fine.

As long as no one asked me to kill anybody.

The hawkers in the streets seemed to step around me more carefully; watchmen tipped their hats to me; even Piers ensured that there were always younger, newer women to see to my needs when I visited him in the stews. All in all, life was good.

It was when I was standing outside the Cardinal's Hat that it happened.

I was pulling off my gloves preparatory to a thoroughly

enjoyable encounter with a lithe young brunette who, Piers assured me, was from Navarre, and who was exotic, wild and desperate to please, when Piers opened the door, looked about me at the street, and then beckoned me urgently. I entered the familiar corridor, with its odours of sweat and perfume to conceal the more odious smells, and followed him. He hushed me when I attempted to speak, and opened a door I had not noticed before. I walked in, and he shut the door behind me.

'Good day, Master.'

It was Atwood, large as life and twice as ugly as sin. I was all for turning, pulling the door wide and fleeing, when I saw he was smiling at me.

'I thought you were dead,' I said.

'I thought you were a fool.'

'How did you escape Wyatt's fate?'

'Ah. Yes, well, sadly, I didn't make it to join him. He rode off with the others to Charing Cross, but I chose to remain. I went to the Thames, found a stable, paid an exorbitant sum for my beast to be looked after, and then clad myself in my city yeomanry uniform before returning to the city. There were questions, of course, but I was able to satisfy all my interrogators. And meanwhile, the madness continued.'

'Yes.'

I knew what he meant. Poor Lady Jane Grey, only seventeen years old. She had been executed a week after the end of Wyatt's rebellion. Lady Jane had watched her husband taken to the scaffold, so I heard, and then his body and head brought back on a cart, before she had herself been taken to Tower Green, where the poor young woman had herself had her head removed.

'And now the Princess Elizabeth is held. Wyatt will be tortured until he admits her part in the rebellion,' Atwood said. 'Even Blount is anxious for her.'

'Did she have a part?' I asked.

'That is a question many will ask. What do you think?' he said.

'Me? It hardly matters to me! Besides, I don't want to know. I have my position in life,' I said with satisfaction.

'A good answer. Such matters are not for the likes of us,' he chuckled. 'Even when our lives are in their hands.'

I didn't know what he meant. I had nothing to do with Princess Elizabeth. 'What do you want with me?' I asked sharply.

He looked at me and gave a shamefaced grin. 'These are uncertain times, my friend. I seek employment.'

EPILOGUE

It was a month later that I heard of Bill's death. His body was found that morning, tangled up in the weeds and detritus that clung to the old, rotten wharf down at the riverside from Deneburgh Lane, and it took three watchmen to pull his sodden body from the water. They tell me that he'd been in there for a while, from the way the skin had pulled away from his body. I didn't want to hear more.

That should have been that, really. I had the distinct impression that no one else was particularly bothered about his death. The watchmen had their own unexplained dead bodies to worry about; the poorer folk didn't care, because who cared about a thief who dies? Everyone who knew how London worked was unbothered, too, because the idea of a famous dealer in stolen goods getting his comeuppance was hardly earth-shattering. Some reckoned that it was because of his offering too little money for some goods, and I could sympathize with them after my own attempt to get a fair price for David's purse; others thought it was simple bad luck. Even the best thief can occasionally step down the wrong street and be murdered in error. But I don't think Bill was greedy enough or enough of a fool for either of those.

No, I was always convinced that poor old Bill died from love. He adored Moll, you see. I was always right about that. I could tell it in his eyes. He may not have been overly bothered about me taking Moll from him, but he would, rightly, have been nervous about her growing to see the benefit of another man rather than him, and she knew how to remove obstacles to her happiness.

Bill would never have been able to cope with that. He loved her, as I said. So when he saw her falling in love with another man, he may have tried to fight the fellow, or, more likely, waylay him and kill him. And Moll might find his actions unacceptable. If she did, she would have found her revenge easy to take, because Bill would never have protected himself against her.

What of the others, you say? Well, I am happy living in my new house, and I have a moderately competent bottler in Atwood. Blount has kept away from me, except to see to it that I have a master of defence to teach me the arts of fighting. I have a good alehouse down my road, where I can meet occasionally with Wat and Ham, and Piers, when he is not so over-drunk that he cannot make the crossing of the river.

Widow Raleigh? I did nothing against her. What would it have served, had I denounced her? She could as easily have accused me of theft of her husband's purse, and even perhaps of killing him. It seemed a better thing to leave her alone.

And Moll? I don't know what happened to her. Wat reckoned she took a boat to Calais, but if she did, I just hope none of the sailors gave her a reason to take exception to their comments. If they did, I only hope she had learned how to sail a ship before she avenged herself.